Francis George Heath

Autumnal Leaves

Francis George Heath

Autumnal Leaves

ISBN/EAN: 9783337365912

Printed in Europe, USA, Canada, Australia, Japan

Cover: Foto ©Andreas Hilbeck / pixelio.de

More available books at **www.hansebooks.com**

AUTUMNAL LEAVES.

BY

FRANCIS GEORGE HEATH,

EDITOR OF THE NEW EDITION OF GILPIN'S "FOREST SCENERY;"
AUTHOR OF
"SYLVAN SPRING," "THE FERN PORTFOLIO," "OUR WOODLAND TREES," "TREE GOSSIP,"
"WHERE TO FIND FERNS," "THE FERN PARADISE," "MY GARDEN WILD," "THE FERN WORLD,"
"BURNHAM BEECHES," "TREES AND FERNS," "PEASANT LIFE,"
"THE ENGLISH PEASANTRY,"
ETC.

WITH TWELVE COLOURED PLATES,

Produced in FACSIMILE *from Leaves collected and arranged by the Author; Four Page and Fourteen Vignette Wood Illustrations of New Forest Scenery, engraved (from Drawings by* FREDERICK G. SHORT) *by* JAMES D. COOPER; *and Twelve Initial-letter Leaf Designs by the Author.*

THIRD AND CHEAPER EDITION.

London :

KEGAN PAUL, TRENCH, AND CO., 1, PATERNOSTER SQUARE.

1885.

PREFACE.

ON THE AVON AT RINGWOOD (*Evening*).

N the preliminary chapter—'The blossoming of Autumn'—the Author has fully explained the object and scope of this volume. In putting it forth as what he believes to be the first attempt ever made in England to reproduce in *facsimile*—if that expression may be allowed—not merely the exquisite tinting but the forms and venation of the most prominent and conspicuous of the leaves whose dying splendour lights up with so much of brilliancy and beauty our autumnal hedges and woodlands, the Author desires to say that the work is the outcome of a minute and careful study of the subject pursued during many years.

It is a singular circumstance that, with all the resources which art possesses in the present day, and in view, especially, of the wealth of illustration that has been brought into requisition in the endeavour to reproduce ' the flowers of the field,' no one should have attempted to reproduce the ' blossoms of Autumn' as represented by autumnal leaves. The neglect, in a literary and pictorial sense, of this most fascinating branch of natural science is doubtless only accidental, and it does not arise from any lack of appreciation of the subject. But the fact remains that, rich as this subject is in itself, and full as it is of attraction for the lovers of Nature, it has, by pictorial art, in the especial phase in which it is here represented, been wholly overlooked.

Merely general references—such as may be found abundantly both in poetry and prose—to the glory and beauty of Autumn,

> ' Thrice happy time,
> Best portion of the various year, in which
> Nature rejoiceth, smiling on her works,
> Lovely to full perfection wrought,'

till leave unsatisfied the desire to know something more of the loveliness which has stirred the enthusiasm and excited the admiration of poets and—in a less degree—of *prosateurs*.   It is true, as one writer feelingly exclaims, that

> 'Not Spring or Summer's beauty hath such grace
> As I have seen in one autumnal face,'

and it is worth an effort to endeavour to catch and stereotype, so to speak, some of the most prominent of the exquisitely beautiful, but transient, features of the season of Autumn.

It is not, perhaps, generally known that transient as these features are in our woodlands—for 'the autumnal forest,' as Gilpin truly says, 'is an instrument easily untuned' by 'one frosty night or parching blast'—yet, as far as the rich and varied tints of autumnal leafage are concerned, they can be retained to charm the eye in portfolios: so that the poet's lament over the 'latest loveliest flowers' which Autumn wreaths 'in many-coloured bowers,'

> ' The rich luxuriance * * of every view,
> The mild and modest tint, the splendid hue,
> The temper'd harmony of various shades,
> Alas! whose beauty blooms at once and fades,'

need not find an echo in the soul of the reader who will but take the trouble to seek for and preserve the coloured gems of the autumnal woods.

Should this volume suggest to any of its readers the collection and preservation of autumnal leaves not merely as objects in themselves of great beauty, but as reminiscences of pleasant autumn rambles, it will, incidentally, it is hoped, serve a pleasant, if a minor, purpose : and if such a pastime should give to the reader half the pleasure the Author has experienced in wandering by autumn hedges and through autumn woods in search of the materials out of which he has wrought this volume, its perusal will, perhaps, in more than one way, be fruitful of good results.

The *modus operandi* by which the outlines of form, the characteristic venation and the tinting of the leaves figured in the coloured plates which accompany the text of Part II., have been reproduced is fully described in the introductory chapter. The Author's best thanks are due to the artists and lithographers—Messrs Emrik and Binger—and to their London representative, Mr. William Day, for the admirable manner in which they have carried out his instructions. The botanical artist employed upon the work is a gentleman of great experience and ability in this especial field.

The eighteen wood engravings of New Forest Scenery have been executed from drawings made by Mr. Frederick G. Short, who, living amidst the most beautiful woodland scenery in this country, has learnt his art from the great book of Nature. Mr. Short makes his first public appearance in these pages, and the Author, with an intimate knowledge of the scenes which he has depicted, will be greatly surprised if those who are equally familiar with these scenes do not recognize in this young artist's pictures a touch which no mere art training could give. Mr. James D. Cooper is the engraver, and it is a pleasure to acknowledge the value of his co-operation. Lovers of English scenery, who like to see what they admire ably represented on paper, owe much to him for his admirable and faithful delineations. The twelve initial-letter leaf designs in Part II. of the volume have been designed by the Author and engraved by Mr. Cooper.

LONDON, *November*, 1881.

LIST OF ILLUSTRATIONS.

Coloured Plates

*Produced in facsimile by Messrs. Emrik and Binger from leaves
collected and arranged by the Author.*

Wood Illustrations

*Drawn by Frederick G. Short, and engraved by
James D. Cooper.*

PAGE ENGRAVINGS AND VIGNETTES OF
NEW FOREST SCENERY.

PAGE ENGRAVINGS.

Initial-letter leaf Engravings

Designed by the Author and engraved by James D. Cooper.

CONTENTS.

Part II.

AUTUMNAL LEAVES

THE BLOSSOMING OF AUTUMN.

B

AUTUMNAL LEAVES.

THE BLOSSOMING OF AUTUMN.

VIEW IN ALUM GREEN.

POETIC fancy has given to the rich tinting of autumnal leaves the name of the blossoming of Autumn, and the designation is most appropriate. There are many real flowers — blossoms of great beauty and of deep tones of colour—in this delightful season: not the almost perennial flowers that open on from spring to summer, from summer to Autumn, and far into winter, nor the vigorous flowers which, coming with the early summer, attain their full splendour in July and August, and linger on into the first few days of September; but the veritable blossoms of Autumn which come with the season and remain open until cut down by the early frosts of winter. Yet these, beautiful as they are and conspicuous, in places, by their abundant presence, appear to be obliterated by the more pervading hues of autumnal leafage.

Content, so to speak, to suffer by comparison, during the summer—whilst they are dressed in their garb of sober green—with the flowers which they bear and serve by contrast to bring into relief, the leaves, in the later season, change colour, and when their early ornaments are faded and gone, blossom, themselves, into tints of mellow beauty, and oftentimes into hues of splendour which enrich the landscape as far as the eye can see.

Pencil and pallet have been industriously employed, since landscape art first commenced to copy Nature, in the work of delineating on paper and canvas the especial, prominent, or typical features of the seasons; and in this work of reproduction Autumn has been fully represented. Photographic skill has, too, been brought into play—and with marvellous and increasing success—to delineate the scenes of Nature in *fac-simile*, and when it shall have succeeded, as it seems not unlikely that it will, ere long, in reproducing not merely the forms but the colours of natural objects, it will have left little else for the landscape painter but imaginative subjects, or imaginative combinations of ' effects,' which it may not be in the power of photography to compass. If ' high art '—as art—should then suffer, it will merely be another instance of the triumph of science and Nature over mere art.

Meanwhile we depend, mostly, for our coloured pictures upon the artist and designer. Yet though these have provided us plentifully with coloured *flowers* we have had few *leaves*, and those which have been drawn for us have been summer leaves. If we look into books we shall find an abundance of coloured representations of blossoms with green leaves added to make pleasant contrast. But in this country, coloured representations of autumnal leaves have never, to the Author's knowledge, been attempted in books, and even the subject itself has not been dealt with except in verse and in a fragmentary way in prose.

But it is full of suggestiveness and beauty, and it has long been the Author's desire to endeavour to give especial prominence to it. How few people take the trouble to study in detail the exquisite conformations of leaves! The fact that the summer leaf is green and the autumnal leaf is yellow, or red, or orange, is the only fact of which especial cognizance is taken. The prominent and conspicuous circumstances of form or colour being roughly noted, the subject is dismissed from sight and from mind. It was in the endeavour to increase the popular appreciation of the beautiful forms of leaves that the Author determined upon the especial character of the coloured illustrations of 'OUR WOODLAND TREES.' In these it was attempted—for the first time, he believes, in the history of colour printing—to give a careful representation of the characteristic *venation* of each leaf. The outlines of form were obtained by the only absolutely exact method—namely by the employment of photography. The artist who undertook the work of filling in the details of venation performed his task with admirable fidelity; the lithographers coloured after Nature. Actual leaves which had been carefully collected by the Author—with their forms and colouring preserved—formed the subjects for draughtsman and colour-printer, and the result was all that the Author could have wished in fulfilment of his design. Amongst many gratifying acknowledgments of the pleasure which this species of Nature-printing gave to the readers of his book, he wishes to refer to one received from an Australian correspondent, who, writing from Melbourne in June 1879, said,—'Having just finished reading "OUR WOODLAND TREES," I feel under such a strong sense of personal obligation to you that I write to thank you even from this distance. . . . I am sure your writings, especially this last work, will awaken, or rather originate, a new and most charming æsthetic *cultus*—the loving study of trees—a subject on which there is the most lamentable ignorance. It is pitiable to see such sources of innocent and, at the same time, exalted pleasure so much neglected, or rather quite unsuspected, even by people who linger lovingly over roses and camellias. I had to learn the little I know of trees under very disheartening circumstances. Nobody appeared to know or care what this or that tree was. . . . I had dreamt, as an almost impossible delight, of the publishing, by some expert, of accurate, tinted delineations of leaves; and your illustrations are almost equal to Nature. Since I have had your book (only in the beginning of this year) I often bring home a score or so of different leaves, and sit down with " Our Woodland Trees" for the pure delight of examining their dainty minutiæ.' . . .

It is unquestionably in the 'dainty minutiæ' of leaves that their charm lies, and it is also the 'dainty minutiæ' which are altogether unobserved and unappreciated by those who simply look at foliage in the mass. Beautiful and impressive as masses of colour appear—arranged and shaded and subject to the gradations and contrasts of wild Nature—there is greater beauty and more elaboration of loveliness apparent, on close examination, in the parts which contribute to the whole; for unless closely and carefully examined the especial beauty of these parts is found to be lost in the general effect.

But the beauty of colour in autumnal leaves is made up, so to speak, of many more elements than is the beauty of the same leaves in spring or summer. As in the mass the later aspect of foliage is more varied and striking than its aspect in spring or summer, it would seem that there should, of necessity, be greater variety in the parts which contribute to the general effect. And so it is in fact. In the mere shades of what is roughly described as 'green,' there is almost infinite variety and far greater charm than the unobservant even suspect. What to the eye, at a distance, seems absolute uniformity of colour is really made up of a large number of insensible gradations. Most of these can be easily seen on close examination. Apart from these differences, which require a certain degree of study to discover, there are the much more broadly apparent changes of hue produced by age. The tender, glossy, almost golden, leaf of spring merges insensibly, through many changing stages, into the deep green of its summer hue. But insensible as is the passage from one stage to another the contrast between the earliest and the latest summer shade is very marked and striking.

It is the varieties of hue and colour on the same leaf that give the striking character to autumnal foliage so apparent when it is closely examined. The effect is doubtless due to the manifestations of the preliminary stages of decay; and yet it is not strictly decay, as will be presently shown, which produces the picturesque changes of colour in the early stages of what is called leaf discolouration. But to whatever cause the change is due, the effect is often singularly beautiful. The normal, or what has previously been the uniform, green is lightened here and there perhaps by varying shades of the same colour, and contrasted in other places by distinct patches or spots, or it may be lines, of entirely different colour—yellow, red, or purple.

We have said that the peculiar colour markings of autumnal leaves, though indicative of approaching decay, are not, strictly speaking, what is understood by decay, or at any rate decay of the kind which, when once commenced, must inevitably lead to a disintegration of parts: for not only can the course and progress of this discolouration be arrested—in the case of most leaves —at any stage, but the effects of the process up to the point reached can be retained and perpetuated by careful management—that is to say, by taking means to alter the conditions which are necessary in order to continue, or merge, mere discolouration into actual decay. It is this possibility which has enabled the Author to obtain the subjects for the coloured illustrations of this volume.

Illustrations of autumnal leaves in this country could, necessarily, be only typical, for notwithstanding the comparative limitation of the extent of our flora the variations of autumnal colouring alone are almost endless. If it had been intended in this volume merely to give the colour of each autumnal leaf when it had reached its final stage of colouring, the task would have been easy and few colours would have been required. But it is in the early autumnal tinting that the charm of colour lies, and it is then that there is the greatest wealth of contrasts. in wild Nature. Hence, in representing, so to speak, in these pages, this especial aspect of Autumn, it has been sought to give the most typical and prominent of autumnal leaves, and these will be found figured in the coloured plates.

The coloured figures have, as already intimated, been copied from Nature—the leaves which they represent having been collected and arranged by the Author, then photographed, and so imitated as to give not merely their natural tints, but an exact representation—no less indeed than a *fac-simile*—of their characteristic venation. This question of the venation of leaves is one that deserves, from its interest and importance, much more attention than it has hitherto obtained. The mere outline of a leaf—though the feature which more immediately strikes the eye—is by no means its only important feature. But artists in general, even when drawing individual leaves, have been content to give little more than the outline. If the reader who has been accustomed to notice only this most salient feature will look at the systems of veins of the first two or three leaves of different species he may encounter, he will be astonished at their variety. The character, too, of the cellular tissue, that forms the epidermis of leaves, and is stretched upon the framework of veins, is very varied— depending much upon the form of this frame-work—and is sometimes smooth and glossy, and at other times dull and curiously crumpled or otherwise relieved from uniformity. Apart, too, from the form and direction of the veins, *colour* is often an element in the difference between one species of leaf and another, and between in-dividuals of the same species at different stages of growth. It is, of course, colour alone which determines the peculiar character of the autumn leaf; but in the illustrations given in this volume the Author has been careful to see that the out-line and venation as well as the tinting are correctly delineated.

In the chapters which follow an endeavour will be made to typify the general aspect or salient characteristics of autumn hedges and autumnal woods, whilst emphasizing the especial charm which is lent to our scenery by the exquisite tinting of autumnal leaves.

PART I.
AUTUMN RAMBLES.

ROUND THE NEW FOREST.

AUTUMN RAMBLES.

1.

ROUND THE NEW FOREST.

BEECHES IN ALUM GREEN.

AUTUMN rambles! There is something exhilarating in the very idea. Hosts of holiday seekers have already returned from sea-shore, country lane and woodland, and the period of *work* —serious, metho-dic, laborious work—has recommenced after their period of relaxation. 'The country,' nevertheless, is not yet deserted; for many tourists are still on foot; but their numbers are greatly reduced, and the charm of quiet is beginning to settle down upon previously frequented roads. The evenings, it is true, are 'closing in;' but the days are bright, as it always is in true autumn weather, the air—though crisp and fresh —is still genial, the sun shines gloriously, and there is, for the pedestrian, a sense of exhilaration, which, in its especial character, is peculiar to this delightful season.

It is at such a season of genuine autumn weather that we form the plan of a pedestrian tour around the New Forest. We determine to proceed by rail from London to Brockenhurst, and to walk thence to Boldre; to return to our point of departure at Brockenhurst; to explore the Brockenhurst lanes; and then to make the entire circuit of the beautiful woodlands, by way of Burley, Ringwood, Fordingbridge, Bramshaw, Stoney Cross, and Lyndhurst, returning, in the direction opposite to that from which we had set out, to Brockenhurst.

Perhaps it would be difficult in any part of these islands to find a route more likely to provide the splendours of autumnal leafage than the one we have indicated. For the greater part of the way the road passes along the verge of the forest—occasionally going through its outermost woods and crossing its heaths and glades. Over a part of the route the opportunity is afforded of contrasting the surrounding cultivation with the wildness of the perpetual forest, whilst from numerous points of view one may see the general as well as at other points are seen the individual features of forest scenery.

AT BROCKENHURST.

AN ENGLISH LANE.

Page 43.

AT BROCKENHURST.

QUEEN'S BOWER STREAM, BROCKENHURST.

T is the end of September; and looking out in the morning from the windows of our inn bed-room we note, in the prospect of leafage beyond and away from the village of Brockenhurst, that the mellow charm of early Autumn has already tinged the trees and hedgebanks. Across the way, on both sides, are white-walled cottages In front, through a wide opening between them a prospect is opened up of garden and meadow enclosures with trees beyond whose greenery prettily contrasts with the roofs and walls of more cottages which peep out from their midst.

Turning from our inn to the right, in our first ramble from this forest village, and then again to the right a few yards down the ' street,' we find ourselves in an elm-and-oak bordered road. Gently ascending, the road crosses the railway whose lines have ' opened up' this woodland district to the world. Just beyond, if we turn round and look towards the north-east, we get a distant view of rolling forest stretching away over uplands, with here and there an open lawn contrasting with the darker hues of the green-wood. The road we are following is soon lost to the pedestrian at the point where it enters a private park guarded by the gilded iron-work of its lodge gate. But close by the gate, and standing in the public road, is an enormous Elm crowning a grassy mound. Passing to the right, under the spreading boughs of this noble tree, we come upon another stately Elm standing out from a half-circle of Oaks and Elms growing within, but on the verge of, a meadow on our right. Just beyond this second specimen of *Ulmus campestris* we reach one of those familiar little patches of triangular turf which are so often found where roadways fork, for the reason that such spaces are large enough to enable them to keep free from the feet of wayfarers, and the wear of wheels. At this spot the road bends, and, taking the left turning, we pass between two ivy-clad cottages fronted by little gardens gay with the bright colours of cottage flowers— that on our right surrounded by mixed flower and fruit ground, shown—as we stop for a moment and peep over the high, quickset, dividing hedge—against a background of tall Elms and Oaks that border its opposite hedge and are in their turn contrasted by the red-walled village houses seen between them and by the great banks of white cloud which float airily in the sky above.

But passing beyond the extreme limits of these garden enclosures we come in sight of a typical English 'lane' which suddenly reveals— as we turn our eyes from the homely *entourage* of our ivy-clad cottages—such an exceeding wealth of quiet and surpassing loveliness that, for a moment, we are constrained to pause in wondering admiration.

Oaks, where we stand, growing from either bank, fling their branches across from side to side, and meet and interlace midway. But at one spot there is an opening in the leafy shroud, and through the 'vignette' thus woven by the natural and untrained garlands of oak foliage we see the blue sky, and though it is but a patch of uniform colour and we cannot now see as we could at night the contrasting beauty of the stars—' the golden nails,' as a pretty fancy loves to consider them, of the floor of heaven—the sunny blue serves to throw out in strong relief the autumnal colouring of the oak leaves.

From looking up at the sky and at the leafy canopy stretching immediately over us let us turn to look at our lane. Its roadway, margined on either side by broad and bright-green bands of grass—the verdant turf now level, now sloping, and now undulating—winds and turns in serpentine fashion as it gently ascends through bands of shadow and bands, or breaks, of sunshine until it is lost in the near distance by overarching trees.

As far as we can see this avenue of greenery is bordered by the wealthy verdancy of its hedge-banks and canopied by foliage, and when the roadway disappears from sight it seems to wind up amongst trees. Going into the lane the pleasant sound of running water falls upon the ear. It flows from a tree-bordered meadow on our right and, passing through a tiny arch under the roadway to the opposite side, its moist banks provide a congenial home for cluster-ing but now flowerless forms of Crowfoot and Daisy. The little stream, passing on by the leaning bole of a large Oak, covered by Moss, grey Lichen and sprays of trailing Ivy, trickles away down the lane in the direction from which we have come and, keeping by the hedgeside, is soon lost from view.

A few yards further on our lane widens out, and, at this spot, is no longer overarched by trees. But the greensward on either side is, in places, brightly starred by the blossoms of the Hawkweed, whilst the clustered foliage of the hedgebanks makes merry with the open sunshine. For the moment the Brambles carry the palm of beauty. The purple of their stems contrasts with their still green leaves and blends with those leaves which have put on their autumnal tints. On the same bush there is the greenish white of late buds, the pink blush of tardy blossoms, and the green, red, and black colours of autumnal fruit. In the bramble stems, too, there is variety; for whilst their prevailing colour is purple they are, in places, overspread by vermilion hues: and, where this hue is spread upon the stem, the adjacent foliage is dyed with the same rich colour. Strongly contrasting with the vermilion leaves are others of bright yellow, approaching gold, and others of greenish white. Now they are sombre in the hue of green, now flushed with crimson, now green and purple-blotched, but always beautiful. The Hawthorns, too, in the same hedgebank, with stems and twigs ashen and purple, are clothed with foliage of varying shades, from golden to dark and shining green, all set off in contrast against the brilliant red of the glistening haws. Dogrose leaves are here just being overspread with their autumnal flush, and do not, as yet, show conspicuously, but the pinkish red of maple twigs and the red flush of the maple foliage attracts attention to this beautiful shrub—half shrub, half tree—whilst the yellowing leaves of the Hazel, standing out from the hedge-top, and the sombre leaves and purple stems of the modest Blackthorn lend their own peculiar features to the scene.

Underneath the mass of outside greenery, where shadows nestle at the base of the hedgebanks, we note the shining tips of the ever-green Hartstongue, the broader fronds of the Male Fern, and graceful forms of *Polystichum angulare* peeping out modestly from their shady habitats—the fronds of these familiar Ferns emerging from the bed of trailing Ivy which forms the innermost covering of the hedgebank.

As the lane begins to narrow again between its verdant banks, two Oaks, on either side of the way, interlace their leafy branches overhead. But the sunlight again comes in, as we pass beyond them, upon the hedgebank shrubbery now rising higher as we continue our way—Field Maples, on either side, with waving leaves of yellow, edged and blotched with brown, standing out in relief against the mass of normal green, their winged samaras, yellowish green tinged with a delicate flush of pink, peeping out in pretty clusters between the leaves. Below the Maples are smaller shrubs of Blackthorn, Bramble, and trailing Dog-rose. A Willow, rising from the left-hand hedge-bank, shows its fast yellowing leaves, tall forms of Bracken, still green and uncoloured, save that the tips of one single pinnule is dyed with gold, grow from the clustering mass, whilst, as before, in the lowermost shady recesses of the bank are verdant Moss and glistening Ivy, the familiar gloss of the Hartstongue and large, conspicuous leaves of the now flowerless Primrose.

Away on either side of our lane are sloping meadows, bordered by and embowered in trees, and opened up to view as the lane widens. Three huge Oaks stand in a line near us in the park on our left, one of them having its great, hollow trunk split down to the ground. The large, mossy and lichen-covered limbs of these noble trees are flung to a great breadth on either side.

The soft geniality of this autumn day—the wind gently stirring the foliage and making music in the tree-tops and the sun burnishing into gold the greenery on which it falls—causes the birds to sing cheerily all around us.

Continuing onwards and upwards our lane, winding under overarching shrubbery and under trees whose tops meet midway and cast the pathway into shadow, we soon reach Brockenhurst Church, standing upon a knoll on the right-hand side of the way, embowered amidst Oak and Ash trees.

Passing up some rude steps and through an iron latch gate we find ourselves in the churchyard, crossing which, along by way of the south side of the church, we reach two enormous trees —an Oak and a Yew, both of which were probably contemporaries of William the Conqueror. Measuring the Yew we find that at three feet from the ground it girths sixteen feet eight inches, whilst the girth of the Oak, at the same distance from the ground, is twenty-one feet; at five feet from the ground one foot more in girth, and twenty-three feet in girth at six feet from the ground. Both trees are hollow and the Oak is supported by props, and, though its enormous limbs bear no branches, young sprays of foliage grow from its ancient bole.

Brockenhurst Church is mentioned in *Domesday*, and is one of the only two churches in the New Forest so mentioned, the other church being that of Milford. The charge against William the Conqueror—repeated by various historians—of having destroyed many villages and some fifty churches to make his royal hunting-ground has, in all probability, been wildly exaggerated. At any rate the mention of Brockenhurst Church suggests the probability that as the two churches of which it is one are the only ones in the forest mentioned in *Domesday*, and both are still standing, the traditionary culpability of William the Norman has been unjustly magnified. Like other churches in the New Forest (the one at Boldre is perhaps the most familiar illustration), the church at Brockenhurst is built upon a hill, and was intended to serve, as doubtless was the case in similar instances, as a landmark in the immediately surrounding forestal district. Its present

situation is a very beautiful one. On the south-
west side of the churchyard, opposite to that we
enter from the lane we have described, we reach
the brow of another lane leading back to the
village between leafy hedgebanks bordering tree-
covered, undulating meadows, and overarched by
Oaks. At its bottom we must again cross the
railway, and from the other end of the village,
opposite that from which we started, pass through
its straggling street to our first point of departure.

When the New Forest, stretching from the
Southampton Water on the east to the Avon on
the west, trenched upon the shores of the Solent
in its southward range, Brockenhurst—a name
which indicated the Badger's Wood—occupied
part of its central area. But the area of this
wild and beautiful tract of country has become
greatly diminished. North and south, east and
west, the woodlands have receded, and Brockenhurst but lingers on their southern borders,
though it is still sufficiently within their area to
remain a true forest village. The time when
herds of deer would, in the stillness of the night,
walk from the forest on either side through its

high street, until startled and urged to retreat by
the barking or pursuit of the village dogs, is gone
into that past so full of pleasant memories of the
ancient and unspoilt beauty of sylvan England.
But beauty lingers yet at Brockenhurst, and
though much of the old splendour has departed,
it still has the charm of leafiness for the lovers of
rural quiet.

FROM BROCKENHURST TO LYMINGTON
AND BOLDRE.

FROM BROCKENHURST TO LYMINGTON AND BOLDRE.

LYMINGTON RIVER.

THE forestal village of Boldre should have an especial interest for all lovers of English woodland scenery, for there lived and wrote William Gilpin. His first impressions of his surroundings and the manner in which he was drawn to take interest in and to note and describe the new scenes of beauty which were opened up to him on his removal to Boldre are simply and

pleasantly told in a letter—dated March 4th, 1791
—to William Mitford, the historian of Greece, who
had presented him to the living of Boldre. The
letter ran thus :—' When your friendship fixed me
in this pleasing retreat, within the precincts of
New Forest, I had little intention of wandering
farther among its scenes than the bounds of my
own parish or of amusing myself any more with
writing on picturesque subjects. But one scene
drew me on to another, till at length I had
traversed the whole forest. The subject was
new to me. I had been much among lakes and
mountains, but I had never lived in a forest. I
knew little of its scenery. Everything caught
my attention, and as I generally had a memo-
randum-book in my hand I made minutes of
what I observed, throwing my remarks under
the two heads of *forest scenery in general* and
the scenery of particular places. Thus, as small
things lead to greater, an evening walk or ride
became the foundation of a volume.'

It is a pretty road which leads from Brockenhurst, southwards, to Boldre. On leaving our
inn-door, in the main street of Brockenhurst, we

turn to the left, in a south-westerly direction, walk through the straggling village and then turn, again to the left, into the Lymington road, running southward after crossing the lines of the South-Western Railway and passing the small post-office. A pretty roadside cottage almost immediately comes into view, low, long, thatched and brick-walled, with four white-framed windows —two below and two peeping out from under the lower slope of the roof—and walls densely covered with climbing shrubs. From a bordering strip of greensward that forms, so to speak, the roadside 'setting' of this little dwelling, a white-posted iron gate leads through a low, quickset bordering hedge, overspread with an embrowning tinge, into the neat garden, and, through it, to a rustic wooden porch almost hidden by greenery.

No dwelling-place so well accords with leafy surroundings as one that is itself covered with verdure. Near a wood or forest a cottage, or other dwelling-house, with square, unadorned brick-red walls, tiled-roof, and straight inclosing iron fence, ill agrees with its surroundings, and strikes the eye as being harsh and inconsistent.

Embowered in trees and shrubs and half-hidden by climbing trailers, clothed, so to speak, like the country around it, it seems to be almost a part of the wild scenes of Nature; for in the wildest of these scenes we cannot, though no human being may be present, forget that man exists and must find a dwelling-place.

On our right, as we follow the high road southwards, we pass a cottage which, were it not for the brightuess of its ivy-mantled walls, would be buried in shadows, so snugly is it ensconced amidst greenery by its garden fronting of Sycamore, Horse-Chestnut, Scotch Pine, and Birch—the embrowning horse-chestnut leaves and the yellowing foliage of the fading Birch contrasting well with the bluish-green of *Pinus sylvestris.* A trickling stream which runs by the side of the road is made bright by the yellow bloom of the Water Ragwort, and the crimsoning of the wayside Sorrel, whilst, from a triangular strip of greensward that borders the road, grow the white and golden crowns of the Wild Chamomile, the yellow flowers of the Hawkweed, and one or two late Buttercups.

Our road winds and gently ascends as it leads further away from the village of 'The Badger's Wood,' passing between meadows upon whose undulating surface and out of whose leafy hedges grow richly-foliaged Oaks, upon the heads of which the sun is shining—bringing out the varying colours of early Autumn. From some of these trees the deep greenness of summer has scarcely given sign of change, though a warm tinge of colour betokens the early commencement of the inevitable transformation. Others appear almost lighted up by the spreading autumnal tints, whilst others again are dyèd with russet hues.

From the point we have reached we can get a pretty view, if we turn round and look back, of the village of Brockenhurst, as it lies at the end of our vista. Just beyond the railway we have recently crossed, a vignette is formed. The roadway beneath, the sky above, and trees on either hand, enclose an enticing picture enriched by colours of red, blue, white, and green. The lower part of this picture is formed by the red-brick and white-walled houses of Brockenhurst, roofed with slate and tile. Above the highest housetop rises the tall white column of a railway signal, and beyond and above stretches—rising against the horizon—the dark-green expanse of the forest. But a bend in our road to the right soon shuts out the view of village and forest, and of all houses, and leaves us only the pleasures of the shady wayside.

Winding onwards and upwards between oak-bordered, undulating meadows and hedgebanks, which, though green with the verdant leafiness of grass, and many other wild plants, are empurpled by the changing foliage of the Bramble—the little stream on the left side of our way making its voice heard, but in very gentle accents, on the incline—we reach the top of the hill. Here, for a moment, there is a homely change in the character of the scenery and one of those pleasant contrasts—between cultivation and wildness—so often afforded in England. One of three ponds by the roadside is occupied by a number of ducks whose presence attests the proximity of a farmstead. The ducks are holding a sort of amateur regatta and, with evident enjoyment, are wildly splashing about, their yellow beaks contrasting strikingly with the green, white, black, and brown of their plumage. Away on the right, across bordering hedgebanks and their adjoining fields and meadows, we can just see the crests of the forest uplands as they sweep around the horizon from the west towards the north.

Taking a turn round to the right, upon what is now, for a short way, our level road, we pass a tiny strip of open forest, with Oaks overspreading undergrowths of Furze and Bracken, of Holly and Bramble, Hawthorn and Blackthorn, twining round the stems and twigs of which White Bryony shows its large leaves, some still green and others richly empurpled, the berries of this beautiful shrub beginning to pass from their early hue of green into a rich shade of yellow preparatory to emerging into the full glory of their final autumnal colouring.

We soon reach the little village of Setley, whose farmhouses, cottages, and homesteads lie along on the left-hand side of our road, the white walls of one slate-roofed cottage standing out in strong relief against its background of woodland and sky, whilst the brown thatch of another cottage is made sombre by the vividness of a great patch of light, golden-green moss which covers nearly half of the roof-surface. Beyond the village we come upon an expanse of open forest which stretches away on our right towards the west until the rise of the uplands, at the near horizon, ends the view. Here the ground is spread, as far as the eye can reach, with Gorse and Heather. The Heather is now on the wane, but its late blossoms still empurple the ground and contrast with the brown of the faded floral cups which, on the same flower-stems, encompass the tiny but expanding seed capsules. The Gorse, though blossomless, pre-serves its hue of green, the sober uniformity of which is enlivened by the blossoms which peep out from beneath its prickly clumps—blue Hare-bells, golden Tormentils, and purple intermingling Heather-bells.

Continuing our way the road dips as we pass through the little hamlet of Battramsley and is here bordered by enclosures on our left-hand side and by the edge of the open forest on our right—the autumnal embrowning of the Bracken, at this point, contrasting with the green of the Gorse and the purple bloom. of the Heather, and with the golden richness of many clustered blossoms of the Tormentil.

Before emerging from the dip in our road we catch sight, away to our left, of a pretty little bit of charming English scenery. To get a view of it we must look over the quickset hedge on our left—a hedge of thickly-matted twigs of Hawthorn, whose stems are grey and gold with encompassing Lichen—green foliage, with purple-brown edges, and vermilion berries. In our line of vision we see meadow, cornfield stubble, and wooded uplands descending into a quiet wooded hollow. On the meadows cattle are quietly browsing, their red, white, and brown markings prettily contrasting with the spreading green turf of the meadows. The cornfields, shorn now of their crops, are made picturesque by the presence of irregularly-scattered wheat stacks. Red-brick, blue-tiled cottages, with whitened fronts, stand here and there half-hidden by screening trees

whilst above the humble dwellings the blue smoke
of the hearth-fires curls up against the white
clouds which overspread the sky. In the foreground, 'pecking' on the meadow near which
we stand, are some fowls gathered in a small
group and in the height, evidently, of quiet enjoyment. Cottage gardens and fruit-trees complete
the rural and pastoral features of the scene. But
there is still left a feature of woodland scenery,
for the background of our picture is formed by
clustered forest-trees which cover the distant uplands and rise against the horizon.

We ascend to the highest point of our road,
which now winds through the remaining portion
of the little village of Battramsley—the roofs of
whose white-walled cottages and farm outbuildings
are stained with Moss and Lichen—and on both
sides of the way beyond we pass meadow and
cornland, the hedgebanks brightened by many
flowers—white, blue, pink, and gold—late blossoms of Crowfoot, Harebell, and Herb Robert
being prominent and conspicuous. The autumnal
foliage of the matted masses of Hawthorn and
Wild Briar add their own richness to the scene,

whilst a Daisy, which we note on the greensward by our way, gives another proof of the truly perennial character of this beautiful little flower that seems to enjoy an almost perpetual spring-time.

Distant now only two miles from Lymington, by way of which we propose, by a rather long *détour*, to reach Boldre, we follow on our way southwards, pass under the shadows of over-arching trees which grow from the hedgebanks on either side—Elm, Oak, and Sycamore whose brown and yellow leaves stand out in relief against the mass of changing green—and then descend over the brow of a gentle declivity. Soon, leaving the leafy overhanging shelter, our road once more ascends through a tree-bordered meadow on our right and an undulated wooded enclosure which stretches away on the opposite side.

Our way now becomes extremely beautiful. We have fairly left behind us, for a time, the open forest and have reached a region of enclosures. But our way winds and turns between them, and as it somewhat rapidly descends is embowered in

leafiness by the overarching foliage of Oak and
Elm. Trees indeed are now everywhere, scattered
thickly upon the undulating enclosures upon
either side of us, whilst the hedgebanks which
border the way are adorned by the fruit of the
now ripening Blackberry, and by the glistening
red berries of the Bryony. At the foot of the
hill, lying away from the road to our right, is a
farmhouse, the very boards of whose outbuildings
are splashed with broad bands of gold from encrusting Lichen. Passing underneath a railway
arch—the railway now crosses what was once
continuous forest—our road winding still, we
presently get a peep on our left, down over some
wooded uplands, of the stream of the Lymington
River or Boldre Water winding away down its
valley to the sea. It is not far from this point
to the quiet streets of Lymington, passing through
which we reach the short stretch of country
between it and the sea by pursuing southwards
the continuous road we have hitherto been
following between leafy hedges, skirting tree-
bordered meadows—a little stream accompanying
us on each side of our way. Taking the left-hand

turning when we come to a point where our road divides into two, we catch sight, between the trees, of the waters of the Solent lying away just beyond us. Presently another road crosses the one we are pursuing, but we keep straight on, and by passing through a wicket on our right we can see the mouth of the now broad and winding channel of the river whose estuary as we reach it is uncovered by the tide and exposes a spreading mantle of seaweed, the prevailing dark green of which is contrasted here and there by patches of richer colour—reddish brown, orange, and gold. To the south flows the Solent, against a background formed by the long, rolling uplands of the Isle of Wight.

When Gilpin was writing his *Forest Scenery*, about the year 1781, Lymington was a forest village, and the country around it was much more wooded than it now is. It is interesting to recall his description of the neighbourhood, part of which description is contained in the opening paragraph of section V. of his second volume, in which he commences the account of his forest itinerary. He says,—'From Vicar's Hill' (his residence at Boldre) 'we passed Boldre Bridge, and ascending the opposite bank, called Rope-hill, to Battramsley, we had a beautiful view of the estuary of Lymington River which, when filled with the tide, forms a grand sweep to the sea. It is seen to most advantage from the top of the hill, a few yards out of the road on the right. The valley, through which the river flows, is broad; its screens are not lofty, but well varied and woody. The curves of the river are marked by long projections of low land, and on one or two of them some little saltern' (the salt works of Lymington, now gone, were in existence so early as the year 1147) 'or other building is erected. The distance is formed by the sea and the Isle of Wight. Altogether the view is picturesque. It is what the painter properly calls *a whole*. There is a foreground, a middle ground, and distance—all harmoniously united. We have the same view, only varied by position, from many high grounds in the neighbourhood, but I know not that it appears to such advantage anywhere as from this hill.'

Further on, in the same section of his *Forest*

Scenery, Gilpin describes the town itself, and again notices the river mouth. Describing his approach to it from the west, in his forest ride, he says,—'A little further to the east stands Lymington, just at the point where the flat country we had been travelling from Christchurch descends to the river which takes its name from the town. The brow and gentle descent of this falling ground the town occupies, forming one handsome street which overlooks the high grounds on the opposite side of the river. It is a neat, well-built town and pleasantly seated. The houses, especially on the side of the street next the coast, have views, from the windows and gardens, of the Isle of Wight and the sea. Across the estuary formed at the mouth of Lymington River, a dam with flood-gates is thrown. The intention was to exclude the salt water from the meadows above, which it was hoped might have become pasturage, but the purpose is not answered. A great beauty, however, arises from the influx of the tide which forms a handsome piece of water above the dam with many reaches and winding shores. We have

already observed the beauty of this estuary when
seen from the higher grounds as it enters the sea.
The scenes are equally interesting which it affords
when the eye pursues it up the stream from its
recesses in the forest. One of the best of them
opens from the stable-yard of the Angel Inn in
Lymington, and the parts adjacent.'

Returning to our own itinerary and to the
forest of to-day—which though beautiful in its
untouched parts has fallen from the splendour of
a hundred years since—we must retrace our steps
to the wicket gate, through which we had passed
to get a better view of the tide-forsaken estuary.
From the gate we follow a path which leads us
along the bank of the Lymington River, passing
the harbour with its shipping. Just beyond we
cross, by the ferry, to the opposite, or eastern,
side of the Lymington River on our way up-
stream towards Boldre, following the road which
runs by the riparian marshy tract. On both sides
of the valley wooded uplands run down to the
river, and the hedgebanks, on either hand, glow
with the colours of autumnal leaves and autumnal
flowers—white bindweed flowers contrasting

with the mellowing bindweed leaves, Tormentil and Thistle, flowering Wild Mint and the ever-present Bramble with red, purple, and deep-green leaves and purple stems.   Late flowers of Bramble contrast with the red and black fruit of the same shrubs, and the maple leaves, so various in colour, here redden, whilst the hawthorn berries encrimson the hedgebanks.

We soon leave our level way in the valley, and the sight of the river-banks, and turn to the right into the ascending course of a lane skirting, on the left-hand side of the way, an upland park. As we near the wooded crest of this slope, the lower part of which runs down to the river margin, we get a pretty peep of scenery over the hedgebank, down into the valley of the Lymington River, and of Boldre—*y Byldwr* of the Keltic (the full stream) and Bovre of *Domesday*—crowning the uplands beyond—the trees which stud the meadow that forms the foreground of the landscape being richly dressed in autumnal colours, red, golden, brown, and green.   At the top of the hill, on the left-hand side of the way, is Vicar's Hill House, and on the right-hand side

Gilpin's 'Vicar's Hill,' the old home of the author of *Forest Scenery*, standing on the crest of a hilly slope, the bottom of which is thickly wooded. Passing beyond, we reach a point where the road divides into two, and taking the left turning and winding up over the uplands, between high banks on either side embowered in leafiness, we reach a triangular bit of greensward where our road dips both to the right and to the left, or on both sides, of the little highway oasis, meeting a road which runs across. Taking the left-hand turning and descending over the hill, under the leafy shadows of large Elm and Oak trees, in another moment we pass a few cottages on either side, and immediately afterwards come in sight of Boldre Bridge, getting a pretty peep just before we reach the bridge, between the picturesquely-contorted branches of ivy-covered Oaks, of the Lymington River or Boldre Water as it is here more appropriately named. The water at this spot is narrowed to a mere streamlet, having low-lying, marshy borders and beyond and above, on its further side, gently rising uplands. On the opposite side of the bridge lies the main part of Boldre village. But, after crossing the bridge and getting a peep at the cottages, we recross the small stream to its eastern side and, leaving the village down and away to our left embowered amongst trees, continue the road we had before been following, which, from the water level, begins to ascend over a hill. From this hill we descend again, and our road again dividing into two, we take the left-hand turning. Uphill and down once more under leafiness until we reach, at length, a winding and ascending road, and away towards the right, at the crest of the hill above us, and up which our road is winding, we catch sight of the belt of trees which surround Boldre Church. The beautifully situated edifice lies really on the left-hand side of the road we are following, as we find when we reach the top.

It seems to be in the fitness of things that Boldre Church and Vicar's Hill should still, as in Gilpin's time, be embowered in trees, and it is equally fitting that the approach to both should be by winding, leaf-enshrouded roads, which are charmingly characteristic of the hedgebank and leafy upland scenery of England. The Church, standing on its hill-top and seen from many distant points—forming in fact a landmark in the district—looks down upon heath and forest which, northwards, lie almost at the foot of the hill upon which it is placed, and from their point of commencement roll away as far as the eye can see. Southwards from the Church the prospect is undulating, but pastoral and agricultural, and the building which was the scene of the spiritual ministrations of the author of *Forest Scenery* during a quarter of a century divides, so to speak, the old from the new—stands between the wild, wide stretch of ancient forest and the meadow, arable, and corn land of modern husbandry.

But walking into the pretty churchyard—with its Norman and Early English Church, one of the prettiest in England—one may easily forget the changes which have marked the period that has elapsed since Gilpin's death, for the sacred edifice and its quiet *entourage* are so closely screened by trees that the sight of the surrounding country is shut out from the level of the graveyard. Here, on the north side near the Church walls and under

the shadow of a beautiful and favourite Maple tree of Gilpin's—a tree to which he himself refers in his *Forest Scenery*—lie the remains of this true lover of Nature, who died in 1804.   His wife died three years later, and was buried in the same grave.   Gilpin had himself suggested the inscription on the tombstone, and it is as follows:—
'In a quiet mansion beneath this stone, secure from the afflictions and still more dangerous enjoyments of life, lye the remains of William Gilpin, sometime vicar of this parish, together with the remains of Margaret his wife.   After living above fifty years in happy union, they hope to be raised in God's due time, through the atonement of a blessed Redeemer for their repented transgressions, to a state of joyful immortality. There it will be a new joy to meet several of their good neighbours, who lye scattered in these sacred precincts around them.'   The dates of death are given on the stone as follows:—'He died April 5th, 1804, at the age of eighty.   She died July 14th, 1807, at the age of eighty-two.'   The poet Southey's second marriage was solemnized in this pretty little Church.   The delightful woodlands

which lie around might perhaps, at some time, have suggested to him his lines on Autumn and have brought up the image of—

> '. . . These fading leaves,
> That with their rich variety of hues
> Make yonder forest in the slanting sun
> So beautiful. . . .'

Instead of looking with melancholy eye upon the temporary decay indicated by the falling leaf, the poet saw beauty in the process itself, and gathered hope from the symbol represented by the natural transformation which it wrought. ' To me they show ' (' the beauties of the autumnal year'), he says in lines which follow those already quoted :—

> ' The calm decay of Nature when the mind
> Retains its strength, and in the languid eye
> Religion's holy hope kindles a joy
> That makes old age look lovely.'

Beautiful to the eye as is the calm (but only transient) decay of Nature as seen in the fading— if that be fading which glows with brilliant colour—of the leaf, the final fall and disintegration of the parts of the late green and glossy foliage of summer are but the forerunners of new and vigorous life—'Death still producing life' as Southey aptly describes the change. The rain speedily carries the essential elements—which are resolved into individuality by decay—into the earth, where they are quickly assimilated by neighbouring roots; and soon the uprising sap of succeeding spring elaborates these beautiful forces of Nature within the hidden mechanism of the cellular tissue, and produces that which once more charms the eye that looks upon the budding loveliness of the vernal season.

BROCKENHURST TO BURLEY AND RINGWOOD.

BROCKENHURST TO BURLEY AND RINGWOOD.

A TRIO OF THE TWELVE APOSTLES.

LEAVING once more the little white-walled cottages of Brockenhurst, standing amongst their fruit and flower gardens, and taking a north-westerly direction for Burley and Ringwood, we pass over Brookly Bridge, and on the other side of the stream turn to the left towards the west. Our road crosses a strip of open common studded with low Furze, between the clumps of which are yellow Hawkweeds in flower, whilst heather blossoms empurple the greensward here and there. The common soon widens out, and we speedily come in sight, as we follow our path, of the embrowned and empurpled surface of the forest as it rolls away westwards, towards Ringwood. Away to our right is an upland meadow bordered by trees, and at its foot a row of little cottages, their white walls, their blue and red tiles and thatch, and the curls of blue smoke which are rising slowly into the air, standing out in relief against the rising ground of the meadow.

We start late in the afternoon, and the sun in the west is already declining behind wreathed banks of cloud. But we hasten our steps, and soon get away from the turf of the common, and from the enclosures of meadow, homestead, and cottage, passing into a region of forest where the ground is no longer green but embrowned by faded leaves and faded Heather-bells, and empurpled here and there by the now blossoming moorland plant. We reach the crest of an upland from which we can see all around us the rolling forest—the brown expanse of Heather stretching away to the north until it is bounded by the dark-green lines of wood on the high grounds; to the east, the village of Brockenhurst; to the south, rolling open heath; to the west, brown, heathery uplands; and, just below us to the south-west, a belt of Oak and Beech wood.

The autumnal colouring of the Bracken is seen with much effect during a long walk across a forest. On its glades, in its depths, and on its open heaths, this beautiful Fern abounds, and in the early Autumn its fronds are variously affected according to the position in which they are growing. Here and there it has not lost the depth of its summer green. But in strong contrast to this verdancy some fronds on the same plants have turned to a dark, rich brown, others are straw-coloured, and others almost golden in their dying glow. Then there are splendid hues of orange, spread, sometimes sparingly and sometimes largely, upon clustering Bracken fronds, and now and then the same plants may include all these shades and colours. Not unfrequently the lower part of a frond is green and fresh, whilst its upper half is coloured brown and orange and gold.

Our road, as we continue it, takes us through a narrow belt of forest—Oak, Beech, Scotch Fir, and Holly—where the ground is spread with Bracken, and the Heather flowers contrast with rich patches of Tormentil blossom. Emerging from the wood we again enter upon a tract of open forest, and ascend its rising ground. At the highest point of the upland we get a fine prospect, away to the north and north-west, of the undulating surface of the forest. The distant woods are irregularly and picturesquely broken— the separate masses of dark verdure being thrown up into greater relief by the mistiness which, as we look, is lying in the hollows between the knolls on whose crests the trees are gathered; whilst, over the foreground of the landscape, the spreading expanse of brown Heather is relieved by the dark-green heads of Gorse. Away in the west a great bank of empurpled cloud appears as if it touched the forestal horizon, whilst, stretch-ing along and over the lower clouds, a streak of

fiery crimson marks the place below which the
sun is setting.

As we pursue our journey the western sky
grows less bright, the empurpled cloud-banks
lose the freshness of their colouring, the streaks
of crimson fire grow duller. No bird voices are
heard near us, the hum of insects has ceased, and
profound quiet, which is almost oppressive, seems
to settle upon the forest. But suddenly the sound
of bells not far distant strikes upon our ears
and reminds us, whilst serving to make the pre-
vious silence felt, that the forest is no longer
what it was, and that villages and enclosures—
house, field, and homestead—now occupy spaces
that were once unbroken wood or continuous
heath or moorland. Yet no houses are in sight
and the ground on either side of our pathway
is genuine, open forest. The spreading Heather
branches are, in places, encrusted with grey
Lichen. Between the sprays of Heather the
ground is occupied by dark masses of the green
glossy blades of the Fine Heath Grass, intermingled with taller forms of the coarser kinds,
whilst from out of the grassy, heathery clusters

flashes the bright gold of the blossoming Dwarf Furze. Tall forms of Bracken from six to ten feet high fringe our path and spread away from us gracefully on either hand. Presently on the open forest our bridle-path divides into two, and we take the right-hand way, and then almost immediately we take another and sharper turning to the right, leaving a Beech wood on our left-hand side and passing by the margin of a forest pool fringed by tall forms of Bracken. Following for some distance a course due west we skirt by a path, through Bracken ten feet high, the entire length of the Wilverley plantation and beyond it look down towards the south-west, into the Holmsley Valley.

Scott used to say that this little valley of Holmsley reminded him of the moorlands of his beloved country, and he greatly admired and was much attached to it. It was doubtless either the scenery of this part of the New Forest—now greatly spoiled by the denudation of trees and by the invasion of the South-Western Railway, whose lines run from east to west across it— or the magnificent woodlands that lie in Canterton

Glen, away to the north, that suggested to Scott the graphically-descriptive lines in 'The Poacher.'

> 'Seek ye yon glades, where the proud Oak o'ertops
> Wide-waving seas of Birch and Hazel copse,
> Leaving between deserted isles of land,
> Where stunted Heath is patch'd with ruddy sand;
> And lonely on the waste the Yew is seen,
> Or straggling Hollies spread a brighter green.
> Here little worn, and winding dark and steep,
> Our scarce-marked path descends yon dingle deep.'

Since Scott wrote these lines the New Forest has greatly diminished in splendour—iron roads and screeching engines have invaded its solitudes; 'proud Oaks' and 'seas of Birch' and many a 'hazel copse' have gone for ever, and south of the railway a wide extent of enclosures now fills the spaces once occupied by Oak and Birch and Holly. The change in very recent times is very great. We do not expect that unbroken forest should extend from Brockenhurst and Ringwood southwards to the sea; nor that the wolf and wild boar should, as of old, roam over its woods. But many noble Oaks and many a grand old Beech that, though contemporaries of the Conqueror, might and should have been preserved intact—trees whose very antiquity and hoariness, so to speak, should have protected them—have been recklessly, ruthlessly destroyed.

But gone as is much of the ancient splendour of the primeval woods of this grand old forest, there yet remain remnants of loveliness precious to the teeming population of our busy island and all the more to be loved and prized because they are the finest of the remains of sylvan England and are justly admired for their beauty, their antiquity and their utility—their utility, that is to say, as objects of beauty.

It is 'the gloaming' as we reach Burley, passing down into the leafy hollow in which the little village is situated. Its straggling houses are almost hidden from view scattered as they seem to be about its undulating, tree-covered meadows, and buried under the shadows of abounding greenery. Here, as elsewhere, cultivation has encroached upon the forest, meadows and 'merry (*mérise*) orchards' being almost mixed with the Oak and Beech and Holly of the woodland wild.

The Cherry is wild in many parts of the New Forest and is a striking and beautiful object whether in blossom or fruit. The name of ' Merry tree ' applied to the Wild Cherry is doubtless a corruption of the French *mérisier,* and ' merry orchards ' a corruption of *mérise* orchards. In one locality of the New Forest—Woodgreen—there is an annual market held for the sale of this half-wild fruit—a *mérise* fair, and locally in fact called ' merry fair.' The Oaks and Beeches at Burley furnish, too, a large proportionate contingent of the great forest fruit crop of ' mast,' upon which still the characteristic Hampshire hogs—whose ancestors could doubtless have claimed close relationship with the now extinct wild boar—are largely fed as of yore. Both acorns and Beech mast are termed ' mast.' But, when both are referred to, a convenient word —' akermast '—gives the mixture a collective expression.

Of the famous Oaks of Burley mention must not be omitted of the ' Twelve Apostles,' once remarkable both for size and beauty. But age has diminished their grandeur and spoilt their name—for though still called the *twelve* apostles, they number only eleven. Nor must the gravelly conglomerate Burley rock escape a passing notice, for the quarries which furnish it forth provided foundations for the older churches of the forest— those at Brockenhurst, at Minstead, and at Sopley. Near Burley the Raven used to build but now builds no more, and its departure, like that of the grand old trees which formerly stood around this forest village, gives another indication of 'the spirit of the age.'

From the leafy depths of Burley we ascend on our way to Ringwood, continuing the road we were following on entering the village. Beyond, towards Ringwood, we enter upon an extensive space of moorland covered by Heath and Gorse. Darkness has now fairly come upon us and our walk is quiet and impressible. Around us on all sides, stretching away until the eye in the near distance loses it, is the wild vegetation of the open forest. Now and then we can dimly discern the pale form of a night moth flitting noiselessly like some visible spirit of the night : or a frog, which we surprise in the middle of our way, begins to hop leisurely to either side, or leaps noisily into some small, glistening pool of water visible by the sparkle of light reflected from the stars. Then amongst the minor incidents which make a night walk impressible there is the sudden and mysterious rustling in some clump of Gorse, Heather, or Fern. Somewhat similar with regard to many of its features is a night walk through a country lane. But a forest walk after nightfall is much more enjoyably impressive, when no light from cottage window meets the eye for many a long mile, and wide-extending heath or moorland is only broken by the black masses of woods which stand out with gloomy grandeur into the night.

But soon to the dim light from the stars is added the radiance of the moon, which, as we continue our way, begins to peep above the hori-. zon and to silver the distant landscape, turning into things of beauty the lighter banks of cloud which, before the rising of the orb of night, had lain black against the sky, shutting out the radiance of many stars. Then at length we hear in the distance the shrill whistle which tells us that we are again nearing that part of the forest which the railway has invaded. We begin to leave the region of wild open heath and pass once more into the region of enclosure. Lights soon gleam from cottage windows, and our road, leading through meadow and corn-land, takes us to Ringwood.

5

RINGWOOD TO FORDINGBRIDGE.

IBBESLEY.

ONCE the boundary of the New Forest in its direction, Ringwood, which, as Rinwede, has mention in *Domesday*, now lies well away, in the heart of its surrounding enclosures, from forestal contact. As William the Conqueror chose Winchester for a royal residence and made the woodlands to the southwards into a great hunting-ground so it has been said did Rinwede at one

time have the distinction for a season of being
the abode of a Saxon king. There is good reason
for believing that Monmouth, on his escape from
Sedgmoor, was making, by way of the New Forest,
for Lymington, the mayor of which place was
preparing to receive him—having raised a troop
of men for his support and assistance. From
Ringwood the fugitive wrote his memorable
letters to the King, the Dowager Queen, and the
Lord Treasurer, craving for the preservation of
his life. Possibly he might have thought he
could successfully, for a time, elude his pursuers
by secreting himself in the forest. Gilpin, writing
just a hundred years after the event, says, re-
ferring to the incident in connexion with Ringwood, 'It was thought that he intended to have
secured himself in the woods of New Forest, with
which he was well acquainted from having frequently hunted in them.' Gilpin adds, 'I have
heard a tradition, that his body after his execution
was sent down into the forest and buried privately
in Boldre churchyard; but I cannot find any
ground for the surmise. The register of the year
is yet extant, in which no notice is taken of any

such burial; unless he were buried, as might possibly have been the case, under a fictitious name.'

The area of Rinwede, as set out in *Domesday*, was tén hydes of land. Of these, four were afforested under the forestal laws of the Conqueror and the remaining six were consequently left out, a proof amongst many others that William did not—as he has by more than one historian been accused of doing—order the wholesale destruction of villages and the ruthless appropriation of the land on which they stood and which surrounded them. A forest by such means, or by any other, could not have been made in his lifetime. He doubtless appropriated with a strong hand for his pleasure all suitable land and most of the woods in the district he had marked out for himself. But he also left most if not all of the meadows and tilled and arable land. Of the manor of Rinwede, for instance, it is seen that he left three-fifths to its former inhabitants and occupiers, including 105 acres of meadow-land. He also left, occupied as before, a mill that paid twenty-two shillings in taxes, and a church to which was attached half a hyde of land. On

the six hydes there were eighty-four inhabitants—
one freeman, six serfs, twenty-one borderers, and
fifty-six villeins; whilst on the portion afforested
there dwelt six borderers and fourteen villeins.
The woodlands in the manor maintained 189
hogs, and were consequently very different in
extent to what they are now.

Standing on the three-arched Avon bridge at
Ringwood we are struck by the pretty and simple
character of the scenery. To the north the eye
follows the river as it broadens out and overflows
the meadows which lie along it. Cattle of different colours—red, black, white, and mottled—
picturesquely contrast with each other, as they
lazily wade, knee-deep, in the water, above which,
in places, are shown patches of grass and great
beds of rushes. Beyond the water-meadows,
northwards, the prospect is bounded by trees
whose tops form an irregular and broken line.
To the south the winding river disappears from
view amongst its tall rushes, and beyond are
meadows and clustering trees. Westwards also
are water-meadows as far as we can see; but the
view is soon bounded by trees which loom up

against the horizon. Under the bridge arches the Avon eddies along over its beds of weeds and by the brown and green clusters of its bordering rushes. To the east is the quiet, half drowsy-looking town of Ringwood—though from our level stand-point we can see little of it—and the Church tower peeping up behind trees fronting a meadow that margins the river. Yet so much of the surrounding foliage which we can see from our point of view is already autumn-tinted with brown and yellow and russet and orange.

We leave the town by a road which runs northwards along by the western side of the Church and follow the up-stream course of the Avon, which, just as we pass beyond the Church, is half screened from view by trees that border it—Lime, Oak, Sycamore and Elm. We now find ourselves in an elm-bordered lane with the Avon on our left and meadows and homesteads on our right. The river is here margined by reedy beds and by clustering shrubs of Alder, Briar, Blackthorn, Elm and Elder—the Alders showing their fruit in yellowish-green cones, which, beneath the leaves, are seen depending in bunches from the

twigs of this abundant riparian shrub; the Elder
fruit, too—green, red, purple and black—contrasting with the still green leaves on the same
branches, whilst leaves, fruit, flower and blossom
are contemporaries on the picturesque sprays of
the Bramble.　Across the river, level meadows,
on which cattle are quietly grazing, extend for a
full mile to the west and are then backed by a
line of trees.　As we pursue our journey the
screen of hedges on our left disappears, leaving
only to interrupt the river view occasional clumps
of interwoven Bramble, Thistle and Nettle.　At
the same time the river winds away from the
road leaving between us and it an intervening
level space of reedy, marshy, meadow-land.　Presently a scarlet Poppy glows out from the hedgebank on our right, and almost immediately we
continue our way under the shelter of overarching
Elms—whose yellowing foliage already distinctly
marks the advancing season—pass by some cottages and gardens, gently ascend, and momen-
tarily lose sight of the river and the surrounding
country.　We are soon once more in sight of the
winding river, of wood, and upland meadows.

We take a turning in our road to the left by a post which points to Fordingbridge, wend on by bramble-woven hedgebanks, pass a farm-house on the left-hand side of the way whose walls and outbuildings are splashed with the green and gold of encrusting Lichen, and then stop for a moment to lean over a little stone-capped, brick-built bridge to enjoy the refreshing gurgle and splash of a clear brook which runs underneath over its clear, stony bed. Presently, as a prospect of wood and meadow opens up before us, away in front and on our left, we pass again on our road. The hedgebanks are now made brilliant by the colouring of the Bramble, brightened by late blossoms of the Bindweed, and graceful by the presence of clustering Brake.

We have quietly wandered perhaps a mile from Ringwood when the prostrate branch of a tree athwart the hedgebank on our right invites us to mount to it and be seated. A moment only we rest, but that moment is quite long enough to get a pretty peep of rural scenery.

Away to the south-west the tower of Ringwood Church appears to rise from a cluster of trees.

Nearer, but in the same direction, are the houses, outbuildings and adjacent cornstacks of the homestead we have lately passed lying together in a picturesque group. In front of us are meadow, corn stubble, hedge and tree. In the nearest meadow a group of cattle are taking their noonday rest, whilst, far away beyond, the horizon is bounded by woods.

We soon pass through the small village of Blashford, a little pastoral and agricultural region with its patches of wayside green starred with the golden blossoms of the Hawkweed and its farm and cottage enclosures of flower and fruit gardens—the familiar Elm being especially scattered about in hedgerow and meadow. We bend round by the left, cross a little bridge spanning a mill stream, follow our road under the shadows of Elm and Ash and emerge from these in a few minutes by a wide space of green on the left-hand side of the way. For some distance trees again on either hand—Ash varying from time to time the familiar Elm—shut out the prospect of the surrounding country except where a peep can be had through meadow gates. Presently we enter an Elm avenue of great beauty, the trees, growing from either hedgebank, meeting overhead and interlacing their tops. Our road winds for some distance under this continuous and living arch of verdure, whilst on either hand, over the bordering hedgebanks, we have perspective glimpses of pastoral and sylvan landscape—on the left the wooded banks of the Avon, on the right meadow and cornfield backed by bordering trees between which we can get glimpses away in the far distance of the embrowned surface of the open forest. The trunks of the Elms of the avenue through which we are going are garlanded by Ivy and Moss whilst the rough surface of the bark is covered by Lichen of varying colours, gold, green, orange and olive. In the hedgebanks on either hand are the great leaves of the Coltsfoot, with Male Fern and Burdock and Bramble and Nettle and masses of the now flowerless Germander Speedwell, whilst from time to time the fiery glow of a Poppy seems almost to illumine the abounding greenery. As we approach the end of the avenue we can see—away to the right—the western edge of the forest, and a little way further on we come to the pretty little village of Ibbesley.

Before entering the fine avenue of Elms through which we have lately passed a road had crossed the one we were following, making turnings to our left and to our right. The left, or westerly, turning leads to the little village of Ellingham— that to the right as we passed it to Moyles Court where Alice Lisle, after Sedgemoor, hid the fugitives Hickes and Nelthorpe. To these fugitives from the law the friendly coverts of the New Forest had no doubt suggested safety; but though now, from the house where Alice Lisle lived, as well as from other points of view adjoining, the forest can still be seen away to the eastward, the woodlands have receded since her time, and farmstead and other enclosures lie between the Avon and the forestal boundaries. In the churchyard at Ellingham Alice Lisle lies buried with her daughter Anne Hartell—the words inscribed on the tomb being 'Alice Lisle dyed the second of September 1685.'

Some seven or eight miles from Ellingham, on the Dorsetshire side of the Avon, Monmouth,

disguised as a peasant, was captured by his pursuers—hiding in a ditch amongst Bracken, Brambles and other wild growths. Gilpin, it has been
noticed, stated in his *Forest Scenery* that Monmouth was well acquainted with the New Forest
from having hunted there, and his suggestion that
the fugitive duke probably intended to hide for
a season amongst the woods of Hampshire is supported by Macaulay who says that Monmouth's
object was to 'lurk in the cabins of deer-stealers
among the Oaks of the New Forest till means of
conveyance to the Continent could be procured.'
All the country eastwards of the Avon was then
doubtless thickly wooded, though now covered by
meadow and pasture for some distance from the
river. Macaulay says that 'men then living could
remember the time when the wild deer ranged
freely through a succession of forests' (he doubtless means woods, for the whole formed but *one*
forest) 'from the banks of the Avon in Wiltshire
to the southern coast of Hampshire.' But Monmouth was arrested when almost within sight of
the forestal coverts whose friendly shelter he
sought.

To revert, however, to our forest itinerary.
We have reached Ibbesley and passing its small
Church on the right-hand side of the way we come
in sight once more, on the opposite side, of the
Avon, winding up through its low-lying meadows
to Ibbesley bridge. The prettily-thatched cot·
tages of this charming little village straggle picturesquely along the roadway on the same side as
the Church, their yellow-washed, brick walls being
almost hidden by Ivy and other trailers, whilst
the little front gardens, bordered by wooden rail-
ings are bright with coloured blossoms—yellow
and pink and scarlet and crimson—windows
peeping out from the deep cosy shelter of their
amply-sufficient eaves. Near the bridge stand
three enormous Elms which crown a sloping,
grassy bank that leads down to the water's edge.

Passing on to the bridge and looking southwards we get a peep of scenery which would
repay one for a journey of many miles to see.
Even the sides of the one-arched stone structure
of the bridge· possess interest and beauty, for
they are blotched with the orange, silver and gold
of spreading Lichen. Growing from the bridge's

base on a mound of earth just above water-level is the graceful form of an Ash. The stream, eddying below us and broadening out beyond the bridge, flows down a little distance from where we stand over a weir and thence on through its water-meadows towards Ringwood. By the weir margin and in the meadow beyond are groups of trees—Elm, Ash and Horse-Chestnuts—the autumnal yellowing of the Elm and the richer and deeper orange and yellow of the Horse-Chestnuts standing out strongly in relief against their darker background of greenery. Across the tree-tops clouds are swiftly drifting, chequering the blue of the sky, whilst the wind, as we look at them, is making music amongst the branches—sweet treble notes to the bass of the weir.

The Avon itself, as we look down at its flowing current, is suggestive of the season, for it bears autumnal leaves on its surface—one, two, three, they go, faster than we can count them—yellow, orange, red and green, borne on the liquid bosom of the stream, which is rapidly running towards the weir and making thence for the sea. It is a pretty sight to watch the Autumn falling of leaves

upon the surface of a limpid river. Looking up
stream it may be that there is a momentary lull in
the wind and the motionless tracery of twig and
spray on riverside shrubs and trees is mirrored
in the clear depths which lie under the banks.
But suddenly there will be sylvan music as a
gentle breeze, which rising far away has been
speeding towards us, airily touches the boughs
around. Gentle as is the touch of the zephyr
it is strong enough to loosen the slender grasp of
departing leaves whose time, before their fellows,
has come. Sailing lightly for a moment on the
wings of the wind and falling at length, as it
would seem, half-reluctantly on the moving surface of the current, they are borne steadily yet
swiftly towards us—mere colourless, characterless
objects as we see them in the near distance; then,
as they are swept past underneath us, veritable
things of beauty; green dashed with gold, orange,
purple, scarlet, crimson. But it is only a fugitive
glance at them that we get. Yet, at the instant of
passing, the eye takes in rapidly the form and
character no less than the rich colouring of the
tiny leaf. Then it is gone—*for ever*—colour,

character, form have vanished into the indistinct distance. The delicate framework of this thing of beauty with its clothing of bright-hued tissue has gone to disintegration and final destruction, only however to enter in a new form into the components of other and immediately succeeding objects of loveliness and utility.

But we must turn from the bridge and from the actual and suggestive beauty of its immediate surroundings and follow the road towards Fordingbridge, taking a peep, however, before we leave, of the prettily-thatched village inn at Ibbesley with its front wall garlanded by trailers and its little garden gay with flowers. The Avon will be our guide to Fordingbridge and we follow its stream as it winds through more water-meadows, northwards up its valley. Our way lies through deep lanes under the shadows of Oak, Elm and Ash, but we get glimpses of the heathy uplands of the forest away over the meadows on our right. We presently reach two Ash trees growing on a green mound by the roadside, where another road crosses the one we are following. But we continue the route we have been pursuing and pass under the shadows of overarching Elms and by hedgebanks dyed with the purple of the Dog-wood. Emerging from our lanes upon a little bridge whose stream runs into the Avon— which we can now see once more across some meadows —we continue past the bridge until we reach some Poplars between the branches of which, away to the left, we catch sight of the houses of Fordingbridge and of the church tower of the little place standing up above all other buildings. After one or two more windings our road takes us into the town itself.

FORDINGBRIDGE TO BRAMSHAW.

THE AVON AT FORDINGBRIDGE.

6

FORDINGBRIDGE TO BRAMSHAW.

THE AVON AT FORDINGBRIDGE.

FROM the bridge of many a town one may often get a pretty peep of scenery. Standing on the one at Fordingbridge, the church tower shows itself over a foreground of orchards and fruit gardens. Under its five arches the Avon flows noisily—gurgling, eddying and splashing, in its hurry to get southwards. In the broad part of the river to the south stands a small island, and beyond are water-meadows in which cattle are peacefully feeding. Beyond again is an irregular headline of woods. But a pretty sight lies close by the bridge where stands a house—the ' George ' inn—fronting the river. Its brick walls are delightfully draped with greenery and adorned by abounding red berries. A hedge of fuchsia and other shrubs borders the river side of the garden, whilst grass-grown, gravelled paths and a gorgeous array of flowers, with its vine-clad outbuildings, make the little inn suggestive of quiet rest after a long journey through country roads.

We have crossed the bridge on our way from Ringwood to get to our inn, but shall need to re-cross it on setting out for Bramshaw. The ancient name of Forde by which this town was known has, in modern times, become Fordingbridge. The manor was mentioned in *Domesday* and then included a Church and mills. Two mills were entered in the record with a rent of fourteen shillings and twopence. The woods of Oak and Beech which then surrounded it, but are now gone, were valued at twenty shillings a year as pannage for swine. They formed, of course a part of the Conqueror's forest : but cultivation has since encroached upon this part of the ancient wild domain, and pasture and cornfield, fruit and flower garden, orchard and paddock, with their necessary accompaniment of hedgebank and green, winding lane, now occupy the space over which, through wood, copse, glade, heath and moor, roamed the deer and wild boar. That it was an important part of the forest in the Conqueror's day is evident from the fact that guard, during the fence months, was held on its bridge to arrest deer stealers and other 'suspected persons' who could only get away with their booty at that part by crossing the Avon at this 'Forde' which formed indeed the north-western entry into the great wood-lands—the lord of the manor being charged with the duty of protecting the king's interests.

Recrossing the town bridge we take the left turning immediately afterwards and then continue in a north-easterly direction, taking another turning to the left at a fork in the road a few yards further on. On either side we pass cottages sur-rounded by fruit gardens—or gardens which are half flower and half fruit gardens. The predomi-

H

nating fruit tree is the Apple which now is burdened with its ruddy, glossy freight whose beauty contrasts prettily with the green, grey and gold of its mossed and lichen-covered twigs and branches and seems to blend with the richly-mellowing autumnal foliage which clings scantily to the picturesquely contorted branches of this delightful tree.

Our way leads us into a winding, leafy, grass-bordered road and under the spreading shelter of Elms, where, upon ivied hedgebanks, masses of Bramble and Nettle are woven by the Bindweed and where, amongst the maze of greenery, we note the great leaves of the Foxglove, pink blossoms of the Mallow, flowerless Dog Violet and thick garlanding hedge Maple just putting on its autumn colouring; whilst straggling through and over all are vigorous sprays of Bramble with fruit—green and red and black—abundantly displayed. We presently pass a homestead on our left and just beyond emerge from our lane by the river at a spot where mossed and ivied Oaks are standing.

On our way, as we continue our route, are

cottages and orchards—one cottage on our left-hand side having its walls nearly covered by rosy and tempting peaches. ' Tempting ' indeed they are, and inquiring at the cottage door we learn from the owner—a peasant woman—that her peach wall is her fruit market and that she will sell us as many as we wish. So we start for our forest walk with a store of peaches for refreshment on the way; and that pretty cottage on the hill with its luscious wall-fruit will long occupy a green and pleasant corner in our memory.

But now our road becomes steep and we begin to climb a veritable hill. We wind on, and, less than halfway from the top, we pass another little cottage fronted, next the road, by a grassy bank, on which the sweet little blossoms of the Daisy are rising amidst the freshest of green, daisy leaves—as freshly as if it were early Spring instead of Autumn. The road gets steeper as we ascend it, and the hedgebanks, on either side of it, get higher and higher. From their shady recesses Ferns now peep out—Male Fern, Prickly Shield Fern and the glossy, beautiful fronds of the Black

Maidenhair Spleenwort. Amidst the mass of greenery, conspicuous amongst which is the foliage of Maple and Briar, the Red Robin is blushing deeply and the leaves of the Meadow Cranesbill are flushing brilliantly with their autumnal colouring. Our road now gets steeper. It is no longer hedges that rise on each side of us but steeply-sloping embankments forming the boundaries of the road where the latter has been cut through the hillside—embankments on which the Brake and Male Fern have room to gracefully outspread their beautiful fronds, mingled with which, here and there, are those of the handsome Broad Buckler Fern. On the left-hand side of our way the steeply-sloping embankment is covered with a thickly-matted mass of Brake, Briar and Hazel, whilst Apple trees growing in the ground above peep out over the hedgebank greenery showing abundantly-crowded, golden fruit flushed with crimson, and mossed and lichen-covered branches. From the hedge mass, too, the Maple shows a tinge of orange red, the Hazel is yellowing and embrowning, and the Dogwood exhibits a profusion of clustering purple. Oak sapling and Beech leaves are reddening and Bracken tips are embrowning, whilst Bramble fruit, Red Robins and Poppies, here and there, peep out into the lane—the Common Polypody growing shyly in the shady recesses of tree stumps embedded in the leaf mould where its roots are hiding.

Near the brow of the hill we reach, on our left, a broken, grassy space where the glossy jet of luscious blackberries gleams from amongst the Brambles. From the roadway, at this spot, we can look down over the hill between overarching trees at the valley we have just left and see the church tower and houses of Fordingbridge peeping out from between the trees. At the top of the grassy space a gateway, crowning the embankment, leads into a meadow which extends over the brow of the hill. From this standpoint we can secure a beautiful prospect of the valley below, where the Avon, winding and turning, flows through the water-meadows in the valley bottom and meanders around the town which, from where we stand, is prettily screened by trees. Looking down towards the north-west there is a fine prospect of fertility suggestive of agricultural industry—the yellow stubble of cornfields, green meadows, trees—thickly clustering in places— and corn ricks, all blended and mingled into one attractive picture, which is spread out in all its largeness before the eye. The tree heads are mellow with autumnal colouring—Oaks on the hill where we stand having the golden tinge which betokens the approaching fall. A murmur of water reaches us from the point, away below, at which the Avon flows over its weir. Following the direction of the sound the eye takes in a prospect of orchard and fruit garden on the slope of the hillside; then, continuing the same line of vision, one rapid glance will include the whole of the smiling valley from where the town, at the foot of the declivity, nestles in its lowest part, away to the dark line of hills that crown the far uplands.

Regaining the road we ascend to the top of the hill, and at a cross road a little further on take a turning to the left in a north-easterly direction, between leafy hedgebanks where Oak, Holly, Hazel and Hawthorn are intermingled with Brake,

Foxglove and Nettle, with Bryony, Honeysuckle and Bramble. Looking towards the east over the hedgebanks we can see the dark edge of the open uplands of the forest whose empurpled surface rises above and contrasts with the lighter and brighter hue of the meadows and hedges which lie between it and our point of view—green meadows and hedges brightened by crimson haws and the glossy berries of the Dogrose.

Slightly ascending, our road now leads us through the little village of Godshill; and here, as elsewhere, the change is marked between the forest of to-day and the forest of the past. From the end of the village, opposite to that we have entered on the way from Fordingbridge, we can see the brown border of the open forest. But there is evidence extant that little more than a hundred years ago Godshill was densely covered by Oaks and Hollies. These have now mostly gone and their place is occupied by farmstead, meadow and corn-field enclosures. Leaving the village at its further end we keep straight on into the forest—our road leading in an easterly direction. The ground now rises and presently we reach a point from which we command a prospect all around us of open forest bounded to the north-west by a dark line of Firs over the tops of which the hill-country lying beyond is pleasantly shown by the light hue of its upland pastures and sunny cornfields whilst down to the west, by a dip in the rolling ground of the open forest, we can look again into the pleasant valley of the Avon.

We must traverse several miles of forest before we reach Bramshaw—and forest, much of which, though open, is probably as wild as it was in the Conqueror's time. To many a wayfarer the route we are now following might appear monotonous; but to one who loves to carefully observe the features of the country it is full of variety and full of beauty and suggestiveness. The rich purple brown of the general surface of the heath is varied by lighter and darker shades of brown. Amidst the masses of autumnal Bracken there are dark green and golden green fronds which light up the fading clusters of this graceful plant. The purple Heather blossoms show richly against the deep green Gorse, and against the brown and withered bells that still cling to the heathery sprays—whilst

the rich flowers of the Dwarf Furze look like golden
flashes from the ground.

For two or three miles our route gives us a
prospect of undulating forest. Here and there
Scotch Firs are sparsely scattered, but no human
habitation breaks the solitariness of the scene.
At some distance further on we pass some cottages,
and just at this spot we get a sight of woods
down away and towards the south. At this point
our road commences to dip over an incline in the
forest where masses of autumnal Bracken of a
rich, reddish brown contrasts with the fresh verdancy of the Gorse and the dark-green glossy
leaves of the Holly, whilst, to heighten the general
effect, we have the rich purple of the Heather
bells, the brilliant blossoms of the Dwarf Furze and
the bluish-green foliage of the Scotch Pine.
Descending into a wooded hollow of the forest we
get a prospect, away to our right and southwards,
of distant wooded uplands whose colours are
brought out in strong relief under the play of sunshine. Our path, now undulating, winds on and
on over the moorlands, opening up, from time to
time, as we continue it, prospects of the woods

towards the south and enabling us to see, as we from time to time reach the crest of an upland, the forestal limits to the north. Beyond these the uplands are abundantly wooded, the bright colour of the corn stubble and the green of the meadows showing strongly against the dark green forms of clustered trees. Foam-white banks of cloud are massed in the blue sky and fling shadows upon the forest, which, deepening the colours of the spreading vegetation that clothes its surface, brings out into stronger relief the spaces of Heather, Gorse and Brake upon which the sun shines. The motion of the wind too, drifting the clouds across the sky and swaying the surface of the far-reaching green, gives play and variety to a scene, which even when still, is of exceeding beauty. The almost golden green of the grass which carpets the forest tracks shows up strongly against the sombre hue of the untrodden moor. As the sun shines upon adjoining Oaks the heads of these monarchs of the forest are burnished into gold and bronze by the effect of the strong light. But away beyond the limits of wild forest another feature is added to the landscape by the brightness of the cultivated uplands where, on the upland pastures, the picturesque forms of cattle—red, black, white and mottled—are strongly shown as the sun shines upon them. Once more ascending to a point of rising ground we can see, away across the forest towards the south-east, the distant housetops of Southampton thrown out in relief against the wooded country beyond. We are now following a road which runs directly towards Southampton, but we presently reach a four-cross way and take the left turning towards Bramshaw, our compass pointing, as we enter it, to the east.

We now go down hill between woods on either hand—between Oak and Beech and Holly forming thickly-wooded forest on both sides of us, bordered by reddening Brake and empurpling Heather. The walk is impressively beautiful, for everything around us is quiet and we do not meet a solitary wayfarer. No sound comes to us, even from the forest, for the sun is sinking below the horizon and the birds are silent. The stillness, broken only by our own footsteps, is delicious. Fatigued by a long walk across the moorlands, we seem, momen-

tarily, to lose the sense of weariness, for the woods
which hem us in on either side exhale an atmosphere that is delightfully cool and exhilarating.
The pedestrian, in vigorous health, knows full well
how keen is the sense of enjoyment when, in walking through a beautiful country—through lane,
heath or wood—no sense of fatigue, no sensation
which can serve to attract one's thoughts to one's
self—interferes with that close attention which
the eye and the ear love to give to the sights and
sounds of Nature. Both senses—sight and hear-
ing—may have full employment, or the one may
be subordinated to the other. The sudden day
notes of the nightingale—which sometimes seem
to flood the woods with delicious harmony, to
obliterate, almost, every other bird song and
command attention—may instantly serve to draw
our sight from the most enticing scenery which
will be *looked at*, but unheedingly, whilst the ear
drinks in the liquid melody of the queen of song-
sters. Or it may be, on the other hand, that
to sounds which have been pleasing the ear and
making us indifferent to the scenery, we may
become suddenly deaf by the bursting on our vision

of some magnificent prospect, the sudden glory of which makes us pause almost spellbound with admiration.

As we turn into the descending road towards Bramshaw it seems as if all the colouring spread upon the wide-extending, open and heathery moorlands through which we have been wandering were compressed into a small space, for the enjoyment here is pre-eminently for the eye alone. It is veritable fairyland. The purple of the bordering Heather; the gold of the Dwarf Furze; the feathery grace of the Bracken, dyed in green and red and amber and orange; the glint of the Holly, the deep, glossy green of which sets off with singular beauty the bright red berries; the gold and green and bronze of the autumnal Oak leaves and the fiery glow of the fading Beech—all unite to make a picture of surpassing loveliness which yet, in spite of its wealth of colour, does not dazzle but charms the eye.

Our way goes down, down, into the very bosom of the woods. And now the silence of Nature is broken by the gurgle of running water along the wayside. Looking down to follow the course of the stream the eye lights upon a prospect, away below and over the golden haze that hovers above the tree tops in the valley into which we are descending, of distant wooded hills lying beyond the forestal limits.

On and down still by a sea of waving Bracken, the setting sun with dying splendour burnishing into brighter glory the gold and amber of the Oak and Beech leaves, making crimson the fronds of Fern and deepening the purple of the Heather bells; flashing on the gold of Furze, sparkling from the Holly, and crimsoning the foliage of wild Strawberry which trails upon the turf.

Down still, and when we reach the valley bottom we still wander on between Oak and Beech and Holly and by forest glades all purple and gold with Heather and Gorse. In the deepest hollow of the charming valley we cross a brook whose banks are gorgeous with the blossoms of Heather and Furze. And as if these colours were not rich enough a light bank of fleecy cloud, which floats in the western sky, is encrimsoned by the setting sun—whilst by it floats a cloudy mass of orange and one of purple, making a combination of loveliness such as is rarely seen even in the glorious sunsets of the New Forest.

Our path now winds on and up but we are still shut in on all sides by woods. To our left a waving sea of Bracken sweeps gracefully upon the hillside to the foot of a wood which crowns the hill, whilst, on our right, forest lawns descend over a slope to woods that lie in the hollow below. Turning round at this point towards the setting sun we note a change in the cloudy mass which a few minutes before had claimed our attention; for from our new point of view the cloud mass is brilliantly empurpled, reflecting upon the woods which sweep over the hill a glow of fiery radiance. In another moment we have left the forest and have entered the long and straggling village of Bramshaw.

AUTUMN FROM BRAMBLE HILL.

I

AUTUMN FROM BRAMBLE HILL.

Page 138.

7

AUTUMN FROM BRAMBLE HILL.

AUTUMN FROM BRAMBLE HILL.

WE are inclined to think that few people properly realize how deep is the debt of gratitude which they owe to the English Press for the powerful support it has given during recent years to the struggle which has been carried on—and successfully carried on—for the preservation of the still splendid remnants of our ancient woodlands. Let those who wish to be fully impressed with this sense of obligation take the opportunity of looking down upon the New Forest from the height of Bramble Hill. Possibly not one person in a thousand has even heard of Bramble Hill, and the number is certainly very small of those who have, from the eminence presented by its southern acclivity, obtained what is probably the finest and most extensive woodland view to be obtained in any part of this fair England of ours.

The day following our arrival at Bramshaw we stand on the brow of this hill, which forms a prominent and conspicuous landmark in what is called the 'hill country' of the New Forest, and which rises—on the northernmost limits of the Conqueror's hunting-ground—from the wooded valley, in the depths of which lies the pretty little village of Bramshaw. In the morning great masses of storm-cloud had swept up over the forest from the sea and discharged some heavy showers. But towards mid-day the sky began to clear, and when we reach our point of view on the hill the clouds have broken up into great foam-white masses, and the sun shines out with singular brilliancy from a large expanse of blue.

Behind us, northwards, the prospect is shut out by trees which cover the hill top—Oak, Beech and Holly. Covering the hilly slope, running down from our feet to the wooded valley below, there spreads a clustering mass of Bracken gracefully waving its still green tips above the lower pinnules which glow in autumnal red. From between the Bracken, as far as the eye can take in the immediate foreground of the landscape, come the purple flush of late blossoms of Heather and flashes of gold from spreading shrubs of Dwarf Furze, the green spines of which, revelling in their autumnal verdancy, sparkle in the sunshine. Following slowly down over the sweep of Brake, Heather and Gorse, letting the eye repose for a moment on the bosom of the woody depths in the valley below, the emotion is one of keen delight as the next moment it is lifted over the vast expanse of green, rolling away wave after wave— now sinking into wooded hollows, now rising over wooded uplands—towards the sea. To the south the distant forest view is hidden by the woods which cover the heights of Malwood Ridge, where trees darkly cluster around the site of Malwood

Keep, the place at which, it is said, Rufus feasted the night before he came to his tragic end in the gloomy depths of the adjoining Canterton Glen. To the right of Malwood Ridge the serpentine form of a forest road stands out vividly from the purple ground of the open heathery upland crest over which it winds its way. But between Bramble Hill and Malwood Ridge lies an unbroken view of wood, its summit bathed in autumnal splendour— splendour characterized not by the pervading, though gorgeous, uniformity of colouring which marks the later season, but by the endless variety of leafy tinting that gives so inexpressible a charm to the early mellowing of the forest. Where the prospect is bounded, away to the south-east, the Southampton Water gleams out from the dark setting of the surrounding wooded landscape, whilst the view between is one of wood-covered upland and meadow—a scene of pastoral beauty, the yellow glow of cornfields strongly contrasting with the sober verdancy of copse and hedgerow. But the middle view from the hillside standpoint has the greatest charm for the lover of sylvan scenery. There the sweep of far-reaching forest rolls on and away in autumnal beauty and grandeur, glowing in colour under the play of sunlight—green and orange, red, purple and gold; the lighter verdancy of open forest glades contrasting here and there with the darker outlines of the woods, and these in turn giving every shade of green—dark where the shadows nestle and golden where Autumn tinting has just commenced. The far horizon is bounded by 'the island hills,' which, beyond the gleaming Solent, loom up against the sky. But the sky itself and the clouds which are floating under the eye of the sun introduce elements of singular beauty in the woody landscape; for a floating mass of white vapour slowly drifting across the sky brings a change at every stage of its progress upon the sylvan prospect—now hiding, now revealing, now darkening, now brightening forest glade and woody hollow. And the breeze which moves the clouds, whilst it gives life to colour and effect to shadow, brings leafy music to the ear.

So much for the mid-day splendour of the forest. But later on we watch the forest sunset, and nowhere in sylvan England is the lustre of departing light more brilliant in its effects than is that which falls upon the great Hampshire woodland. As the round, fiery orb slowly declines, flooding the western sky and the western landscape with its parting beams, its slanting rays, bringing the hill-side into the brightness of its waning glory, deepens the purple of the Heather blossoms, flashes from the twisted leaves of Holly, burnishes into gold the flowering Gorse, and heightens the fiery glow of the withering Bracken; whilst Oak and Beech around lend a dozen tints of autumnal leafage to multiply the pervading hues. And then the clouds catch the dying splendour of the sun, and seem, too, as if they were reflecting the glowing colours of the autumnal forest, for the masses of vapour which at mid-day were of spotless white are now flushed with crimson and delicately empurpled. Lower and lower in the west sinks the great golden disc, heightening the beauty of the western landscape, but deepening the shadows which creep over from the eastern horizon, until at length the glory of the day has quite departed, and the streaks of fiery red which for awhile have hovered in the western sky melt into darkness.

Less beautiful perhaps to the eye which delights in the play of colour, but not less grand and impressive than the scenes we have attempted to describe, is the prospect which a few hours later we obtain from the same high standpoint. There is the most profound silence. Not even the cry of the owl or the harsh note of the nightjar! Even the wind is perfectly still, and there is not the slightest rustle of foliage, though an ocean of leaves rolls away for miles into the night. It is still the forest over which we look, and the trees are sleeping under the moonbeams. Moonbeams? Never in our recollection has the silvery radiance of the queen of the night excelled in brilliancy the splendour of this evening. The sky, as we have said, had been cloudy. But the clouds begin rapidly to disperse as darkness creeps on, and soon after the last fiery glow of the sun has departed and night has fairly stolen over the landscape, there is not one tiny speck of cloud to dim the ethereal blueness of the vault of Heaven. Then the great round moon in its full-orbed grandeur slowly rises into the blue firmament, paling the light of the stars and throwing a flood of radiance over the expanse of rolling wood.

We look from this height down upon the sea of green, from the heathery slope on whose crest we stand, where the Bracken spreads out its graceful fronds, and the prickly spines of Gorse sparkle in the moonlight—down, down to the leafy hollows below, where the dark shadows of night creep under the trees whose heads are steeped in silvery lustre.   We cannot help thinking that the birds might have wished to keep awake to enjoy the exceptional beauty of this night; and earlier in the year nightingales in chorus would, at the same place, have made the woods ring with their sweet music.   But as we look no sound breaks the pervading stillness, and nothing moves but the tiny forms of the flitting night-moths.

Surely in this age of hard work, when tired bodies and overwrought brains need, more than they ever did before, the relaxation which nothing can afford so perfectly as a quiet country ramble, we should prize as a treasure beyond price—for our own present enjoyment and as a precious inheritance for posterity—the solitude and beauty of our woods.

A RETROSPECT.

8

A RETROSPECT.

TWO SENTINEL TREES IN MARK ASH.

COMING down from our hill-side stand-point it is curiously interesting and instructive to reflect that the Heather and Bracken upon which we tread now clothe what was once covered by the sea. Instead of the vast expanse of wood, upon which we have just looked, stretching away from near the southern border of Hampshire to this its highest ground, a sea of waters rolled inwards from the deeps beyond, and, many miles to the north, dashed against cliffs which are now the chalk hills of inland Wiltshire. Then the sun shone with equal splendour on the waste of waters and with equal brilliancy and beauty the moon rose over the horizon of the sea. Where the Hawk now hangs motionless above green hollow and wooded valley, over ferny glade and heathery moor, watching keenly for its prey, the seagull screamed over the restless bosom of the deep. Where now roll away, dressed in leafage dyed with autumnal beauty, wood and copse and hedge, giving life and enjoyment to myriads of their inhabitants—inhabitants of the sun-loving world upon which we ourselves delight to live and move —creatures of the sea moved in the great watery world which was to them a home of joy. No Holly then, as now, grew to sparkle in the night under the moonbeams upon the wild steep we are descending; but even in the blackest night, when clouds blotted out the faintest ray of light from the stars, the marvellous phosphorescence of the sea shone more luminously than the brightest leaf dancing under the noonday sun in the forest of to-day. Then too had begun, and was continuing, the silent work—the work of life and of death—which caused the slow but sure accretion of substance—by the agency of legions, incomprehensively vast in number, of infinitesimal mollusca, that produced the solid formations of strata under our feet.

Abundant evidence has been forthcoming from all parts of the area of the New Forest that this retrospect is no mere fancy but is founded on indisputable fact : and of these facts—the facts of geology—we will give one interesting illustration from the testimony of Mr. Wise, who records his discoveries in his own valuable and interesting work on the New Forest. This record will have especial interest here because it relates to the Brook Beds which lie in the very valley into which we are descending : and we will give the account in the discoverer's own words. 'The Brook Beds,' says Mr. Wise, 'I can best describe for the general reader by an account of a pit which Mr. Keeping and myself made. It was sunk about twenty feet from the King's Gairn Brook and measured about six yards long by

four broad.   We first cut through a loamy sand,
measuring three feet, and then came upon nineteen
inches of gravel, where at the base stretched the
half-fossilized trunk of an Oak, and a thick drift
of leaves mixed with black peaty matter, the
remains of some primæval forest.   Three feet of
light-coloured clay, unfossiliferous, succeeded;
and then came the *Corbula* bed, with its myriads
of *Corbula pisum*, massed together, nearly all
pierced by their enemies, the *Murices*.   Stiff light-
coloured clay, measuring eighteen inches, followed,
revealing some of the shells which were to be
found so plentiful in the next stratum.   Here, at
the *Pleurotoma attenuata* Bed, our harvest commenced, and since Mr. Keeping has worked these
beds, no spot has ever yielded such rich results.
Every stroke of the pick showed the pearl and
opal-shaded colours of the Nautilus, and the rich
chestnut glaze of the *Pecten corneus*, whilst at the
bottom lay the great thick-shelled *Carditæ plani-
costæ*.   Inside one of these were enclosed two
most lovely specimens of *Colyptræa trochiformis*.
Mr. Keeping here, too, found a young specimen
of *Natica cepacea* (?), and had the good fortune to

turn up the largest *Pleurotoma attenuata* ever yet discovered, measuring four and a half inches in length and three and a quarter inches in circumference round the thickest whorl.

'We were now down no less than eight feet. And at this stage the water from the brook, which had been threatening, began to burst in upon us from the north side. We, however, with intervals of bailing, still pushed on till we reached the next bed of pale clay, measuring from seven to eight inches, containing *Cassidariæ* highly pyritized, and sharks' teeth, amongst which Mr. Keeping discovered an enormous spine, measuring at least ten inches in length, but we were unable to take it out perfect. The water had all this time been gaining upon us, in spite of our continued efforts to bail it with buckets. We, however, succeeded in making the *Voluta horrida* bed which seemed, at this spot, literally teeming with shells. Each spitful, too, showed specimens of fruit, carbones, fish-palates, drift-wood, and those nodular concretions which had gathered round some berry or coral.

'At this point the water, which was now.

pouring through the side in a complete stream, and a rumbling noise, showed danger was imminent.   Hastily picking up our tools and fossils, we retreated.   In a moment a mass of clay began to move, and two or three tons, completely burying our bed, fell where we had stood. Founder after founder kept succeeding, driving the water up to higher levels. We procured assistance, but precious time was lost. Night began to fall, and we were obliged to leave unworked one of the richest spots which, in these beds, may, perhaps, ever be met.

'As it was we found no less than sixty-one species, including in all two hundred and thirty good cabinet specimens, which, considering the small size of the pit, and our limited time, and the great disadvantages under which we worked, well showed the richness of these beds.'

These Brook beds—which were found so rich in fossils—and other and similarly low-lying parts of the New Forest where fossilized marine remains have been discovered and prove the presence in remote ages of the sea upon the ground where ancient Oaks and stately Beeches now add sturdy beauty and vigorous grace to these Hampshire woodlands—formed the depths of the pre-historic sea which rolled over the land. But chalk flints and other marine deposits, which lie on the 'hill country' of the Norman hunting-ground, prove also that even these heights were covered, at that era, by the briny waters of the deep.

BRAMSHAW TO STONEYCROSS.

9

BRAMSHAW TO STONEYCROSS.

POND AT BRAMSHAW.

RAMSHAW, though now on the forestal borders, is nevertheless a genuine forest village. Its great feature of interest is Bramble Hill, and there is little else to relate of it beyond that it is pretty, quiet and rural. Here, as elsewhere, enclosures of orchard, garden and meadow have encroached upon the forest in modern times, though doubtless, in the Norman period of our history, it was densely

wooded.   From the woods in its vicinity were cut
the shingles for the roof of Salisbury Cathedral.
But though its annual crops of acorns and beech
mast have diminished with its herds of swine,
which ran wild amongst its glades and thickets, it
has an abundant store of Apple-trees in its orchards
and gardens, and, as we pass through the little village on our way to Stoneycross, we note the green
and gold and red of the fruit with which they are
heavily laden.   We take the road, at a four-cross
way, that leads towards Southampton and Cadenham Green and go down hill under leafy shadows,
reaching in a few moments the pretty hamlet of
Brook, getting pretty peeps of common, forest, and
farm and cottage enclosure as our road slightly
ascends. We cross the stream (that doubtless gave
its name to Brook) and pass from Hampshire into
a little corner of Wiltshire, walk a little way under
the shadows of Oaks, bordering either side of our
winding way, and presently, again crossing the same
stream, find ourselves once more in Hampshire.
We follow what is now a winding road through the
forest, with Oaks on both sides of the way—the
woods and glades being wild and the surface

picturesquely broken and covered by empurpled Bramble clumps, by Bracken, green and red, and by flowering Gorse—until we reach the village of Cadenham. Here we turn to the south-west, by a turning on our right at the entrance to the village, and follow a road which, winding up hill towards Stoneycross, presents an appearance of singular beauty. On either side is the forest, and from our point of view the serpentine form of the road through it makes it look, as it climbs the distant hill, as if it were cut through the tree tops. From the top of the first hill there is a dip into the hollow of the woods, and then the road again appears to rise amongst the trees. As we pursue our journey the sun is setting, and the reflected light, thrown slantwise, sparkles brilliantly from the glossy leaves of Holly and brings out vividly all the rich colours of the wild and beautiful woodlands. The ground is carpeted in some places by Moss, green and sometimes almost golden in the richness of its hue; in others by small-leaved Ivy; by the pretty clustering leaves of the Wood Sorrel and by the dwarf and beautiful foliage of the Wood Anemone, whilst Bramble leaves are in many places dyed blood red by autumnal colouring. The woods, on either hand, are glorious with Oak and Beech which crowd the uplands of the forest—leaving small intervening spaces, here and there, for Holly, Bramble and Bracken—until they have reached the hill on the crest of which, on the road we are following, is Stoneycross.

STONEYCROSS TO LYNDHURST.

STONEYCROSS TO LYNDHURST.

A PEEP AT DISTANCE FROM CASTLE MALWOOD.

STANDING upon the high ground—a part of the 'hill country' of the New Forest—that runs by the inn at Stoneycross, the eye can take in a glorious prospect whether it turns to the south or to the north. A level space of Furze and Fern runs from east to west along this commanding ridge, to the heights of which come alike the briny air of the English Channel and the invigorating breezes from the Downs of Wiltshire as season or temperature moves them.   As we leave our comfortable inn quarters, on our way to Lyndhurst, proceeding for a short distance eastwards along the breezy ridge of Stoneycross, we can see, away to our right, if we turn our eyes southwards, a cultivated valley lying just beneath us; away over the uplands that rise from the valley a sweep of far-reaching forest; and then, beyond again, forming the distant horizon, the hills of the Isle of Wight rising, like a great blue line, against the sky and high above all the Hampshire mainland. On our left, and away to the north, the eye takes in a line of wood-covered hills which rise from a wooded valley formed by a slope in the forest that begins almost at our feet.   Looking down into this valley and letting the eye take a north-easterly direction we get a view of the beautifully-wooded Canterton Glen, in which stands the stone supposed to mark the spot where stood the Oak by which Rufus fell.   The woods in this romantic glen are of singular beauty and splendour and as wild and weird and rugged as they could ever have been in the Conqueror's day.   The glen itself is surrounded by wood-covered uplands, and above and beyond these the eye can follow, to the north-east, a long extent of pastoral and agricultural country—meadow, cornfield, and their dividing hedges, rolling away, over undulated country, to the far horizon.

Turning round by the gateway which leads into the enclosure of Castle Malwood we take a south-easterly direction over the brow of a hill, passing, immediately afterwards, on the left-hand side of our way, a wild and beautiful bit of forest, and then, as we make a bend in our road, getting a delightful prospect, away to the east, of the wooded depths of the forest below and the distant sweep beyond of undulating country, and, to the south-east, of the town of Southampton.

Our road still descends by orchard and fruit garden by way of Minstead Green, with its clump of large Oaks, through the leafy valley of Minstead—a smiling region with its undulating meadows and trees and its enclosures of cottage and farmstead, Oaks, overspread with autumnal hues, overarching the hedgebank and making chequered shadows on the road. Our way leads us on past cottages garlanded by roses and trailing Ivy, and turns and winds through the straggling village, now gently rising, now descending. Under the deep shadows of Oaks which, on either side of the way, filter the sunshine through the leafy screen of their branches, we pass out and away from the village and, ere long, reaching the limit of enclosures, again come upon the open forest. Coming soon upon a road running to the right and to the left, we turn to the right and for a short distance pursue a level way. At a point where two stalwart Oaks, growing from opposite sides of our path, commingle their branches over our heads the road makes a general and sweeping descent, and, at its lowest part, rises again through the forest until, in the far distance, it appears almost to touch the sky. Arrived at the top of this distant hill our road falls once more, and again rising with a graceful sweep leads into Lyndhurst, whose houses can now be seen embowered in trees.

LYNDHURST TO BROCKENHURST.

FOREST ROAD FROM LYNDHURST TO BROCKENHURST.   *Page* 173.

STREAM IN QUEEN'S BOWER WOOD,
BROCKENHURST.

NTERING Lyndhurst —the 'Lime wood'—and ' Linhest ' of *Domesday* book, many of the picturesque associations of the past come to the mind and touch the fancy with pleasant suggestions. Through its winding, straggling street the Conqueror and the hunting members of his family must often have ridden, sometimes perhaps in hot pursuit of the deer, or it may be wearily after a day's hard running,

L 2

or with eager pace and flushes of expectation on the morning of the hunt. Lyndhurst was in fact a royal manor and has mention, as such, in *Domesday;* for William of Normandy retained it in his own hands. There was doubtless good reason for his retention of this particular manor, because in his day it occupied a central and very important position in the forest, being in fact 'the capital' of the forestal district. The hall where the courts of attachment—the ' wood motes '— a remnant of the machinery of the ancient forest laws, were held, still stands in the village. Though Lyndhurst at one time, as we have seen, when the New Forest extended its boundaries from the Avon in the west to the Southampton Water in the east and rolled away southwards to the Solent, was nearly central, it no longer occupies that position. Yet it is surrounded still by forest and by much of sylvan loveliness. The approach to it from the Lyndhurst Road Station of the South Western Railway is by a road cut for two miles through the forest, having glades and woods on either hand and entering the village from the north-east. Then, from the village itself, southwards to Brockenhurst, northwards to Brochis Hill, Cadenham, Canterton, Brook, Bramble Hill and Bramshaw, eastwards towards Langley Heath and westwards to Mark Ash and Boldrewood, the route is through forest.

For the completion of our forest itinerary our way lies to Brockenhurst. At the top of the hill, which we ascend after passing through the leafy outskirts of Lyndhurst, we shall, if we turn round, get a beautiful peep of houses and foliage the white-walled dwellings of the pretty village peeping out from their green framework of trees. Then, as we again turn to continue our way, the forest begins to open up in all its beauty. The road we are following descends over a hill, and then, from our point of view, appears to be lost in the trees as it bends round towards the right. On the left-hand side of the route enclosing rails shut out the forest for a short distance ; but we soon get beyond them, and then the open forest spreads out on both sides, showing at the point where the enclosure ends a glow of yellow and gold from the foliage of Birches contrasting with the hue of autumnal Beeches. We pass on by bordering turf and a fringe of graceful Bracken rich in its changing colours—Holly, Birch, Beech and Oak above and Tormentils below lending their contrasting foliage to heighten the picturesqueness and beauty of the forestal scenes. Reaching the crest of our road we can look down beyond us upon the autumnal forest which again hides our road as it bends away round to the left.

The sun has already commenced to sink in the West and the sky seems almost to reflect the colours of the spreading woods, for the fleecy clouds, shown against the blue, are tinged with orange and gold and pink and purple and crimson. Presently the trees cluster less thickly and give place to glades of singular beauty. Our road, first descending, again rises. One moment it is lost as it gently ascends a little way in front of us and then suddenly dips as if it had lost itself in the leafy depths of the trees away beyond. Reaching the point beyond which the further course of the road is hidden from view we look down over its slope, stretching far away into a leafy hollow of the forest, the road losing itself midway on the hill as it ascends on the opposite side and then reappearing again above the tree tops as if it had climbed through the mass of distant greenery. Beyond its utmost limit, as far as we can see its course, a great mass of woods rises against the sky and makes the distant horizon.

The crimson of the Hawthorn berries adds a distinct element of beauty to the forest on either hand and enriches the tangled clumps of Bramble and Brake. The setting sun brings out in strong relief the warmer colours of the landscape—the purple Heather blossom which is clustered on the glades where autumnal Fern is spread out to the light, and the massed heads of Beech and Oak which glow under the dying radiance with red and orange and purple.

Descending again into a leafy hollow of the forest we can follow with the eye the picturesquely-winding course of our road until it dimly melts into the far distance, its farthest extent being concealed by the misty blue mass of the woods which end the sylvan view.

By glade and wood our way leads on, the trees now advancing upon the extremest edge of the forest border and casting shadows upon the road, and now receding in order to open glades of Fern and Heather to floods of sunshine and to reveal purple vistas from out of which gleam the crowded berries of the Hawthorn. Then, as we near our journey's end the way is straight, bordered by grassy strips, with glades on either hand of Gorse and Brake fronting their background of Oak and Birch and Beech. We soon reach the little bridge of the Boldre Water, and, crossing it once more, it is sunset as we quickly walk into the village of Brockenhurst.

PART II.
AUTUMNAL LEAVES.

OAK, ELM, ASH.

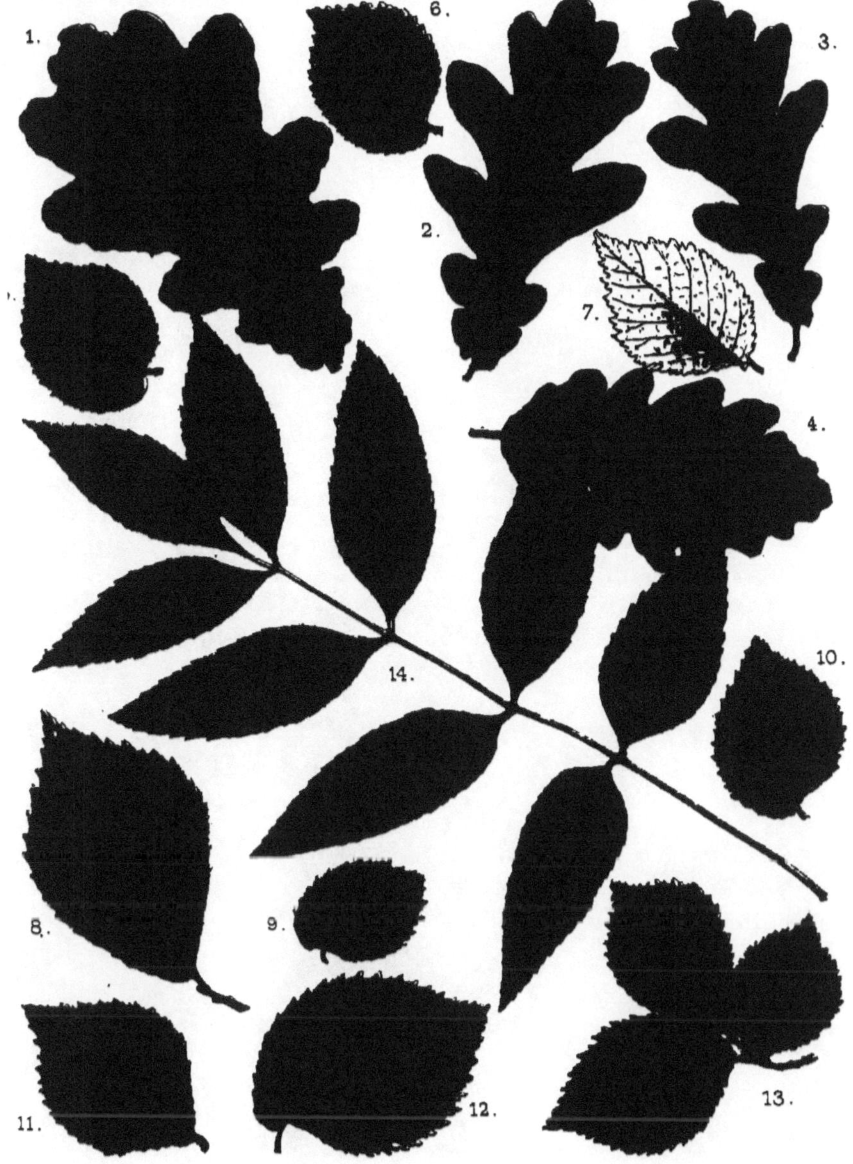
1.
6.
3.
2.
7.
4.
14.
10.
8.
9.
11.
12.
13.

AUTUMNAL LEAVES.

1.

OAK, ELM, ASH.

PLATE 1. FIGURES 1 TO 14.

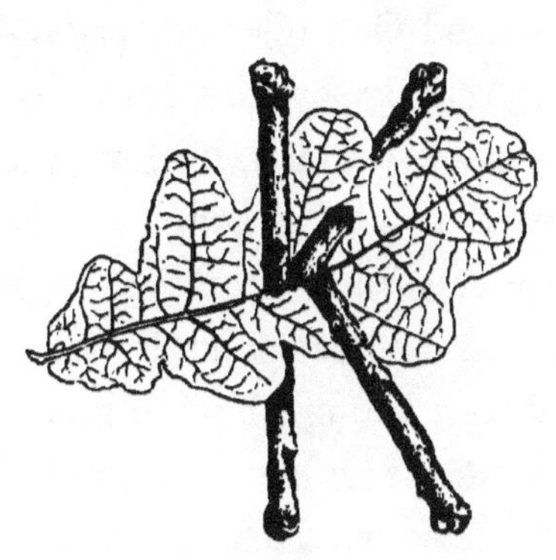

ING of the forest by virtue of qualities of strength and endurance which give it real pre-eminence, the foliage of the Oak lends a preponderance of leafy beauty to the autumnal forest and strongly attracts the eye by the charm and variety of its colouring, wherever, by roadside, in meadow, or on upland, its sturdy form adorns the landscape.

> ' The Oak when living, monarch of the wood ;
> The English Oak, which dead, commands the flood.'

The leaves of our two species of native Oak, though very similar in form and general outline, differ by distinctly-marked characteristics. The leaf of the Wavy-leaved Oak (*Quercus pedunculata*) is known most readily by the entire or partial absence of a leaf-stem—which, however, is distinctly possessed by that of its congener the Flat-leaved Oak (*Quercus sessiliflora*). But though the first-named species has no leaf-stem it has a fruit-stem, whilst the latter, though having stems for its leaves, has either no stems or very imperfect ones for its acorns. The waviness of its leaf surfaces and leaf margins has given origin to the specific name of *Quercus pedunculata*, and this waviness gives a rugged and somewhat wrinkled look to its leaves, whose large-lobed margins are less regular and symmetrical than are those of the larger, glossier, and handsomer leaves of the Flat-leaved Oak. The venation, too, like the general form and contour, is more symmetrical in the stemmed than in the stemless species. But, having thus noticed the prominent differences between the two kinds, it is interesting to mark what is common to both—the particular character of the venation and the beauty of the autumnal colouring. The leaf is traversed by a prominent and slightly-waved mid-vein from which waved veins alternately diverge, on each side, at an acute angle—each branch vein proceeding to the apex of a lobe. From these branches contorted veinlets run irregularly, almost at right angles, and give origin to a thick network of venules which, anastomosing, cover the entire surface of the tissue and provide the elaborate and beautiful system by which life and vigour are carried into the spreading foliage of the king of the woods.

But as, on the wane of the year, the vital forces of the tree become weakened, the full, deep green hue loses its hold and the mellow tints of autumn advance upon the leafy tissue. Plants may be said to live by drinking and breathing. Their roots, with the moisture which they extract from the earth, absorb the chemical substances which conduce to their life, health and beauty: their leaves, through their almost countless *stomata*,

or breathing pores, take in the carbon of the
atmosphere to form their solid parts. How beautifully adapted are these processes to the requirements of the animal world we have shown, with
some elaboration, in ' OUR WOODLAND TREES.' Here
let it suffice to say that the carbonic acid gas, un-
wholesome to man and rejected by all breathing
animals, is absorbed by leaves for their benefit
and for the benefit of the animal kingdom, whilst
the leaves give off, as their contribution to the
vitality of the world, the life-giving oxygen which
man and the animals around him require, performing thus a function by which a compound gas is
made to serve the plant-use and the needs of
the animal world.   But there are, of necessity,
times and seasons for the performance of this.
useful and beautiful function—and these again
are admirably adapted to the requirements and
for the happiness of mankind. It is mostly during
the daytime that man is occupied out of doors, and
then it is that the plant world, under the influence
of the sun, is giving off its oxygen for his benefit.
At night when man is asleep, oxygen is largely
absorbed by the green parts of leaves.   When

these are performing healthy functions and are in full vigour the action of sunlight causes them to part with their oxygen. But as they approach the season for their fall the active functions of assimilation and exhalation become retarded. The oxygen absorbed at night is not freely given off during the daytime and its retention in the cellular tissue causes, under the sun rays, the exquisite tinting of Autumn. How much these striking effects of colour may be partly dependent upon chemical substances, other than oxygen, absorbed into the tissues of plants from their roots towards the approach of the season for the fall of the leaf, and how much upon the action of light upon all these substances, science has not yet been able to accurately determine. It has been discovered that there are a number of distinct pigments or colouring matters of the nature of chlorophyll in the tissues of plants. The presence of chlorophyll in the superficial cells of leaves causes them, under the action of light, to assume their green hue; and similarly the presence in varying proportions of the other pigments, to which Mr. Alfred Russell Wallace gives the collective name of chromophyll, occasions the almost endless shades of other colours.

In relation to this subject of the colouring pigments of plants—a subject which is one of great interest—the accomplished naturalist and writer whose name has just been mentioned has an able chapter on 'the colours of plants and the origin of the colour-sense'* in his work ' *Tropical Nature;*' and as he there epitomizes so much on the question as recent science has discovered, it will be well to make a short extract from the chapter in question.   Mr. Wallace says :—' The recent investigations of Mr. Sorby and others have shown that chlorophyll is not a simple green pigment, but that it really consists of at least seven distinct substances, varying in colour from blue to yellow and orange. These differ in their proportions in the chlorophyll of different plants ; they have different

* The origin and development of the colour-sense is a subject of considerable interest and importance. It is, however, too extensive to be pursued in these pages, and is, moreover, outside the purpose and object of this volume. But the reader who desires to study it is referred to the writings of Mr. Alfred Russell Wallace and to the able and interesting volume on ' *The Colour-sense* ' by Mr. Grant Allen.

chemical reactions; they are differently affected by light; and they give distinct spectra. Mr. Sorby further states that scores of different colouring matters are found in the leaves and flowers of plants, to some of which appropriate names have been given, as erythrophyll which is red, and phaiophyll which is brown; and many of these differ greatly from each other in their chemical composition. These enquiries are at present in their infancy, but as the original term chlorophyll seems scarcely applicable under the present aspect of the subject, it would perhaps be better to introduce the analogous word *chromophyll* as a general term for the colouring matters of the vegetable kingdom. Light has a much more decided action on plants than on animals. The green colour of leaves is almost wholly dependent on it; and although some flowers will become fully coloured in the dark, others are decidedly affected by the absence of light, even when the foliage is fully exposed to it. Looking therefore at the numerous colouring matters which are developed in the tissues of plants, the sensitiveness of these pigments to light, the changes they undergo during growth and development, and the facility with which new chemical combinations are affected by the physiological processes of plants as shown by the endless variety in the chemical constitution of vegetable products, we have no difficulty in comprehending the general causes which aid in producing the colours of the vegetable world or the extreme variability of these colours.' Further on Mr. Wallace remarks:—' The different colours exhibited by the foliage of plants and the changes it undergoes during growth and decay, appear to be due to the general laws already sketched out, and to have little if any relation to the requirements of each species. But flowers and fruit exhibit definite and well pronounced tints, often varying from species to species, and more or less clearly related to the habits and functions of the plant.'

But to return to the autumnal leaves of the Oak. Gilpin, in his *Forest Scenery*, says :—' Of all the hues of Autumn, those of the Oak are commonly the most harmonious. As its vernal tints are more varied than those of other trees, so are its autumnal. In an oaken wood vou see

every variety of green, and every variety of brown;
owing either to the different exposure of the tree,
its different soil, or its different nature; but it is
not my business to enquire into causes.' Those
who have not stood under the spreading boughs
of an Oak in the early Autumn, and carefully
looked up through the tree towards the light in
such a manner as to bring into view the various
hues of the foliage, can have little idea of the
almost infinite variety of tints, not only on the
same tree and on the same branch but on the
same twig. On the same tree are the full green
leaves of summer untouched by the slightest
shade of autumnal colouring, and leaves which
have almost reached the last stage of their discolouration—as it is called; and between the
extremes there is almost every possible tone and
shade. Yet all is, as Gilpin so aptly puts it,
'harmonious.' Except where some accident has
caused the breaking of a branch and the killing
of the leaves upon it there is no harsh contrast.
Next to the deep green summer leaves we shall
perhaps find others enriched by a slight glow as
of golden light, but a glow so spread upon the

leafy surface as to give an indefinable sense of
richness without enabling the eye to detect where
the invading hue begins and where it ends.
Others will have their leafy lobes just touched
with the lighter colour, as if they were under the
rays of the sun; and the hue from its starting-
point spreads inwards, merging so insensibly into
the green that it is impossible to discover the line
of demarcation. Sometimes the upper half of a
leaf is dyed with a russet hue which ceases midway, giving place to the normal green, or the
autumn tinting may be spread in larger or
smaller patches which are, so to speak, insulated
by the surrounding verdancy. It may take the
form of spots which, with never-ending irregu-
larity, are spread upon the green. Sometimes
one lobe of a leaf has changed to its autumnal
colour whilst all the other leaves are of a vivid
green hue. From these stages the process of
autumn tinting advances until the gold, or russet,
or orange, or bronze, or it may be red, colouring
has almost overspread the surface and driven out
the green which lingers until finally extinguished
by the prevalence of the dead uniformity that

marks the final stage of autumnal leafage. To note in detail the almost endless variation from what has been described would be impossible, so let us pass on.

The Elm leaf affords a pretty study, and is well worthy of careful examination. Its most striking peculiarity—the inequality of its base—is much more strongly developed in some specimens than in others. The principal vein, which continues the very short stalk, cannot be strictly called its mid-vein because it divides the leaf into two unequal parts, the base of one part extending further down and along its side of the stalk than the other and smaller part. The leaf margins are very prettily cut into small, sharp-pointed segments, or rather serratures, for the margins are distinctly saw-edged though the serratures are of two kinds, a smaller and more acute series running between the larger series. Very prominent veins branch on either side, and in alternation with each other, from the principal vein, and run straight to the points of the serratures or fork near their apices—one of the forks entering one of the marginal teeth and the other entering the adjoining one. It is interesting to note, in different leaves, the different manner of the forking of the veins. Sometimes it commences almost close to the principal stem, sometimes midway between that stem and the leaf margin and sometimes almost close to the latter. Held against the light the venation can be seen with great distinctness, but the aid of a magnifying-glass will be required to note the ramification over the leaf surface of the minute veinlets; and it is noticeable that, in the Elm leaf, there is not the same gradation, as in some leaves, between the principal veins and the ultimate veinlets, for the latter are almost imperceptible to the unaided eye where they ramify in the spaces formed by the course of the almost parallel veins.

There are three principal stages of colouration of the Elm—by which we mean the familiar and best known *Ulmus campestris*—or Small-leaved Elm of the field and hedgerow. There is the light green of spring, the dark, and almost sombre, green of the summer and the yellow of the Autumn. So bright sometimes is the autumnal yellow of the Elm that it wears a golden hue; and one of the prettiest sights in the early season of change, when yet the mass of foliage of this delightful tree still retains its normal verdancy is the falling to the ground of tiny leaves which are veritably golden. Down they come, slowly and gracefully, looking so delicate and beautiful that it is almost a saddening reflection that they must speedily be trodden into the earth, blackened, disfigured and destroyed.

Between the normal green and final yellow of the Elm leaves there are many, various and beautiful gradations. The more symmetrical form of the foliage gives greater elegance—if we compare it with the leaves of the Oak—to the autumn tinting of *Ulmus campestris*. The invading yellow will sometimes begin at the serrated margins. It will, at other times, extend itself in longitudinal bands in the spaces between the parallel veins— the course of the veins, in this case, being indicated by their green lines of tissue which serve to bring out into relief the enclosed bands of yellow. Occasionally the tinting encroaches broadly upon one side of the leaf and then diminishes gradually

over the rest of the surface. Other stages may
be noticed showing the greater or less advance of
the yellow and the retiring of the green. The
effect is often very striking when bands or
splashes of uniform yellow occupy the centre or
one side of the leaf, all the rest of the surface
being of the normal shade of green. Now and
then there are three colours in the Elm leaf, the
ordinary green and yellow being varied by red,
which spreads sometimes in spots small or large
and sometimes in splashes or bands. It not unfrequently happens that one twig within arm's
reach will contain more than a score of variations
from the uniform green or yellow which forms
the extreme of colouring.

Very graceful is the foliage of the Ash by reason
of its pinnate character ; for what is strictly a leaf
subdivided into leaflets looks like pairs of leaves
set on the stem on opposite sides and ended by a
single leaf. It is this symmetrical arrangement
and the individual smallness of the Ash leaflets
that give the drooping, graceful and pretty
character to the Ash foliage. There are generally

four or five and sometimes six pairs of leaflets on the common stem of the Ash leaf besides the single and independent leaflet at the stem apex. Each leaflet is oblong, is attached by a narrow point to the stem, is then somewhat broadened and ends in an acute point. The margins are sharply-toothed and the venation is very regular and symmetrical, a straight mid-vein giving origin to alternate, though sometimes opposite, pairs of veinlets which, branching from the parent vein, proceed thence to either the points of the serratures or to the crenatures lying between them. The minute anastomosing venules are very beautifully arranged and will well repay close attention, though to see them properly the eye must be aided by a magnifying-glass.

The early loss of its foliage is one of the disadvantages of the Ash. It is on this account that Gilpin says it 'falls under the displeasure of the picturesque eye.' He adds :—' Its leaf, is much tenderer than that of the Oak, and sooner receives impressions from the winds and frost. Instead of contributing its tint, therefore, in the wane of the year, among the many-coloured offspring of the woods, it shrinks from the blast, drops its leaf, and, in each scene where it predominates, leaves wide blanks of desolated boughs, amidst foliage yet fresh and verdant. Before its decay we sometimes see its leaf tinged with a fine yellow, well contrasted with the neighbouring greens. But this is one of Nature's casual beauties. Much oftener its leaf decays in a dark, muddy, unpleasing tint. And yet, notwithstanding this early loss of its foliage, we see the Ash, in a sheltered situation, when the rains have been abundant and the season mild, retain its green (a light pleasant green), when the Oak and the Elm in its neighbourhood have put on their autumnal attire.'

There is more 'casual beauty' in the Ash than Gilpin appeared to think; for though oftentimes it decays in what, by comparison with its richer hues, may be described as an 'unpleasing tint,' it, not unfrequently, assumes a very beautiful glow on the approach of the fall—a glow so bright as to resemble sunlight on the leaves. Sometimes the autumnal hue of the Ash assumes the form of

a uniform brightness which pervades the entire
leaf and, deepening, leads on to the final yellow
that immediately precedes the fall. But at other
times—and this is its most striking and beautiful
appearance—a bright hue, as from a ray of sunshine, falls upon the bases of two or three leaflets,
bathing, so to speak, with golden light, the whole,
or nearly the whole, of one of them and extending,
but with less of intensity, and with a gradually
diminishing area, upon the others, the glow of
light finally—at the leaflet last affected—merging
almost insensibly into the normal green. Occasionally a broad area of yellow is tinged at its
margin with red, and orange spots, and splashes of
dark purplish red are not unfrequently spread
along the margins or over the whole surface of
the leaf. Even when the brown, instead of the
yellow, hue prevails the approach of the autumn
tinting is not unfrequently well worthy of close
examination, for the discolouration advances in
spots, splashes, or bands which, before it has
spread so as to cover the whole leaf, contrasts
strikingly with the still existing green. As with

the Oak and the Elm, all these hues and markings may be found on the same tree—oftentimes on the same branch—in the earlier part of the season of Autumn.

BEECH, LIME, IVY.

1.
2.
3.
4.
5.
6.
7.
8.
9.
10.
11.
12.
13.

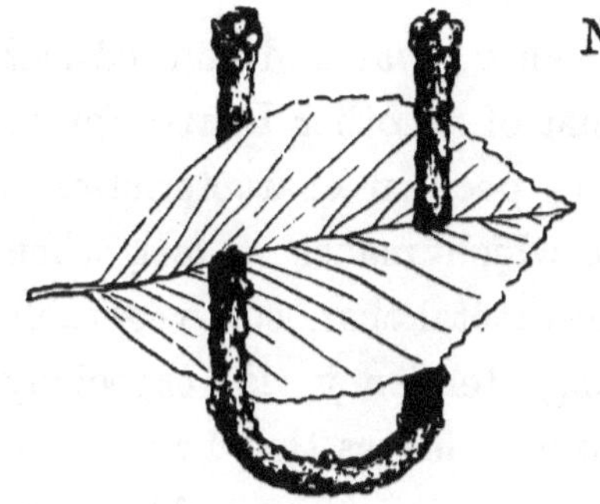

NDER no forest tree is the ground more dry than under the Beech, and leaves which have fallen lie in a thick stratum that crackles as the foot presses them. The lowermost are fast passing into the earth which provided much of their elemental substance; those immediately above are dry and brown, whilst the leaves which strew the surface of the layer, if the 'fall' have commenced, are still painted with patches of colour which have not yet changed into the uniformity of hue of the dead season.

The thin, hard, polished, oval and pointed leaf of the Beech is like that of no other British forest tree ; and amongst its peculiar characteristics is its crackling texture which makes it feel, when handled, more like thin metal than soft vegetable tissue. Its crackling tendency is especially noticeable in the autumnal leaves that have fallen from the tree and lie dry and unmoistened beneath it. Even more prominent than the venation of the Elm is that of the Beech, the mid-rib, continuing the short stem, giving origin, on each side of it, to branch veins which run to the slightly waved margin with marked regularity and in nearly straight and parallel lines. Very often the opposite branches start from the same point of the mid-vein each opposite branch forming, with it, an acute angle and giving a very symmetrical appearance to the venation ; but more frequently opposite vein branches proceed in alternation from the central vein. There is a slight variation in the character of the venation ; the veins and branches being sometimes almost straight and at other times more or less wavy.

Speaking of the beauty of the autumnal hues of the Beech Gilpin says :—' Sometimes it is dressed in modest brown, but generally in glowing orange ; and, in both dresses, its harmony with the grove is pleasing. About the end of September, when the leaf begins to change, it makes a happy contrast with the Oak, whose foliage is yet verdant. Some of the finest oppositions of tint, which perhaps the forest can furnish, arise from the union of Oak and Beech. We often see a wonderful effect from this combination. And yet, accommodating as its leaf is in landscape, on handling it feels as if it were fabricated with metallic rigour. In its autumnal state it always crackles :—" Leni crepitabat bractea vento " (the light metal crackled in the wind). For this reason, I suppose, as its rigour gives it an elastic quality, the common people in France and Switzerland use it for their beds.'

Perhaps there are no forest leaves better adapted in every way for couches than those of *Fagus sylvatica* on account of the dryness as well as the elasticity of the mass; for the accumulated leaves, in a Beech wood, are, whilst foliage hangs upon the tree, singularly well protected from the rain. The author of *Forest Scenery* thinks that in the beechen grove 'you seek in vain' for the variety which characterizes the Oak in Autumn; but in this respect, as in others, he is, we think, somewhat unjust to the Beech. Gilpin does admit that this variety is sometimes present in the wane of the year. He says:—'In the early Autumn, indeed, you see it, when the extremities only of the tree are just tinged with ochre; but, as the year advances, the eye is generally fatigued with one deep monotony of orange; though, among all the hues of Autumn, it is, in itself, perhaps the most beautiful. The painter imitates it the most happily by a touch of terra de Sienna. But the eye is palled even with beauty in profusion and calls for contrast.' 'The same uniformity reigns,' Gilpin continues, 'though of a different hue, when Ash, or Elm, prevails. No fading foliage, indeed, of any one kind that I know, produces harmony, except that of the Oak. The hues, however, of the *distant forest*, when most discordant, are often harmonized by the intervening trees in the *foreground*. We can bear the glow of the distant Beech wood, when it is contrasted, at hand, by a spreading Oak, whose foliage has yet scarce lost its summer tint—or by an Elm or an Ash, whose fading leaves have assumed a yellowish hue.'

The especial admiration of Gilpin for the Oak and his strange prejudice against the Beech must have greatly tinged his estimation of the Beech foliage in Autumn—for though, like all foliage which has reached the final state of its autumn hue, there is a degree of monotony in the pervading uniformity of one colour, it has—much more than Gilpin appeared to think—the charm of variety. His prejudice probably prevented him from carefully studying the Beech in early Autumn; for the variety of its shades of colour, at that season, is almost endless. Sometimes, as with the foliage of the Oak and Elm, a flush of golden colour appears to suffuse, as it were, the green surface of the leaf. At other times the tints are so graduated that green lines or bands appear to lie together in parallel and alternate order—the

bands or markings generally taking the direction
of the veins—that is to say a direction diagonal to
the mid-vein, and giving a sort of striped appearance to the leaf.   In this, as in other cases, it is
generally noticeable that the autumn tinting first
commences in the parallel spaces which lie between
the veins—the veins themselves, and the cellular
tissue which covers them, being the last to give
up the normal green hue.   Hence the alternate
appearance of green and orange or light brown or
reddish fiery brown—for the green lines of the
veins separate the other and discolouring portions
of the leaf.   At other times the tinting begins at
one end or at one side of the leaf and spreads
thence to the opposite end or side until uniformity
of hue prevails over the whole surface.   But
between the kinds of colouring just indicated
there are others giving, as we have said, almost
endless variety—and variety which may be observed by close examination upon not merely the
same tree but upon the same branch.   The natural
lustre of the Beech leaf, its gloss and finish, lend
additional attraction to the loveliness of its autumn
tinting.   But when all these delicate shades are

gone—melted in the pervading and final hue—the fiery colour of the brown is still striking and beauful in the mass, especially when thrown out in strong relief against either the still green leaves which may chance to clothe the stems of neighbouring Beeches or against the more persistent verdancy of adjoining Oaks.

Though amongst the earliest of trees which impart their beauty to the spring, the Lime is the first to show symptoms of change. All the stages of this change are beautiful—for the colouring which indicates the coming fall and the final departure from the twigs, though more rapid, by comparison with leaves of other trees, in spreading over the leafy surface than the ordinary progress of autumnal discolouration, advances, at first, with sufficient slowness to permit of the fullest appreciation of the contrasts afforded by the association of varying tints. The Lime leaf is usually supported by a rather long stalk and is more or less heart-shaped at the base and sharply pointed at the apex, whilst the body of the leaf is rounded in form. These general features vary in different individuals. Sometimes the depression at the base, which makes the heart-shape, is deep and at other times so shallow as to be scarcely perceptible. One of the two lobes which make the heart-shape ordinarily descends lower than the other, sometimes on one side, the right or the left, and sometimes on the other; and the edges of both lobes, in what may be called the bay of the depression lying between them, are unindented; but the whole of the remainder of the leaf-margin is finely and regularly serrated. When the base of the leaf is but slightly depressed it is still free from serratures. The venation is very beautiful, and consists of a mid-vein and branch veins which fork from it to the margin, the two larger of these diverging at an acute angle—one on each side—from the base of the mid-vein and traversing nearly the entire length of the leaf: the others diverging at acute angles from the mid-vein, higher up, and making for the top of the leaf. All the principal veins are again forked once or twice and give origin to a very elaborate and beautiful ramification—veinlets running across the longitudinal veins in roughly parallel lines which take a general crescent-shaped direction from side to side of the leaf—forming an appearance, which can be plainly seen by the unassisted eye, like the meshes of a net.

The peculiar, and exceptionally beautiful, golden-green hue of the Lime foliage in spring changes in the height of summer to a deeper and more sober shade of verdancy: and the change is one that serves to withdraw from particular attention a tree which is conspicuous in the earlier season by the luxurious softness of tint of its leafy clothing. But its withdrawal from notice is for a short period only. It soon claims a renewal of attention by the speedy arrival of the period of its autumn painting. It has, in fact, an early Autumn of its own; for before the end of summer a slight russet tint begins to overspread the tree. The general effect of the commencement of autumnal colouring is expressed in this tint. But if individual Lime leaves be examined, the general hue will be seen to arise from the presence of small, yellowish blotches which cannot easily be individualized, but appear to spread over and

blend with the normal green of the leafy surface.
Along the course of the veins and veinlets the
green retains its darker hue—darker, no doubt, in
appearance, by contrast with the suffusing yellow.
This colour (which ultimately becomes the final
hue of the Lime) like spots of subdued sunlight,
commences in the spaces—each in form like the
figure of a rough parallelogram—lying between
the veinlets which traverse the leafy surface
inside the lines of the principal veins that branch
from the mid-stem of the leaf.   Here and there
are blotches of withered tissue dead brown in
colour, and these contrast effectively with the
yellow and green of the leaf.

As decay advances the colouring is intensified.
The spots of brown increase in size and in
number.   The yellow merges from an indistinct
hue into concentrated and independent blotches
and patches of colour which, in conjunction with
the darker brown, are picturesquely disposed over
the surface of the leaf—sometimes occurring upon
the margin—at the sides, apex or base—and
sometimes in mid-leaf.   At times the yellow
blotches occur independently of the brown ones.

At other times they are merged into them; and sometimes this merging is very picturesque, as when a patch of brown occurs in the centre of a patch of yellow—the dead surrounded by the dying portion. Occasionally a mottled appearance is occasioned by the blending of brown, yellow and green in alternate blotches, and then the effect, so far as the individual leaf is concerned, is strikingly picturesque.

But the assemblage of leaves on a Lime tree, in this the season of its early autumnal colouring, produces an effect to which the individual markings of each leaf contribute. If on different trees only were shown the differences of colouring the effects of contrast would only be manifest in the grove. But it is not so. An individual tree will often-times show nearly all the stages of decay, and all the gradations of colouring. Why the leafy cover-ing of one branch should give symptoms of decline before that of another on the same tree it would be extremely difficult to explain: and why parti-cular twigs on the same branch or particular leaves on the same twig should proclaim the advance of Autumn some time before their fellows

it is not easy to understand. But the result contributes to the infinite variety which constitutes
much of the charm of Nature. Upon the same
tree we may see the almost unchanged summer
leaf, the leaf with the suffusing sunset glow, the
brown-patched leaf, and the leaf with yellow
blotches.

The contrasts, beautiful in themselves, afforded
by these varying colours, are, further, affected—
and deepened or lessened—by the weather : and
of all weather effects that produced by sunshine
is the most powerful. In the summer foliage of,
for instance, the Lime there is only the change of
shade produced by sunshine. What, under a cloudy
sky, was but a mass of uniform green becomes
lighted up by varying hues of verdancy as the sun-
rays penetrate the leafy maze of the tree head.
Yet it is only close inspection that can enable us
to discern the varying tints of green. But in the
Autumn the multiplication of colours and shades
—dark green, pale green, fading green, orange,
russet, yellow, brown—and the modifications of
shade of all these, are powerfully affected by the
advent of sunshine.

How the colours of masses of leaves are influenced by the setting sun is interestingly discussed by the author of *Forest Scenery*. Speaking of the effect upon scenery produced by the weather he says :—'A depth of shadow, hanging over the eastern horizon, gives the beams of the setting sun such powerful effect, that although in fact they are by no means equal to the splendour of a meridian sun, yet, through force of contrast, they appear superior. A distant forest scene, under this brightened gloom, is particularly rich. The verdure of the summer leaf and the varied tints of the autumn one, are all lighted up with glowing colours. The internal parts of the forest are not so happily disposed to catch the effects of a setting sun. The meridian ray, we have seen, may dart through the openings at the top and produce a picture : but the flanks of the forest are generally too well guarded against its horizontal beams. Sometimes a recess, fronting the west, may receive a beautiful light, spreading in a lengthened gleam amidst the gloom of the woods which surround it ; but this can only be had in the outskirts of the forest Sometimes, also, we find in its internal parts, though hardly in its deep recesses, splendid lights, here and there, catching the foliage, and running among the branches which though in Nature generally too scattered to produce an effect, yet if judiciously collected may be beautiful on canvas. We sometimes also see, in a woody scene, corruscations like a bright star, occasioned by a sunbeam darting through an eyelet-hole among the leaves. Many painters, especially Rubens, have been fond of introducing this radiant spot in their landscapes. But, in painting, it is one of those trifles which produce no *effect*. In poetry, indeed, it may produce a pleasing image. Shakespeare has introduced it beautifully where, speaking of the force of truth entering a guilty conscience, he compares it to the sun, which

> " Fires the proud tops of the eastern Pines,
> And darts his light through every guilty hole."

It is one of those circumstances which poetry may offer to the *imagination*, but the pencil cannot well produce to the *eye ;* and, if it could, it were better omitted, as it attracts the attention from what is more interesting.'

The lover of Nature is not concerned for the mere *effect* which what he admires may produce on canvas : nor does he care much whether what he loves does or does not 'produce a pleasing image' in poetry. All painting and all poetry is false which does not reflect Nature, and it is the egotism and conceit of art which makes it profess—as it sometimes does if some of its votaries are to be allowed to speak on its behalf—to rise superior to Nature. The pleasure which we experience in looking at the painting of a landscape or in reading a poem descriptive of scenery is derived from the picture called up to the mind's eye of the subject represented by the artist or the poet : and the greater the fidelity to the original the greater is our pleasure and the greater our admiration. But though the artist cannot represent in detail the smaller effects of colour produced by an autumn sun upon autumn leaves in the interior parts of the mass which forms a tree head, the lover of Nature can and does enjoy the contemplation of the beauty of shade and tinting which close examination reveals.

Though poetry has had little to say of the Lime, it has had much to say of the Ivy and its leaves, which have suggested various reflections, embodying conflicting sentiments—of pleasure and dislike—and have given rise to widely differing feelings and ideas.   Mrs. Hemans says:—

> ' Oh! how could fancy crown with thee
>   In ancient days the god of wine,
> And bid thee at the banquet be
>   Companion of the vine ?
> Thy home, wild plant, is where each sound
>   Of revelry hath long been o'er ;
> Where song's full notes once peal'd around
>   But now are heard no more.'

The prettily descriptive lines of Mant aptly give the characteristics of the plant :—

> ' Its verdure trails the Ivy shoot
>   Along the ground from root to root ;
>   Or climbing high, with random maze,
>   O'er Elm and Ash and Alder strays ;
>   And round each trunk a network weaves
>   Fantastic, and each bough with leaves
>   Of countless shapes entwines, and studs
>   With pale green blooms and half-form'd buds.'

And further :—

> ' The Ivy, fairest plant to seize,
>   And promptest, on the neighbouring trees,

O'er bole and branch, with leaves that shine
All glossy bright, tenacious twine,
And the else naked woodland scene,
Clothe with a raiment fresh and green.'

But it is much more than 'fresh and green.'
Delightful as is this its characteristic it revels in
the loveliness of other colours, and none are finer
than those seen on the sunny sides of autumn
hedgebanks; for there, when much of the summer
vegetation has gone and fallen leaves give room
for the display of the beauty of the glossy trailer,
it may be seen in perfection, dark green, light
green, bluish green, red, orange, purple and yellow,
with shades and markings and blendings of all
these which make variety that is very beautiful.
As with many leaves, so with the Ivy the veins
give play, so to speak, and variety to the tinting,
for the reason that the tissues of which they are
composed and the tissues immediately surrounding
and investing them longer retain the normal green
colour of the leaf. Very frequently after the
leaf-stalk has turned reddish purple or purple the
principal veins and adjacent tissue remain green
whilst the smaller veins and the spaces of tissue

between them have turned yellow or red or orange or purple.

The venation of the Ivy is very elaborate and beautiful. The form of the leaf is marvellously varied, though rarely departing from the three-lobed or five-lobed form, but the rounding or elongation of the lobes is very various in different individuals. A principal vein runs from the apex of the leaf-stalk through the centre of each lobe, and from these veins the forking and branching of the veinlets is very elaborate, resembling indeed very much the contorted and twisted ramification of the Oak.

It is upon the upper surfaces of the Ivy leaves that the most beautiful tints are to be seen, and as it is the upper surfaces which are exposed to the sunshine the circumstance furnishes another proof that it is to the action of sunlight upon the chemical substances contained in the superficial plant cells that is due the marvellous hues which contribute to the splendour of Autumn.

CHESTNUT, WALNUT.

o

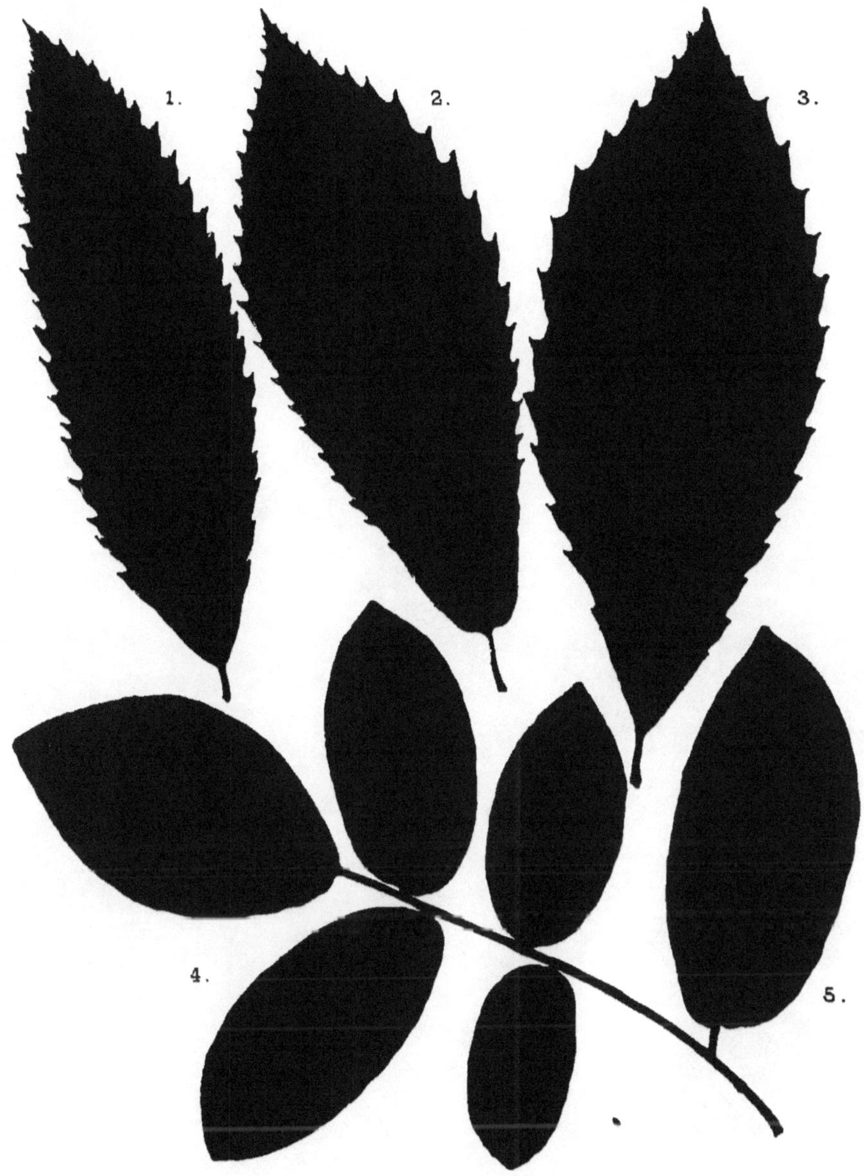
1.
2.
3.
4.
5.

CHESTNUT, WALNUT.

PLATE 3.   FIGURES 1 TO 5.

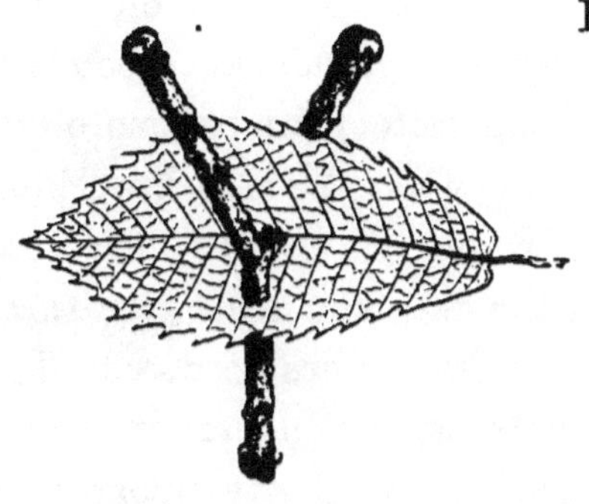

IELDING fruit whose taste is as agreeable to the palate as the glossy beauty of the cosy case that encloses it is pleasant to the eye, the Chestnut has foliage that makes a fine display of autumn colour. In spring and summer the green and shining leaf is a thing of beauty. The mid-vein, continuing the short leaf-stalk, sweeps by a graceful curve through the centre of the long, handsome, tongue-shaped leaf to the sharply-pointed apex. From it, on either side, run almost equally prominent secondary veins, sometimes in opposite pairs but more frequently in alternation. Each of these branching side veins runs by a gentle, upward curve, to one of the points of the deep and acute serratures by which both sides of the leaf are bordered. The points of these serratures, which are ordinarily arranged with beautiful regularity along the margins—commencing usually at about an inch from the base of the leaf—are so acute as to resemble bristles. The branching side veins run parallel with each other—being only occasionally forked—to the very apices of the bristling points of the serratures, and the minute veinlets, that elaborately intersect the leafy tissue lying in the intervening spaces, can only be seen by close examination of the surface or when the leaf is held against a strong light.

The advance of autumnal colouring upon the green, glossy tissue of the Chestnut leaf makes contrasts of great variety and beauty. Sometimes it commences at the edges of the leaf in such a way

as to form a sort of blended but irregular border
of a pale, [illegible] or yellowish-green colour. As
the change extends upon the forces it [illegible] the
direction of the space between the parallel wires
which run from the mid-wire to that margin;
light spots of the same colour being intermingled
with the working green. At other forces the
extreme colour will commence in form of yellow,
orange, or light brown immediately next the mid-
wire and spread them towards the margin or
other side, having the edges all round that half
green. Occasionally a [illegible] brown haze will
begin to develope itself at the base, at the space or
at one side of the half, and, spreading gradually [illegible]
[illegible] will strongly contrast with [illegible] of green
and yellow and orange. Sometimes a [illegible]
half will exhibit a [illegible] tint which, when slowly
examined, will prove to be an effect produced by
minute [illegible] over the whole surface, of green,
orange, yellow and [illegible] brown. In other
[illegible] all these colours are present in the same
half, but instead of such open or [illegible] the
[illegible] consist of [illegible] and yellow-green
spots, the tiny ones, being occasionally left in [illegible]

the midst of pervading yellow, or orange, or
reddish brown. Frequently the tissue along the
course of the veins retains its green hue after the
other parts of the leaf have turned yellow or
orange, and this circumstance often gives rise to
a very beautiful appearance. When the ultimate
colour, which may be yellow, orange, or russet, is
almost uniformly spread upon the surface of the
leaf, remnants of the former hue may often be
found spread in a multitude of small green spots,
giving a mottled appearance which is very attractive. All these phases of change are beautiful
and provide almost unending variety.

Few trees are so valuable in every part as the
Walnut. Wood, leaves and fruit have long been
held in great estimation. Though its shade was in
ancient times thought to be injurious to man and
to the vegetation which might grow under or near
it, its fruit, both for food and medicine, was highly
prized; and notwithstanding that its supposed
prejudicial influence is still greatly believed in
—the 'drip' from its leaves being regarded as
hurtful to plants growing under them—the esteem

in which it is held for its useful and valuable qualities remains as strong as it ever was. Whilst the Romans called it Juglans or 'Jupiter's mast' to distinguish it pre-eminently from all other kinds of mast, the Greeks likened its kernel to the human brain. It was also, by the ancients, called 'the kingly tree.'

But it is of the foliage of the Walnut that especial mention must here be made. Its odorous leaf is large and consists of a common stem supporting two or three nearly opposite pairs of short-stemmed, large, oval leaflets with a single terminal leaflet at the apex of the common mid-stem. The venation is very symmetrical—a prominent, raised mid-vein giving off, on each side towards the leafy margin, parallel branch veins which, running diagonally outwards, are curved upwards, as they approach the entire, unindented edge of the leaf. This curving upwards is a noticeable peculiarity of the Walnut leaf, as the veins of most leaves follow the general direction taken from the mid-vein thence to the margin. In the spaces enclosed between the parallel branch veins there are no prominent veinlets, but a network of

minute venules may be observed on holding the
leaf against a strong light.

The normal hue of the foliage of the Walnut is
dark green.   Speaking of the tree Gilpin says :—
' The Walnut is not an unpicturesque tree.   The
warm, russet hue of its young foliage makes a
pleasing variety among the vivid green of other
trees, about the end of May ; and the same variety
is maintained, in summer, by the contrast of its
yellowish hue, when mixed in any quantity with
trees of a darker tint ; but it opens its leaves so
late, and drops them so early, that it cannot long
be in harmony with the grove.   It starts best
alone, and the early loss of its foliage is of the
less consequence, as its ramification is generally
beautiful.'

The autumnal foliage of the Walnut, though not
possessed of the attraction and the rich colouring
and variety of that of many other trees, is nevertheless interesting and worthy of study and attention.   The normal summer hue deepens into an
olive green, upon which markings of yellow—spots,
splashes, and mottlings—soon make themselves
apparent, whilst a reddish hue begins to over-

spread the leaves. Then, frequently, deep, reddish-brown spots, or spots of a rich rust colour, appear on the tissue which is discoloured by them through its texture—the staining being discernible, though with less intensity, on the under as well as the upper surfaces. A deep olive brown, or russet brown, is the final and least attractive autumnal hue of the Walnut foliage.

HORSE-CHESTNUT, SYCAMORE.

1 and 2 Horse Chestnut. 3 Sycamore.

4.

HORSE-CHESTNUT, SYCAMORE.

Plate 4.   Figures 1 to 3.

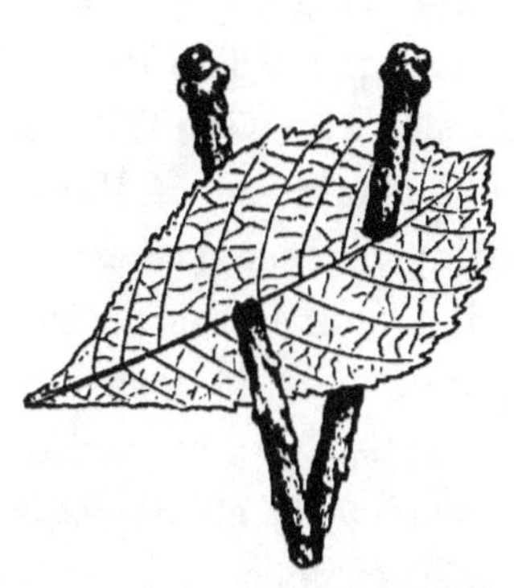

ERY few trees can give so magnificent a display of colour in their autumn tinting as the Horse-Chestnut which was curiously considered by Gilpin to be 'a heavy, disagreeable tree'—a remarkable opinion for so keen a lover of Nature. In speaking of the Horse-Chestnut he says :—' It forms its foliage generally in a round mass, with little appearance of those breaks which, we have observed, contribute to give an airiness and lightness, at least a richness and variety, to the whole mass of foliage. This tree, is, however, chiefly admired for its flower, which *in itself* is beautiful; but the whole tree together in flower is a glaring object, totally unharmonious, and unpicturesque. The Park of Hampton Court, planted I believe by King William, is a superb specimen of a plantation of Horse-Chestnuts. In some situations, indeed, and among a profusion of other wood, a single tree or two, in bloom, may be beautiful. As it forms an admirable shade, it may be of use, too, in thickening distant scenery, or in screening an object at hand, for there is no species of foliage, however heavy, nor any species of bloom, however glaring, which may not be brought by some proper contrast, to produce a good effect.'

Though in the absence of lightness of form the Horse-Chestnut strongly contrasts with many other trees it is not for that reason 'disagreeable.' On the contrary its contrasting characteristics give it variety which is pleasing. With some inconsistency even Gilpin, whilst condemning the

form and general appearance of the round mass
of the tree, and approving it only when serving
as a contrast, yet speaks of the specimens which
stand alone at Bushey Park as 'superb.' Heartily
as we agree with Gilpin in his keen appreciation
not only of the loveliness of forest scenery in
general, but in his particular admiration of the
beautiful forms of individual trees, we cannot en-
dorse his opinion of the Horse-Chestnut, either in
respect of its trunk, its ramification, or its foliage.
But it is our province here to speak only of its
foliage.

In spring when its leaf is golden green, in
summer when it has acquired a darker and a deeper
tinge, and in Autumn when the departing green is
set off by orange and yellow and golden brown—
it is beautiful: and the leaf of no tree is more
beautifully symmetrical. From the apex of a leaf-
stalk of varying length grow from five to seven
large, pear-shaped leaflets attached at the same
point and arranged in a circle or whorl around it.
The base of each leaflet is narrowed towards the
point of attachment to the common foot stalk—
and each leaflet has a straight prominent and

slightly curved mid-stem which runs from the base to the sharply-pointed apex. From each mid-vein a series of prominent, parallel branch veins run on each side to the serrated leaf margins, sometimes in opposite pairs and sometimes in alternation— the spaces between being almost equal to each other over the greater part of the leaf. Occasionally the parallelograms formed by the almost equidistant branch veins are traversed by short veinlets which fork from the latter; and occasionally, also, the normal division of each leaflet into two about equal parts by the mid-vein is varied—one part being distinctly smaller than the other.

The veins of leaves are always more prominent on the under sides of their surfaces than on the upper surfaces, and on the reverse of the Horse-Chestnut leaf not only can the mid-veins, and the branch parallel veins, be clearly seen, but the entire ramification can be traced without the aid of a glass. The venation is very elaborate and beautiful, the course of the veinlets, as they cross the parallels of tissue, being rendered particularly prominent by the thickening of the parts of them adjacent to the branches from which they diverge.

The leaves of the Horse-Chestnut are variable in the hue and richness of their autumn colouring on different trees in different situations, even in the same season—the variations depending on soil and aspect and on the greater or less exposure of the tree to the action of the sun's rays. But oftentimes the display of colour in the early season of Autumn is very striking and beautiful. At first the deep green of summer is, with scarcely perceptible lightness, tinged at the tips of the leaves. It is merely a slight paling of the green. Soon the touch of invading brightness deepens in intensity —the pale green turning to golden brown at the tips, whilst the adjoining tissue near the mid-vein, and previously dark green, becomes slightly paler and finally takes a hue of golden brown. Sometimes the whole leaf is lightened in hue almost uniformly over its surface, every leaflet being equally affected. But frequently, yellow, orange, or golden brown, will advance down the tissue between the parallel spaces formed by the principal branch veins on one side only of a leaflet—it may

P

be on the top of the right-hand side of the leaflet
or at the bottom of the same side: or the new
colouring may begin on the opposite side. Two
or three parts of leaflets may be thus—though
never uniformly—affected by the autumn colouring, whilst the others remain green and unaltered.
The top of one leaflet and the base or sides of
another may be tinted at the same time, though
never in the same way. From their normal
green the principal veinlets themselves will turn
to russet or to brown, and a very beautiful contrast
is afforded when the embrowned veins are surrounded by lines of deep green tissue. Oftentimes when the parallel veins themselves are
russet or brown and nearly the whole surface of
leaf—including the venules—in the spaces between them are also thus coloured, lines of tissue
along on either side of the parallel veins will
remain green, giving an appearance as of green
stripes arranged diagonally, along on either side
of the mid-vein. Russet spots will not unfrequently appear at the top, at the side or at the
bottom of the leaflets upon the pervading golden
brown, and at other times the same leaflet will

exhibit green lines of tissue and golden brown spotted with russet. But all these rich colours, very beautiful in the earliest part of the season of change, will merge into the uniformity of a dark brown hue in the stage preceding the final decay.

We must not

> 'Unnoticed pass
> The Sycamore, capricious in attire;
> Now green, now tawny, and ere Autumn yet
> Has changed the woods, in scarlet honours bright.'

Frequently large and handsome, but various in size, the five-lobed, indented leaf of the Sycamore is remarkable for the beautiful character of its venation. From the top of its long leaf stalk a principal vein runs to the apex of each of its five lobes, and gives origin to curved and opposite or alternate branch veins which run to the margins of the lobes. On close examination of the surface of the tissue it will be seen that the roughly and unequally parallel spaces formed by these branches are crossed by veinlets which, running from branch to branch, divide the whole of the leafy tissue into small, irregularly-shaped spaces that are, in turn, covered by a minute network of still smaller veins.

The Sycamore leaf does not present the variety or possess the attraction of many other leaves for the lover of Autumn. The change of colour is generally indicated by the advance upon the tops of the lobes of a very light brown or drab tint— sometimes merging into brown and occasionally red enough—though only occasionally—to warrant Cowper's designation of ' scarlet.'   Set off against the dark green hue of the summer leaf the effect is often picturesque—the tinting penetrating the tissue, and although shown most prominently upon the dark, upper surface of the leaf, also, though less conspicuously, noticeable on its paler under-side.   As the discolouration advances it takes possession of the spaces between the principal veins, the lines of tissue however on either side along the course of the principal veins remaining green longer than any other portion of the surface and forming an effective contrast with the decay-ing brown.

WESTERN PLANE, ORIENTAL PLANE.

2.
1.
3.
4.

5.

UICK as its growth is, the foliage of the Western Plane is none the less beautiful; and one of its most useful characteristics is its capacity for giving pleasure to towns-people by growing in the heart of densely populated cities. It seems indeed almost to thrive with greater luxuriance in the smoke and dust generated by crowded manufacturing districts; and numberless examples could be furnished of the marvellous growth and vigour of this tree under circumstances which would be depressing to many species of vegetation.

Very beautiful in spring and summer is the handsome leaf of the Western Plane—for the golden green of spring scarcely loses its verdant lightness with the arrival of the riper season: and it is delightful then to look up into the luxuriant mass of foliage that shuts out the scorching sun-rays. But fair to the eye as are the external form and colour of the leaf of the Western Plane the framework upon which the beautiful tissue is so attractively spread is equally pleasing. If a rough comparison were instituted it would be found that the Plane leaf is not unlike that of the Sycamore; or rather it should strictly be said that the Sycamore somewhat resembles the Plane, having in fact, received the name of *Acer pseudo-platanus*, or the 'False Plane.' Whilst, however, the one leaf is dark green, as we have seen, the other is almost golden. Like the Sycamore the Plane is more or less distinctly five-lobed, though the lobes are pyramidal instead of rounded, and sometimes the two lowermost lobes are not very prominent. Unlike the Sycamore the leaf edge of the Plane is almost unindented, but, like it, a principal vein runs from the top of the leaf stalk to the apex of each lobe and gives out branches which fork alternately from it on either side. From veins and branch veins diverge veinlets which traverse the entire leafy surface and form a minute system of reticulation.

The early autumn colouring of the Western Plane is very striking and beautiful—hues of yellow, orange, russet, and sometimes red invading the yet green summer leaf. The advance of the change often produces fine contrasts. Sometimes, unlike the progress of early colouring in most leaves, the principal veins, and the tissue immediately adjacent to them, become tinged with yellow or orange or light golden brown, whilst the rest of the tissue remains green. In the instance of leaves we have already described, we have seen that the contrary is the case, the veins and adjoining tissue being the last instead of the first to receive the impressions of Autumn. The peculiarity that has just been noticed gives an appearance as of yellow stripes upon the leaf. At other times the whole of one lobe—it may be the upper one of the leaf—will become suffused with a fine orange colour upon which a glow of light red may be cast, whilst the rest of the lobes are either green or green and yellow-veined. Sometimes two or more lobes are thus affected, or one may be orange and reddish orange and another, or others, green, or russet. Again the middle of a lobe or the middle of the leaf only may be dyed with orange or yellow over an irregular space, whilst all the tissue outside and around it may be still of the normal green. Variations from all these species of colouring is provided by the entire surface being mottled and splashed and spotted and stained with golden brown, orange, light red, russet and green, whilst upon the same tree which bears all the varieties that have been enumerated we may find leaves untouched by the faintest hue of autumn colouring.

In speaking of the two species of Plane which grow in this country, Gilpin calls them 'noble trees.' Of the Western Plane, which came to us from America—a tree which, though only naturalized in this country, has become singularly attached to the soil of its adoption—the author of *Forest Scenery* says that 'no tree forms a more pleasing shade.' He adds;—'It is full-leafed, and its leaf is large, smooth, of a fine texture, and seldom injured by insects. Its lower branches, shooting horizontally, soon take a direction to the ground; and the spray seems more sedulous than that of any tree we have, by twisting about in various forms, to fill up every little vacuity with shade.'

The Oriental Plane so much resembles its congener just mentioned that it is scarcely necessary to do more than note the points wherein its leaves differ from those of its western relative. The points of difference lie in the more acute and attenuated form of the five lobes into which the leaf of the Oriental Plane is cut. It is also more distinctly five-lobed and the indentations between the lobes are deeper, giving a very pronounced palmate or hand-shaped form to it. The summer leaf, too, of the Oriental Plane is somewhat less golden in its hue than that of its congener. But

in other respects the resemblance is very close.
The venation is similar, and the autumnal hues
of yellow, orange and russet are equally varied
and beautiful.   On the subject of this tree Gilpin
has the following passage :—' Kempster tells us
that at Jedo, the capital of Japan, he found a
species of this tree, the leaves of which were
beautifully variegated like the tri-colour, with
red, green and yellow! An appearance of this
kind is so contrary to Nature's usual mode of
colouring the leaves of forest trees that I should
rather suspect that Kempster saw it either when
the leaves were on the wane, or blasted, or in
some other unnatural state.' Doubtless it was
the Plane under its autumnal colouring that
Kempster saw, for it does—sometimes with
great beauty and magnificence—assume the
colours of red, green and yellow, often adding
to these hues tints of russet and orange.

Of famous ancient Planes Gilpin gives several
interesting descriptions. Let us quote one which
especially well shows the delightfully simple and
graphic manner of expression which was characteristic of the author of *Forest Scenery*. Gilpin
relates that, ' One of the most celebrated trees

on ancient record was an Oriental Plane which grew in Phrygia. Its dimensions are not handed down to us, but from the following circumstances we may suppose them to have been very ample. When Xerxes set out on his Grecian expedition his route led him near this noble tree. Xerxes, it seems, was a great admirer of trees. Amidst all his devastations in an enemy's country it was his particular order to save the groves. This wonderful Plane therefore struck his fancy. He had seen nothing like it before, and, to the astonishment of all his officers, orders were despatched to the right and left of his mighty host to halt three days, during which time he could not be drawn from the Phrygian Plane. His pavilion was spread under it, and he enjoyed the luxury of its delicious shade, while the Greeks were taking measures to defend Thermopylæ. The story may not speak much in favour of the Prince; but it is my business only to pay honour to the tree.'

The falling leaves of the Planes reveal a beautiful provision of Nature for the protection of the young buds of the succeeding season during the possible cold of Autumn, and in their tenderest stage from the heat of summer and from dust, from smoke or other injurious influences. The buds of the Plane instead of being produced in the axils of the leaves—the angles made by the leaf-stalks with the twigs on which they grow—are formed at the bases of the leaf-stalks which are hollowed at the foot to cover them. Only, therefore, when the old leaves drop off are the newly-formed buds underneath them revealed. The base of each leaf-stalk is, in fact, a case which neatly and exactly covers and protects the young bud. Before this stage arrives—at which the new leaf-buds are left to the rigours of winter by the fall of the protecting leaf-stalks—Nature has been busily engaged in swathing the tender tissue of the buds with soft, cold-resisting, silky down, upon which has been placed fur-lined scales. So much has she done to ward off the cold. But the rain and injurious dampness of winter have not been forgotten; for resinous, waterproof cases enwrap the whole, and when the last sere leaf has fluttered to the ground the forerunners of the young foliage are cosily armed against all wintry dangers.

MAPLE, SPINDLE TREE.

1.
2.
3.
4.
5.
6.
7.
8.
9.
10.
11.
12.
13.
14.
15.
16.
17.
18.

MAPLE, SPINDLE TREE.

PLATE 6. FIGURES 1 TO 18.

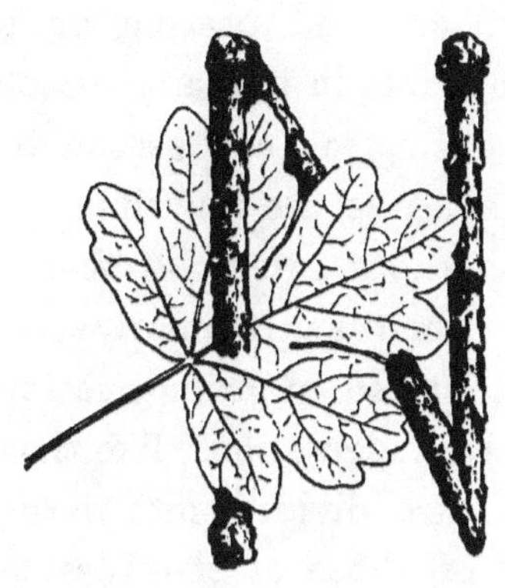

O shrub or tree lends more beauty to autumn hedge-banks than the Maple—the Field Maple, or the Maple of the hedgerow, as it must be called to distinguish it from its larger congener the Sycamore. Though sometimes a tree, it is more commonly seen and recognized as a shrub, and, as such, it frequently almost monopolizes

Q

the lane-banks in rural districts. In spring, summer and Autumn, its foliage is extremely beautiful, turning from its early golden green to a mellow hue of verdancy and passing on to richer and more striking tints in the later season.

Apart from its colouring at any season the form and texture of its leaves are beautiful. In general shape the Maple leaf resembles that of the Sycamore, being somewhat similarly five-lobed. But the lobes, instead of being cut into numerous, small, rounded indentations, like those of the Sycamore leaf, are divided into larger lobes more suggestive of those of the Western Plane, though, unlike the Plane lobes, they are rounded and not acute-pointed. To the apex of each of the five principal lobes a principal vein runs from the top of the leaf-stalk, and smaller veins, branching from the longer and larger ones, run to the apices of the smaller lobes, the spaces of tissue between the lines made by these principal veins being traversed by a sort of double network of veinlets—a large-meshed net-work—if the expression may be used—of veinlets giving origin to a smaller network within it. If the back of the leaf be closely examined it will be seen that the larger of the two sets of veinlets are embossed upon the surface, their course being distinctly traceable from principal vein to principal vein. They form, in fact, irregularly-shaped figures and enclose spaces that are traversed by the still finer set of veinlets forming the still finer network already mentioned, the configuration of which cannot be readily seen without the aid of a magnifying-glass.

When seen in the summer hedgebanks the Maple is often tinged with pink or light red upon its stems and upon the under sides, and sometimes upon the upper sides of its smooth-looking, glossy leaves. The advance of Autumn is shown sometimes by a suffusing hue of pink, sometimes by deep red, and sometimes by a deep golden glow. But, whatever the colour, the whole of a hedgebank will often be found dyed with it.

So much for general displays : and no shrub can better produce a striking effect when seen in the mass. But it is only upon a close examination that the charm of the Maple hedge can be fully appreciated; for the variety of tinting is

marvellously striking and beautiful. Upon one
and the same twig we may see deep green, pale
green, and golden green leaves: a sere and yellow
leaf and a pink or bright red one. But inter-
mediate between all these we may find an almost
endless variety of tinting. The almost uniformly
green surface of a leaf may have a sort of golden
lustre shed upon it, so equally spread that it is
impossible to say where the lightness begins or
where it ends. On another leaf, whilst the centre
is subjected to this species of light, the lobes all
around will glow with orange, with a deep golden
hue, or with a hue of golden brown. Another
leaf will be dyed through with a deep rich orange
colour, excepting a spot or patch or other space
of vivid green, which will be found in the very
centre of the almost pervading orange. Leaves
may also be found with green bordering their
edges, and orange or gold or golden brown in
their centres; others again will present lobes of
deep red side by side with other lobes on the
same leaf of a bright orange or golden brown,
whilst others still will have gold and pink and
green, in spreading patches, merging so insensibly

the one into the other, that no dividing line can be traced.

The especial charm of Nature is its never-ending variety. There is no possibility of exhausting these varieties, even in the Maple hedges one may pass during a single walk. If the walk be rapid we shall lose more than half of the enjoyment. We must continually be stopping, pressing aside the sprays which form the outside clothing of the bank, and peering into the innermost recesses, if we would fully appreciate the beauty of the autumnal Maple hedge.

Poisonous leaves and fruit have oftentimes a fascinating brilliancy of colour. Thus it is with the Spindle Tree, both in fruit and. foliage. As commonly seen in our hedges and woodlands this species assumes more nearly the form of a shrub than that of a tree. Twigs and leaves are noticeable in the spring and summer by a remarkable greenness; but the autumnal hue of the leaves largely surpasses, in the splendour and attractiveness of colour, even the especial verdancy of the earlier season. The form of the leaf may be

described as being somewhat broadly lance-
shaped, but drawn out to a point at the apex.
The margin is finely serrated, but the serratures
are inconspicuous. From a prominent mid-vein,
continuing .the short leaf-stalk, alternate veins
branch towards the margin, which they do not
quite reach, merging near it into the irregular
network of veinlets that traverse the entire leafy
surface.

The vivid green colour of the summer leaf
changes into brilliant hues of red or crimson and
yellow, which are spread in almost endless variation upon the tissue. Sometimes the top of a
leaf will glow with a golden tinge, whilst the
whole of its remaining portion will be deeply
dyed .with crimson; or the lower part will be
golden, whilst the upper portion is crimson. A
crimson centre to a deep yellow margin is another
variation; or yellow spots, or splashes, or bands,
will break the monotony of red or crimson on the
leafy tissue. Now and then a brilliantly crimson
leaf will hang on a twig side by side with one of
spotless yellow; or a leaf may be mottled, or
splashed, or spotted, with a trio of colours—

crimson, yellow, and green. A fine effect is produced when, as not unfrequently happens, a crimson leaf is traversed by golden veins, or a golden leaf by bright green veins, and one shrub, of moderate size, will oftentimes present a combination of glowing crimson and green and gold, the brilliancy of which is heightened by the splendour of the crimson fruit that, though fair to the eye, is poison to the tongue.

MOUNTAIN ASH,
GUELDER ROSE, WAYFARING TREE,
CHERRY, BIRD CHERRY.

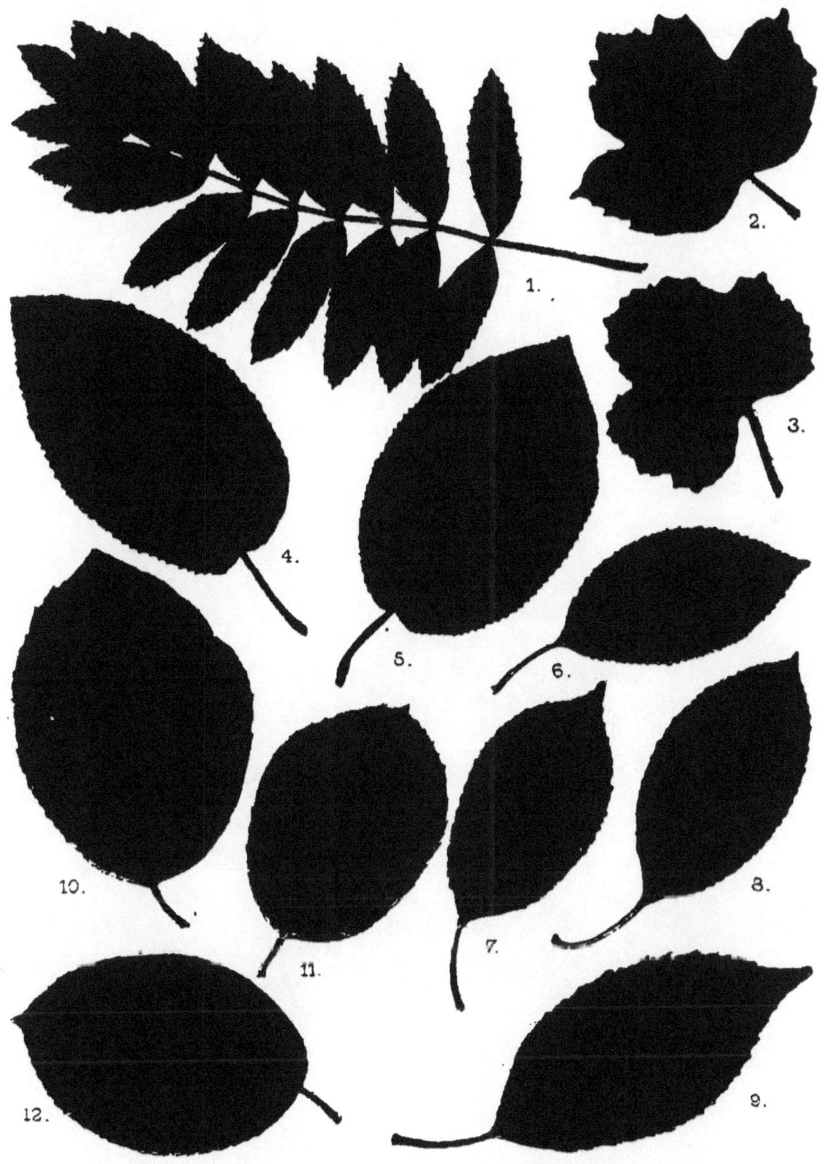

1 Mountain Ash. 2 and 3 Guelder Rose. 4 and 5 Wayfaring Tree.
6 to 9 Cherry. 10 to 12 Bird Cherry.

7.

PLATE 7. FIGURES 1 TO 12.

UTTING knolls and the crests of forest uplands owe often-times much of their beauty to the Mountain Ash, which loves an airy position, and adds the charm of leaf, flower, and fruit, to the attractions of the woodlands where they grow :—

'The Mountain Ash
No eye can overlook, where 'mid the grove
Of yet unfaded trees she lifts her head,

Deck'd with autumnal berries, that outshine
Spring's richest blossoms; and ye may have mark'd
By a brookside, or solitary tarn,
How she her station doth adorn: the pool
Glows at her feet, and all the gloomy rocks
Are brighten'd round her.'

Its name of Mountain *Ash* is a misnomer, for it has no relation whatever to the Ash, and only resembles it in the pinnate form of its leaves. Gilpin fell into the error of considering it ' a beautiful variety ' of the common Ash; but the genial author of *Forest Scenery* made no pretension to be a botanist. He has, however, a characteristic passage on the Mountain Ash, Roan Tree, or Fowler's Service Tree, of which he says:—
' Its name denotes the place of its usual residence. Inured to cold and rugged scenes, it is the hardy inhabitant of the northern parts of this island. Sometimes it is found in softer climes; but there it generally discovers, by its stunted growth, that it does not occupy the situation it loves. In ancient days, when superstition held that place in society which dissipation and impiety now hold, the Mountain Ash was considered an object of great veneration. Often, at this day, a stump of

it is found in some old burying-place; or near the
circle of a Druid temple, whose rites it formerly
invested with its sacred shade. Its chief merit
now consists in being the ornament of landscape.
In the Scottish Highlands it becomes a considerable tree. There, on some rocky mountain
covered with dark Pines and waving Birch, which
cast a solemn gloom over the lake below, a few
Mountain Ashes, joining in a clump, and mixing
with them, have a fine effect. In summer, the
light green tint of their foliage, and in autumn,
the glowing berries which hang clustering upon
them, contrast beautifully with the deeper green
of the Pines; and, if they are happily blended,
and not in too large a proportion, they add some
of the most picturesque furniture with which the
sides of those rugged mountains are invested.'

Virgil says :—

> 'Nature seems to ordain
> The rocky cliff for the wild Ash's reign.'

The leaf of the Mountain Ash consists of a
series of elongated, oval, sharply-indented leaflets,
arranged, ordinarily, in opposite pairs upon the
common mid-stem, a single leaflet terminating the

stem. Upon the base and upon that part of each side of each leaflet next the base, there are no indentations. But the remainder of the edge is so sharply incised that the points of the serratures resemble spines or bristles. The mid-vein divides each leaflet into about two equal parts, and from it proceed, in alternation to each margin, a series of waved branch veins, a branch vein running to the point of each of the marginal spines. It is interesting to note, in the venation of leaves, that the principal branch veins which run through the tissue from the mid-vein to the margin sometimes run to the points of the segments, into which the margin is cut, and sometimes to the base of the crenatures; and that whilst sometimes, and more frequently, a separate branch vein will run direct from the mid-vein to the bases or apices of the serratures, at other times one principal branch vein will, by forking near the margin, run to two of the divisions into which the margin is cut. The network of veinlets which traverse the tissue of the Mountain Ash leaf, between the lines formed by the principal veins, is very elaborate and beautiful.

The autumn tinting of the handsome foliage of the Mountain Ash commences with a delicate flush of crimson, which appears to suffuse the edges of the leaflets, from which it spreads towards their centres. But the tinge is at first so delicate and so slight that it almost insensibly merges into the prevailing green hue. The tips of the leaflets have sometimes a bright and almost lurid glow of red or reddish orange, whilst on the edges immediately below them on either side a faint and almost imperceptible tint of the same kind spreads along towards the base. As the season advances the hue increases in intensity and the whole leaf is oftentimes suffused with a fiery glow that, seen against the still lingering green and in conjunction with the crimson flush of the beautiful berries, presents a spectacle that is often magnificent.

In ancient times the Mountain Ash was considered to provide an antidote to witchcraft; and even yet, in some parts of England, the superstition lingers. It has been, for instance, related that in Yorkshire, not many years since, a peasant cut some twigs from a 'Roan Tree,' and nailed them up against a cowhouse to prevent the evil influence to which the cow kept in it was believed to be subject from a ' witch ' who had ' over-looked,' it. The exclamation in Macbeth 'Aroint thee, witch ! ' has been supposed by some persons to be a corruption of ' A *Roan* Tree witch ! ' and the following verse from an old song will give probability to this supposition :—

> ' Their spells were vain : the boys return'd
> To the Queen in sorrowful mood,
> Crying that " witches have no power
> Where there is Roan Tree wood." '

The palmate leaf of the Guelder Rose bears some resemblance to that of the Western Plane. In its normal form, however, it is ordinarily three-lobed, each lobe having a waved, indented margin. From the waved mid-stem of the leaf, continuing the somewhat short leaf-stalk, wavy branch veins run to the apices of the two side lobes. These start, like the mid-vein, from the apex of the leaf-stalk; but higher on the mid-stem, and from the lower side of the two principal branch veins, other branch veins proceed in alternation to the margin, each running to the apex of one of the smaller lobes into which the three principal parts of the leaf are divided. The whole of the leaf surface, thus intersected by the principal lines of the venation, is traversed by veinlets which form irregular-shaped figures. On the tissue and within the framework thus, so to speak, formed, a fine and elaborate network of still smaller veinlets is spread.

It is not so much by the variation of tints that the Guelder Rose is distinguished in the Autumn as by the magnificence of its hue of empurpled crimson. The deep green leaf oftentimes, on the wane of summer, assumes a darker green tint than it had shown before. Upon this a hue of red begins to appear and, deepening, suffuses the whole leaf. Sometimes one and sometimes two of its lobes may be first affected, whilst the other lobes on the same leaf are green. But the colour soon spreads and, in a very short time from its original appearance, the entire leaf becomes a glowing crimson or purple or purplish crimson; or leaves may be found with purplish crimson centres and golden margins, or gold, purplish crimson and green may be found intermingled—

a very beautiful effect being sometimes shown when a bright golden tinge on the leaf margin sets off against dark purple and green in the middle of the leaf.

Its dense clothing of short, white hairs on its under side gives the mealy, dusty appearance which has doubtless gained for the Wayfaring Tree its common name. These hairs are so thickly scattered upon the under surface of the leaves of this half shrub half tree as to make it soft and velvety to the touch. On some leaves the hairs are much more thickly scattered than upon others. The leaf is large and oval in shape, somewhat bluntly pointed at the apex, slightly heart-shaped at the base and finely serrated along the edges. On its under side the course of the veins can be very prominently seen, and they strongly resemble the ramification of a vine. The rather short leaf-stalk is continued by the mid-stem which takes a slightly waved course through the centre of the leaf, giving off, alternately on each side of it, a series of waved branches each of which is prominently forked as it approaches the leaf margin. A prominent series of veinlets run in a diagonal direction, but irregularly, across the rough parallels of tissue formed by the branch veins, and the thick, soft substance of the leaf is further traversed, between these prominent veinlets, by a close network of venules.

The normal hue of the foliage of the Wayfaring Tree is a dull, deep green. At the commencement of Autumn this gives place to tinges of orange, yellow and red, but the yellow is ordinarily of a deep tint approaching orange. Sometimes the deep green hue turns uniformly to a golden green; at other times to a golden brown. The autumnal change is sometimes indicated by patches of orange that, bright in the centre, become gradually merged and finally lost in the surrounding green. At other times a reddish orange tint is given to the tissue and, if minutely examined with the aid of a glass, it will be seen that the effect is due to the presence of small spots of red in the midst of slightly larger spots of orange. Great richness is given to such an appearance when small spots of the fast departing green still linger on the surface of the tissue. The entire edge of a leaf, to the depth, inwards, of an eighth of an inch, is occasionally found of a rich crimson, whilst yet the summer green is spread upon the rest of the surface. Markings of red or crimson or reddish brown— sometimes also of golden brown and orange—are often splashed upon one and the same leaf and interspersed with patches of green. A fine effect is produced when an almost encrimsoned leaf is mottled with bright yellow or golden brown; and the principal veins will sometimes remain bright green whilst the whole of the adjacent tissue is coloured red or orange or golden brown. We are of course indicating only the prominent and, we may say, the representative shades of autumnal colouring; for a volume could not exhaust the catalogue of the actual variations which may be found in our woodlands.

Fruit and not foliage has given its reputation to the Cherry: and the glossy freshness of the pendant clusters has served to draw the eye from the beauty of the leaves. Even when in Autumn they are dyed with glowing colours, Nature is consistent in every part, and we seldom, if ever, see beautiful fruit and unattractive foliage. Our present subject, at least, proves our rule, for the leaf of the Cherry is as beautiful in its way as its fruit. In shape it is nearly oval, but it is pointed at the apex, and not quite equal at the base; for one of the parts into which the leaf is divided by the mid-stem is slightly longer than the other. The mid-stem, which, with the leaf-stalk that it continues, is generally red in colour, is very prominent on the under side of the leaf. From it branch, in alternation, other prominent veins, which observe a wavy course to the margin, near which they are frequently forked. The spaces formed between the principal branch veins are traversed by an irregular series of thickened veinlets which take no well-defined course, but run sometimes from the mid-stem to meet other and similar veinlets crossing from branch to branch of the principal vein, and sometimes simply cross the space from branch vein to branch vein. The course of these thickened veins can be clearly traced on the under side of the leaf or when the latter is held against the light. The network of smaller veinlets which fill up the rest of the tissue forms a distinct feature, as we shall presently see, in the autumn colouring of the Cherry leaf.

If the foliage of the Cherry be closely examined it will be noticed that the fresh green of each leaf is usually overspread with a slight reddish tinge. The leaf-stalks, as we have seen, are red, as are also the mid-veins, and the wood of the tree itself is red in colour. As Autumn approaches the green of the leaf begins to turn to a light golden hue, whilst the redness deepens both in shade and richness and instead of remaining spread, as in the summer, uniformly over the surface, shows itself around the edge, at the top, at the bottom or on either side of the leaf, in such a way as to contrast with the green or rich yellow tissue adjacent to it. In many leaves the autumn colouring is shown most plainly if not entirely upon the upper surface only, which is the side most exposed to the action of sunlight. In the Cherry as in some other leaves the tissue is stained through by the reddening pigment. A very beautiful variety of the autumn tinting of the Cherry leaf is seen when the whole series of veins and veinlets deepen into a rich red colour, whilst the tissue, which they traverse, turns a deep yellow. Very frequently a fine russet hue will overspread the waning Cherry leaf and produce, with reddened veins and veinlets, a fine effect.

Allied to the tree last mentioned the Bird Cherry shares with it much of the charm of its autumnal colouring : but the form of the leaf is different, being rounder and somewhat less pointed at the apex. The leaf-stalk of the Bird Cherry is short and from the mid-stem, which traverses the leaf, thin and not very prominent veins branch alternately towards the finely serrated margin near which they fork into branches that run into each other. The venation is, in fact, peculiar in the leaves of the Bird Cherry—each pair of parallel veins on either side of the mid-vein forming together a sort of narrow arch. From the outer sides of these arched veins, veinlets run to the margin of the leaf. The remainder of the venation is inconspicuous unless with the aid of a glass or when the leaf is held against the light.

A reddish tinge overspreads the summer green on the approach of Autumn; and soon, as the red hue deepens in intensity, the green merges into a full, rich yellow. Not unfrequently a red glow suffuses one side of the leaf whilst the other side is brightened by a deep tinge of orange or yellow. Standing by a tree in the early Autumn, and looking in amongst the foliage, the variety of tinting is often seen to be very beautiful. Fresh green leaves side by side with red and yellow and reddish yellow and reddish orange—the green merging insensibly in some leaves into the yellow or orange—the orange into pale red and the pale red into glowing crimson, and presenting a picture which is singularly attractive.

WILD SERVICE TREE, APPLE, WHITE BEAM.

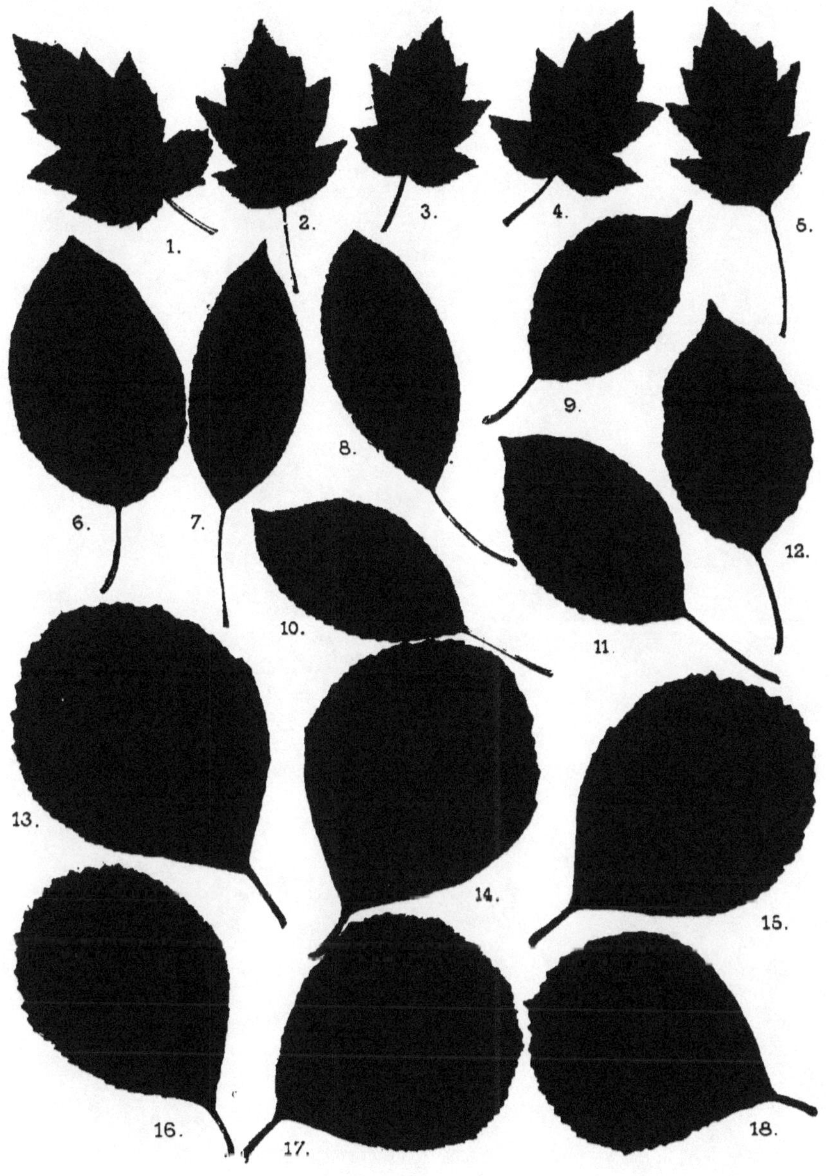
1.
2.
3.
4.
5.
6.
7.
8.
9.
10.
11.
12.
13.
14.
15.
16.
17.
18.

WILD SERVICE TREE, APPLE, WHITE BEAM.

PLATE 8.   FIGURES 1 TO 18.

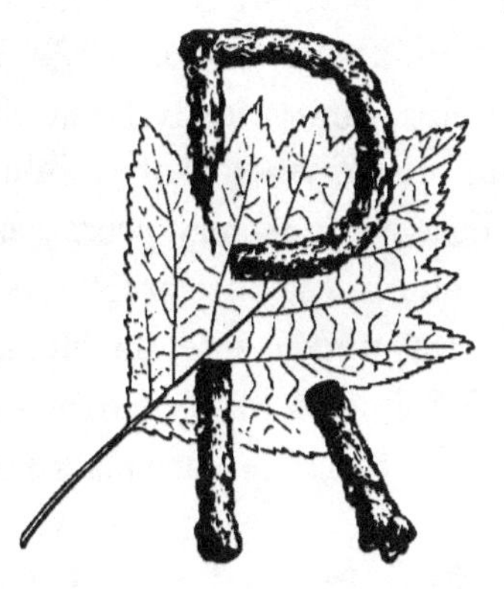

ELATED closely not only to the Mountain Ash, but to the Pear and the Apple, the leaves of the Wild Service Tree differ widely from the foliage of both of those more familiar trees. Their form is somewhat pyramidal, the margin being cut into from five to seven sharply-angled lobes, four or six small ones and a larger, terminal one. The margins

are finely and sharply serrated and the venation is
very symmetrical.   From the mid-vein, which
traverses the centre of the leaf, branch veins
diverge, either in opposite pairs or in alternation
and run to the extreme points of the lobes. From
either side of these veins—but chiefly from the
sides towards the leaf margins—a few veinlets
are thrown off; but these are not very prominent
and cannot be seen well unless the leaf be held
against the light, or its under side be closely
examined.   The ramification of venules over the
rest of the surface of the tissue is very elaborate
and beautiful.

In Autumn the fresh-green leafy surface
changes to a light golden brown, which is relieved
here and there by patches of brighter colour.
The colouring is subject to few striking variations,
but the handsome form of the leaf, under rich,
mellow shades of gold, and light, delicate brown
upon green that has not yet faded, presents an
appearance, in the earlier part of the season of
change, which contributes not a little to the loveliness of autumnal foliage.

In the familiar Apple, the charm of the fruit blinds us, commonly, to the beauty of the foliage. A green Apple leaf is very fresh and delightful, and when the young tissue has fulfilled its office and ministered to the full fruition, the fading leaves are none the less attractive, though they ordinarily drop, unnoticed, to the ground.

The form of the Wild Apple leaf is ovoid; but it is pointed at the apex and the margin is rather finely serrated. A mid-vein divides it into two equal portions, and from that a few prominent branch veins, five or six on each side, run to the margin and are usually forked before they reach it. Some thickened, but smaller and less conspicuous, veins also diverge from each side of the mid-vein and are merged into an irregular network of veinlets that enclose spaces traversed by a very fine and elaborate system of venules. The venation of the Apple leaf is indeed characteristic, in its irregular form, of the tree itself, which, in trunk and ramification, is curiously rugged and contorted.

On the approach of Autumn a mellow hue overspreads the light green Apple leaves, sometimes of yellow merging into gold, sometimes of orange, and sometimes of russet or golden brown. The same leaf may have patches of deep, rich brown, orange, russet and yellow upon green which has not yet disappeared. The autumn colouring usually appears in either spots, splashes, or blotches which affect both the veins and the tissue at the spot where it commences; and it does not, as in some leaves, affect the veins alone or the adjacent tissue alone. The variation is almost endless upon a single tree. We may see, at one and the same time, deep green leaves, orange, yellow, dark brown, light brown, golden brown, and almost every gradation between them—orange leaves with patches or spots of green or yellow; or green with patches or spots of yellow, orange and brown. The markings are of all sizes and appear in varying parts of the leaf: in the centre; along on one side of the mid-vein; at the top, at the bottom, or on either edge; but all merge into final tints of russet or of light, yellowish brown.

The White Beam or ' white tree,' though not a very familiar tree, is distinguished by the singular beauty of its autumnal foliage. The fine white hairs which densely clothe its twigs, its leaf-stalks, and the undersides of its leaves, have suggested its common name. In form its leaf is somewhat roundly ovate, the margin being rather irregularly crenated. The venation is exceptionally prominent, on its mealy underside, an almost geometrically straight mid-vein giving off symmetrically regular, opposite pairs of branch veins which run, in an equally straight course, to the margin. These branch veins are forked, near the leaf margin, and give origin to a very fine, but irregular, reticulation of veinlets which are connected both with them and with the mid-vein.

Though the underside of the White Beam leaf is whitened by the presence of the closely crowd-ing hairs which cover its surface, the upper side is, ordinarily, a deep, dark green, upon which autumnal colouring is very variously shown. Occa-sionally the whole leaf will turn almost uniformly to a bronze hue; at other times to a light brown or a dark brown, or an orange, or a golden brown or green, or to a rich russet hue. But the inter-mediate kinds of colouring are often very striking by the strong contrasts which they produce. Whilst the whole of one side, along the line drawn by the mid-vein, is a deep green the other side will be coloured with bands of dark brown, of light brown and of orange; or one side may be brown and golden green, whilst the other is brown and orange. Deep, rich russet blotches will be found on golden brown leaves, or golden brown blotches may be found on dark russet leaves. One bright, large spot of orange, or deep brown, may lie in the middle, at the side, or at the top or bottom, of a leaf; or there may be bands along the spaces—symmetrically and regularly parted off by the parallel course of the veins—of green and gold and orange and brown and russet. These variations may be seen at the same time on the same tree; and when, as often happens, a considerable mass of still green leaves remains upon the tree, a fine effect is produced by the deep contrasting hues of russet, orange and brown, all of which colours are, not unfrequently, overspread by a deep tint of red or reddish russet.

HORNBEAM, HAZEL, BIRCH, BARBERRY, ALDER.

s

1 to 4 Hornbeam. 5 to 9 Hazel. 10 to 12 Birch. 13 to 20 Barberry. 21 Alder.

HORNBEAM, HAZEL, BIRCH, BARBERRY, ALDER.

PLATE 9. FIGURES 1 TO 21.

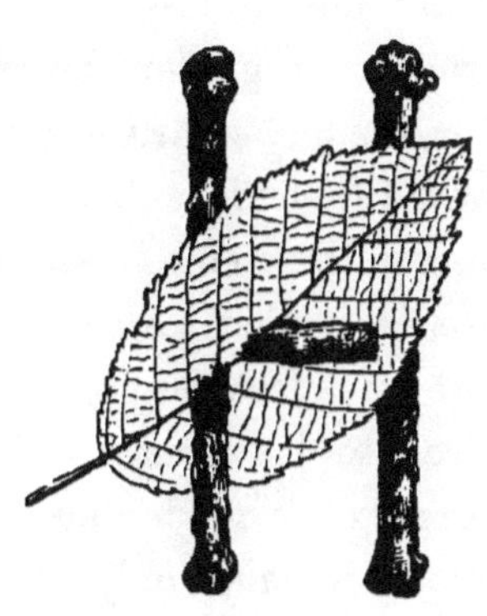

ARDNESS of texture of its woody fibre has given rise to the common name of the Hornbeam, which, by the beauty of its foliage, adds much to the attractions of the forest. Its long, oval leaf is very symmetrically veined, straight parallel branches running from the mid-vein to the sharply-serrated margin. The margin is cut into short

s 2

bays—but the entire edge is indented—and the branch veins run to the ridges of the crenatures.

A bright, glossy green is the normal summer hue of the Hornbeam leaf: but as the Autumn approaches, a bright orange, or golden brown, tint suffuses the entire leaf edge, sometimes extending in places towards the leaf centre along the parallel spaces between the veins. As the colouring increases it spreads further towards the mid-stem, and a very pretty effect is produced when the green has retired to the centre and is surrounded by glowing orange or golden brown. Sometimes the green colour remains only along the veins whilst all the remainder of the tissue is orange, yellow, or light golden brown.

About the time when cosy bunches of nuts begin to peep out from the thick shrubbery of wayside hedges, the Hazel foliage, always of a light, cheerful green, begins to turn to a golden hue. The Hazel leaf will repay close examination: for though in the hedgebank it may sometimes seem to wear a rugged edge, it will be found when held in the hand that its outline is cut

into scollops, and is sharply, and prettily, indented. The form of the leaf is rounded with a
slightly indented base, and a sharp, abrupt apex.

Brown green and russet, are the tints that contrast in autumn woodlands with the green of the
Hazel: and it is in the picturesque disposition of
these tints that the charm of its colouring lies.
A green centre may be immediately surrounded
by golden brown, and that in turn edged by an
irregular line of dark russet; or dark splashes of
russet may interrupt the uniformity of golden
green. Nearly the whole of the leaf may be dyed
with a stain of bright yellow, with just one central,
or nearly central, spot of green: or green and
golden yellow may spread in alternate bands upon
the greater portion of the tissue, whilst at the tip
of the leaf, at the edge, or at the bottom, there
may be a large patch of bright green. These are
some of the variations which, in a single hedgebank, may be numbered by ten thousand.

Very small but very elegant is the leaf of the
Birch. It may be said to be nearly four-sided,
sharply pointed at the apex and acutely serrated

on two of its four sides.   The margin is scolloped into a series of little bays formed by prominent points, which, so to speak, bound them—the bay between each two points being sharply indented, whilst the base of the leaf, which may be said to form two short sides of it, is unindented.   To each of the prominent points of the serratures branches run from the midvein in straight, parallel lines and in opposite pairs—the venation between them, inconspicuous to the unaided eye, being very finely reticulated.

The Birch foliage does not offer a great variety of tints as a contribution to the splendours of autumnal colours, but the motion of its pretty little, glossy leaves which are always ' twinkling ' in the sunshine, adds life and intensity to their hue.   The normal colour of the summer leaf is a bright, fresh green.   As the wane of the year commences, freckles of yellow and orange begin to appear upon the verdant tissue, and, gradually spreading, form many pretty effects and give rise to varied contrasts.   Sometimes one side of a leaf will remain green whilst the other is fast changing into yellow, golden brown, or orange, though the last two tints are much more common in the Birch leaf than yellow. Then, whilst one side may remain green in the centre the margin of the same side will turn perhaps to a golden orange, the other side having an orange ground with green spots or freckles. At other times a whole leaf will be found to have turned to rich, golden brown with the exception of a final freckling of green—the remnants of the departing colour—equally spread over all the surface. Blotches of russet, too, on a ground made up of green and orange, or patches of green on a golden brown, or orange, ground are variations from the colouring already indicated. But the gradations of colouring are too numerous to indicate in detail.

Speaking of the motion of the Weeping Birch foliage Gilpin says :—' Its spray being slender and longer than the common sort forms an elegant pensile foliage, like the Weeping Willow, and, like it, is put in motion by the least breath of air. When agitated it is well adapted to characterize a storm, or to perform any office in landscape which is expected from the Weeping Willow.'

Small and club-shaped in form, the leaves of the Barberry are very beautifully spined upon the margins and very curiously and beautifully veined throughout their tissue. From the mid-vein a series of branches take an irregular, contorted course, spreading over every part of the tissue and presenting an appearance which may be likened in form to a species of irregular mosaic work. It is like, in fact, few other leaves, as a glance at our illustrative figures, in which the artist has excellently rendered the venation, will show. Between the veins prominently shown on both sides of the leaf—for they are raised or embossed on both the upper and under sides—there is a still finer and more elaborate system of venation occupying the spaces which the larger veins enclose.

Hues of yellow, orange, and red are the prominent characteristics of the autumn tinting of the Barberry, and in the early season of change these colours are oftentimes spread very beautifully over its leaves. Whilst some will turn uniformly from the green to a bright golden yellow, others will become yellow at the sides or the top or the bottom, whilst upon the centre a bright red tint is developed. In other cases whilst the green remains in its ordinary shade, upon the leaf edge or in the centre of the leaf, a bright, red tint will overspread the centre or the edge. A pretty effect is produced when golden green and red and orange are mingled so deftly upon the leaf surface that it is impossible to define the limits of either. Now and then the same leaf will exhibit a patch of light brown, another of green, one of yellow and another of red; or there may be mottlings of yellow upon a green ground or mottlings of green or red upon a yellow ground. A patch of red upon the upper side of a leaf will be represented on the under side by a similar patch of yellow, but a yellow or orange upper side produces a similar, though sometimes paler, shade on the other side. A small Barberry bush will, indeed, furnish variations of colour and tinting that, in the early season of Autumn, are almost endless.

The Alder is not subject to much of what Gilpin calls 'picturesque beauty' in its autumn colouring but a fine shade of reddish brown oftentimes overspreads it. The margin of the Alder leaf is waved and slightly crenated, its form is almost round, and it has, ordinarily, a slight depression at its apex. The venation is especially prominent at the back of the leaf and consists of a waved mid-vein and parallel branches which run alternately on either side of it to the apices of the short lobes into which its wavy course divides the margin. Across the parallels formed by the principal branch veins, run, at right angles to the latter, a series of nearly parallel veins and between these the tissue is traversed by a dense network of venules.

Comparing the Alder with the Willow, Gilpin says that the first-named is 'the more picturesque tree, both in its ramification and in its foliage; perhaps, indeed, it is the most picturesque of any of the aquatic tribe, except the Weeping Willow.' 'He who would see the Alder in perfection,' continues the author of *Forest Scenery*, 'must follow the banks of the Mole, in Surrey, through the sweet vales of Dorking and Mickleham into the groves of Esher. The Mole, indeed, is far from being a beautiful river; it is a silent and sluggish stream. But what beauty it has it owes greatly to the Alder, which everywhere fringes its meadows, and in many places forms pleasing scenes, especially in the vale between Box Hill and the high grounds of Norbury Park.'

LOMBARDY POPLAR, WHITE POPLAR,
BLACK POPLAR, ASPEN, WILLOW,
ALDER BUCKTHORN.

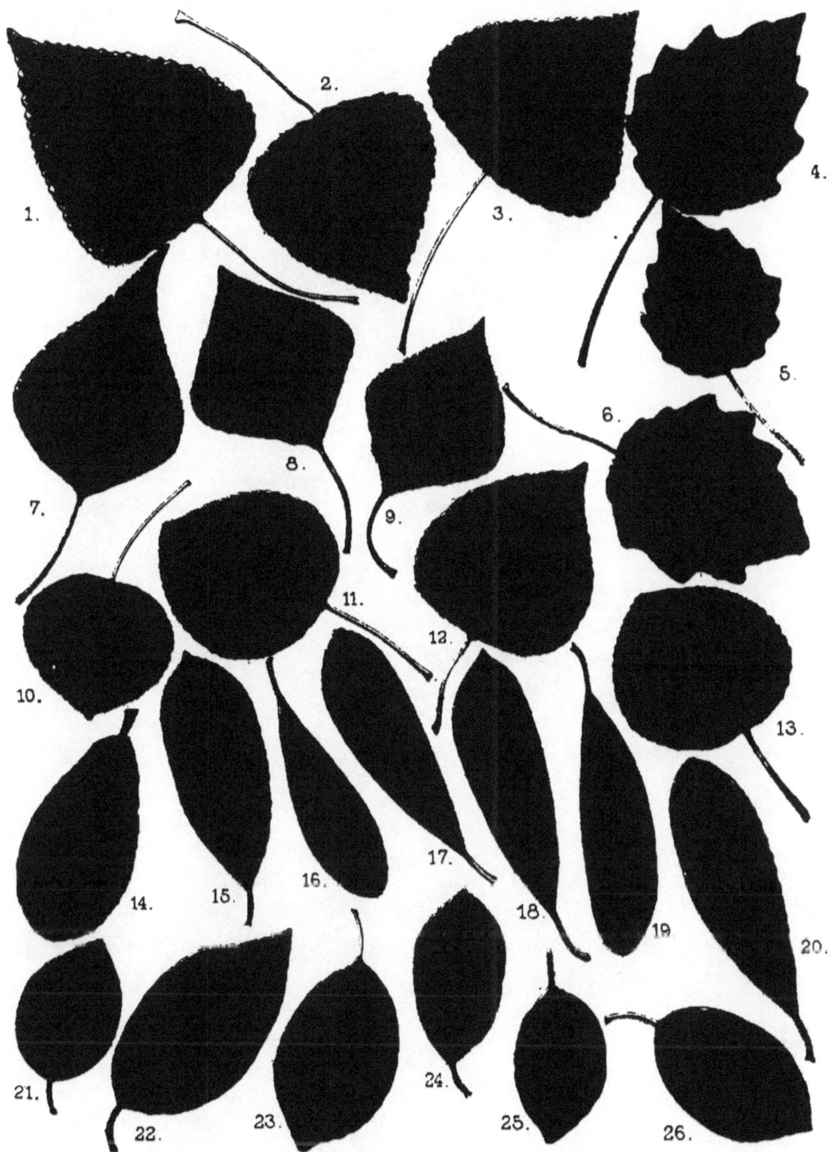

1 to 3 Lombardy Poplar. 4 to 6 White Poplar. 7 to 9 Black Poplar. 10 to 13 Aspen.
14 to 20 Willow. 21 to 26 Alder Buckthorn.

10.

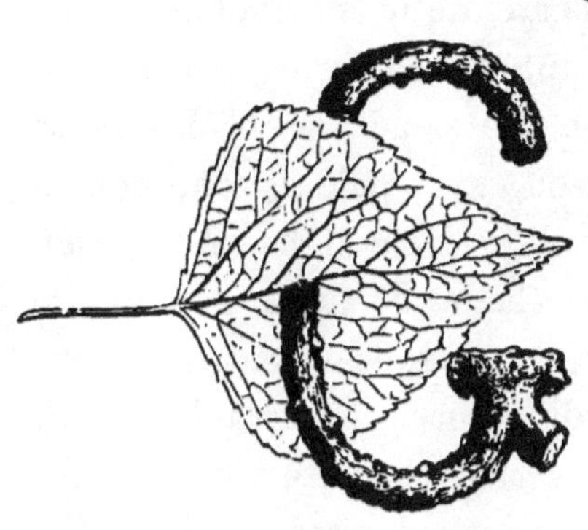

OLDEN almost in hue in its final stage of colouring the Lombardy Poplar presents many shades and markings which give it 'picturesque beauty' in the early season of Autumn. Its leaf is almost triangular and its edges are somewhat broadly indented. The venation consists of a wavy mid-vein which divides the leaf in two, and an irregular series of waved, much-forked veins, branching from it. Running across the course of these principal veins are a second series of smaller ones, and, within these, there is a close network of venules.

The variations of autumn colouring are shown by the presence upon the same tree of leaves of normal summer green, and pale green, golden green, orange and yellow, with light and golden brown. Contrasting shades of these colours are sometimes shown on the same leaf; but it is more frequently in the differences observable in an aggregation of leaves that the autumn character of the Lombardy Poplar is exhibited.

The foliage of the White and Black Poplars and the Aspen is distinguishable by very clearly marked characters. The white underside con-trasting strongly as it does with the glossy green upper surface, has given rise to the common name of the first-named of these three Poplars. The general form of the leaf is more or less rounded, but it has a pointed apex, and its margin is broadly waved, or cut into short, rounded lobes.

The principal veins which, diverging from the midvein, are forked as they near the margin—a vein or fork proceeding to the apex of each lobe—are crossed by a series of veinlets that run nearly at right angles with them in a course which can be plainly traced on either side of the leaf; and these veinlets enclose, between them, an elaborate network of venules.

Though the final colour of the autumnal leaves of the White Poplar is a dark brown, there are several preliminary stages of tinting which are interesting and beautiful—such as the normal dark green contrasting, on the same or adjoining leaves, with light brown, upon which a distinct hue of red is discernible. Pale green, pale brown and red, may be seen on the same leaf, and one branch may show at the same time a rich array of various shades and markings. But the colours are very transient and extremely difficult to preserve—when the leaves have been gathered—from merging into the final and less interesting stage of dark brown.

In its general form, venation, and autumnal

colouring, the leaf of the Black Poplar so nearly resembles that of the Lombardy Poplar that a lengthened separate notice of it will be unnecessary. The points of difference lie chiefly in the longer and more pointed apex of the leaf of the Black Poplar, and in its almost four-sided form, a distinction that will be readily noticed on reference to the coloured figures.

The pretty little, rounded leaf of the Aspen, which has a crenated margin, is veined very much like that of its congeners just mentioned, and its stages of colouring—giving contrasts of green against golden brown, yellow and orange— are, too, much like those of the Lombardy and the Black Poplars, though it takes oftentimes, like the White Poplar, a final tint of dark brown. Dismissal with mention is, therefore, all that need be said of the Trembling Poplar.

Of the prolific family of the Willows, very various in their autumn colouring, mention will be made and illustration given of one of the broad-leaved kind whose venation—a mid-vein with alternate parallel branches proceeding to the margins, crossing veinlets and a reticulating network of venules,—can be plainly traced on its under side.

The ultimate autumnal colour of the Willow leaves is yellow or orange; but the gradations of tint, from the normal green to the final hue, present oftentimes very beautiful contrasts. Minute spots of rich, golden orange, overspreading the decaying green, produce an almost bronze tint in some leaves. In others the whole of one side will be orange whilst the other is green; or the top or the bottom may be yellow, golden brown, or orange, and the rest of the surface green or green spotted with yellow or orange. Pretty effects are produced when an orange leaf is freckled with tiny green spots, as also when a green leaf is freckled with yellow or orange. But all these changes, and many more, can only be noted on close examination.

The smooth, oval, unindented leaf of the Alder Buckthorn bears a not altogether remote likeness, in the character of its venation, and of its autumn tinting to that of the Willow we have described. and figured. The principal veins sweep upwards from the mid-vein, in curves, towards the margins on either side and are very prominently shown on the under side. Across these, smaller veins run enclosing tissue which is traversed by a fine network of venules. The final colour of the Alder Buckthorn is a deep yellow, or orange; and these tints, commencing sometimes upon the edges of the leaves, sometimes at their tops and sometimes on either side, will advance upon the normal hue in an almost endless variety of ways, giving occasion for many beautiful effects of contrast.

HAWTHORN, BLACKTHORN, DOGWOOD.
MEDLAR, QUINCE.

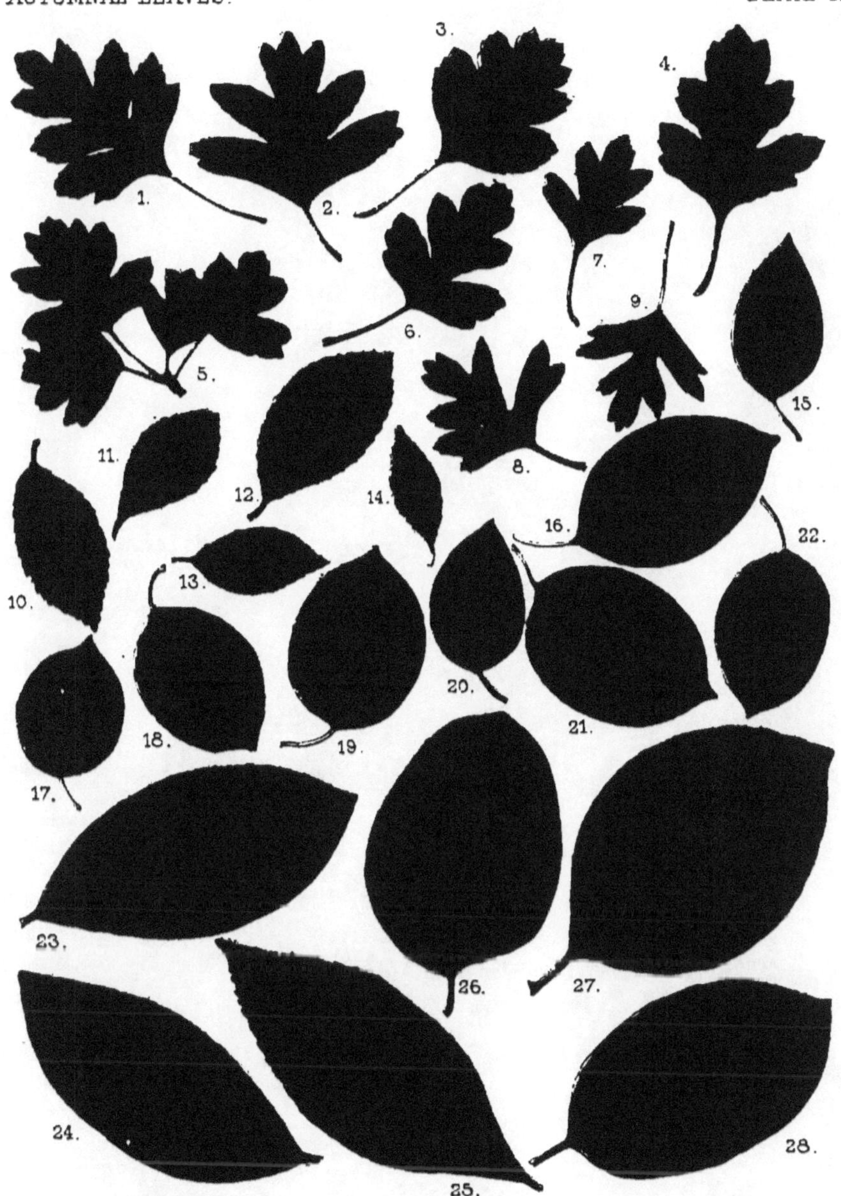

1 to 9 Hawthorn. 10 to 14 Blackthorn. 15 to 22 Dogwood.
23 to 25 Medlar. 26 to 28 Quince.

HAWTHORN, BLACKTHORN, DOGWOOD, MEDLAR, QUINCE.

PLATE 11.   FIGURES 1 TO 28.

ELIGHTFUL reminiscences of the sunniest of sunny days in the dear 'country' come to the mind at the mere mention of the Hawthorn, which in leaf, flower and fruit is ever beautiful. But delightful as this familiar plant is when its leaves are golden green in spring and its blossoms perfume the vernal hedges, its autumnal foliage vies with its crimson berries in feasting the eye with the charm of colour.

The Hawthorn leaf is very various in form, being sometimes almost triangular and sometimes four-sided, and it is deeply cut into lobes which vary in number from three to seven, and are more or less acute or rounded. From the mid-vein a principal vein runs to each principal lobe, and veinlets branch from the principal veins to the smaller lobes, whilst a network of venules traverses the spaces lying between the lines of the more important veins.

Probably—excepting the Bramble—there is no other hedge shrub or woodland tree—for the Hawthorn is both—that presents so great a variety and such magnificence of colours in the early season of Autumn: and one of the most interesting of country rambles, for any one who loves the beauties of leafage, is a walk at that season by Hawthorn hedges. The pure pleasure of noting the really marvellous varieties of tinting of this delightful plant is very great, and it is well nigh inexhaustible. Side by side, upon the same bush, we may find deep, dark, glossy green leaves and leaves whose upper sides are dyed a dark rich crimson ; and we may find crimson and green, crimson and orange and bronze leaves. Walking on by the same Hawthorn hedge we may chance upon dark, golden, and light, pale green, and upon golden and dark brown leaves; upon leaves of orange, yellow and russet ; and upon leaves which are reddish brown, dark red, crimson, purplish red, and rich deep orange. It would require literally more than the space of a volume to enumerate all the variations of these colours which are found blending, contrasting and uniting with each other on the same or on adjoining shrubs.

In one short walk through a country lane not two hundred yards long, bordered, on either side, with Hawthorn, we have seen, on individual leaves, the colours respectively indicated in the following enumeration, in which the tones predominating on any leaf have priority of mention : —dark green with dark brown ; dark green with dark crimson and orange; pale straw colour with green and russet blotches ; golden green with orange and crimson ; bronze with deep red ; golden green with orange ; orange with russet blotches; yellow with orange and green blotches; deep red with orange and green spots; golden green with dark brown splashes; bronze with crimson and orange; deep red with orange red and green; pale green with pale straw colour and brown; pale green with light red and orange; pinkish red, with orange and green; and crimson with reddish orange and green. And these are less than a tithe of the tints which any one may discover who takes the trouble to study the Hawthorn hedgebanks in the early season of Autumn.

To such marvellous variety of individual tinting the Blackthorn cannot lay claim; but it often, in the mass, presents pretty combinations of green and yellow and russet, with, occasionally, light reddish hues, and its forked, principal veins, which branch alternately from either side of the mid-veins to the serrated margin, give origin to a beautiful and elaborate system of reticulating venules.

To the splendours of autumnal hedges the Dog-wood largely contributes. Its symmetrical, oval leaf which is ordinarily pointed at the apex, possesses a very characteristic venation. A small number of prominent veins branch from the mid-vein—alternately on either side of it or in opposite pairs—to the margin—each branch taking a curious upward curve. Running across these principal veins, from edge to edge of the leaf, are a few waved veinlets that cannot be easily seen unless the leaf be held against the light.

Sometimes autumnal hedges are dyed deep red and sometimes rich purple by the clustered foliage of the Dogwood; but these general or massed effects, beautiful as they are, can bear no comparison with the loveliness of the varied and contrasting tints which are conspicuous in the early season of leafy change. Deep crimson, light red, orange, and almost golden leaves may be found, side by side on the same bush, with the vivid green leaves of summer. Green and brownish red, green and purple, green and red, orange and green, and crimson and yellow, are merely the tints which are spread in endless variation, upon the tissue—presenting shades and markings which are far too numerous to indicate in detail.

Striking and picturesque contrasts of green, yellow, russet and red, are often furnished by the autumnal foliage of the Medlar, the venation of whose large, soft, somewhat lance-shaped leaf can be plainly seen on its hairy under-side where alternate, waved, forked branches diverge from the very prominent mid-vein. On the same branch one may find deep green, yellow, reddish-orange, brown, russet, and golden-brown leaves: but on the same leaf may sometimes be found nearly all these colours. Light red and dark brown, and orange with bright green spots, will be found on one; russet and orange and green on another; on a third golden brown and green; on a fourth golden green with deep green spots. All these variations on the same tree and many more that could be indicated, oftentimes produce effects of colour which are very beautiful.

Somewhat similar in the character of their tinting, though the contrasts of colour are even more striking, are the leaves of the Quince. The leaf of the Quince is of varying size, and is oval in shape. It has a very elaborate and beautiful system of venation. From the central and somewhat rigid mid-vein a number of prominent branches are given off irregularly on each side, and are two or three times forked near the margin. Across these branch veins, taking a wavy course, run a series of veinlets between the lines of which there is a close reticulation of venules.

On the same tree one may pick deep green leaves, bright yellow, deep orange, golden green, golden brown and red inclining to black leaves; green leaves with golden or orange veins; golden green with orange and blackish red; green and dark brown with orange and dark red; green and orange with light red veins, and many other markings and shades between all these—the mass of colour on the whole of a tree in the early season of Autumn being frequently very striking.

BRAMBLE.

BRAMBLE.

PLATE 12.   FRONTISPIECE.

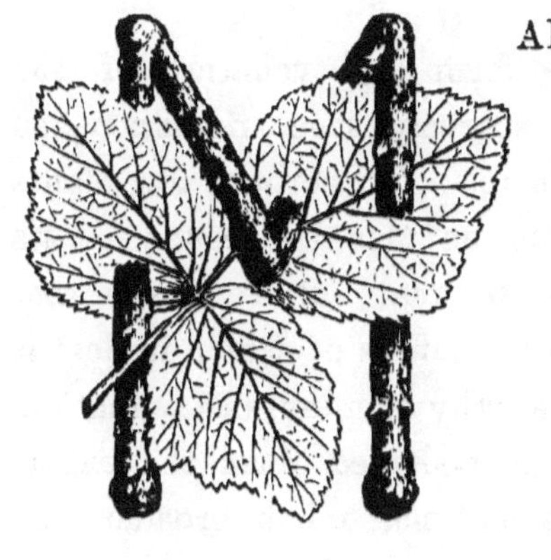

ARVELLOUS is the diversity of colouring which suffuses stem, leaf, blossom and fruit in the Bramble.   Indeed there is probably no other hedge or woodland shrub that equals it in the extraordinary and almost endless tints which it wears during the course of the year.   But the variations of colour assumed during the early period of leafage

U

and during the various stages of fruition by this charming plant, are far exceeded by the diversity of its autumnal hues.

To describe the form and venation of the Bramble leaf may scarcely seem necessary, so common ' is the shrub. Yet perhaps few plants are so little noticed as this by reason of its ' commonness ;' and we may, at least, say that the three, four, or five leaflets of which its leaf is composed are well worthy of minute examination. From the general pear-shaped form the leaflets vary much, being sometimes much broader than they are at other times ; sometimes more or less pointed at the apex ; sometimes slightly depressed at the apex, and now and then nearly round in general form. Occasionally, and indeed not unfrequently, a leaf will be found to possess two normal leaflets and an abnormal or double leaflet, or one normal leaflet and two double leaflets ; or, it may be, three normal leaflets and one double leaflet. The margins of the leaflets do not much differ in the character of their serratures, which are ordinarily acute and almost spinous. From the mid-vein, slightly waved branches run, on either side, generally in alternation and occasionally in opposite pairs, towards the leaflet edges. These branches are forked near their apices and are traversed by a series of rather prominent veinlets which run in a straggling direction across them. In the spaces of tissue between the lines of these veinlets the eye, aided by a magnifying-glass, can trace the course of a very beautiful network of venules.

We can only indicate the prominent features of the colouring which overspreads the foliage of the autumnal Bramble. To give the mere colours and shades would require a long enumeration : to describe the really endless combinations of them would be impossible. We will mention some of the colours and leaf-markings which we have found in a single lane, premising that these are not one-hundredth part of those which might easily be given. Of colours and shades we have found pale green, deep green, golden green and dark green; yellow, straw colour, orange, pink, light red, blood red, dark red, purple, light brown, golden brown, reddish brown, russet and bronze. Of colours, grouped on the same leaf,

we have seen those which we will indicate in the
following enumeration, giving priority, as we do
so, to those shades or markings which predomi-
nate :—pale straw. with a few green spots, and the
tips of the serratures on the leaflet margins a
pinkish red; pale green, with the principal veins
brown, giving an appearance of brown stripes on
the leaflets; orange with dark red spots and
freckles, green spots and pinkish red serratures ;
rich, golden-orange with pale red, orange red and
deep red spots and blotches, an overspreading
hue of pale red merging into the orange ground,
and serratures of deep red and pale red and crimson; dark green with dark purple bands (in the
spaces between the principal veins) blotches,
splashes and spots and a few reddish spots ;
purplish red with golden green, orange and yellow
spots and other small markings ; dull, almost
bronze, green, with blood-red bands edged with
orange and dark purple blotches; golden russet,
nearly covering the entire leaf, but having dark
brown veins and spots of deep red and green
with an almost indefinable hue of red overspreading the russet; orange with pale, golden green,

red and russet edges, and dark brown blotches;
golden yellow with touches of bright orange
upon it, and bands (in the spaces between the
veins) of dark red; russet edged with brown and
with blotches of pinkish red; deep purplish red
with the principal veins on the upper side of the
leaflet green and golden; pale green with dark
brown, dark red, light red, and orange and gold
blotches; bronze green with pinkish red blotches;
pale green with golden green overspreading the
sides of two leaflets, a splash of bright yellow, and
an edging, along the serratures, of brown and deep
red; dark green with bronze bands and reddish
brown edgings; reddish, golden brown in bands
and splashings in the spaces between the principal veins, golden yellow along and on either
side of the veins, and green spots in places; rich
red densely overspreading dark green, with bright,
vivid green tips and nearly black veins; purplish
black in the spaces between the principal veins
with the veins themselves a bright green; pale
golden green with slight touches of orange and
pale reddish brown spots; pale green, dark green,
and orange gold with reddish brown spots; and

finally deep blood-red with dark brown tips, and a slight golden tinge upon some of the veins.

These colours and markings of the Bramble, noted upon foliage which we ourselves have not only passed and closely examined but have gathered and carefully preserved, are, as we have said, only representative of the wealth of beauty which this charming trailer adds to the abounding and surpassing loveliness, in lane, field and forest, of autumnal leaves.

THE END.

PRINTED BY GILBERT AND RIVINGTON, LIMITED, ST. JOHN'S SQUARE.

A LIST OF

KEGAN PAUL, TRENCH, & CO.'S

PUBLICATIONS.

1 Paternoster Square,
London.

A LIST OF

KEGAN PAUL, TRENCH, & CO.'S

PUBLICATIONS.

CONTENTS.

A. K. H. B.—FROM A QUIET PLACE. A New Volume of Sermons. Crown 8vo. 5s.

AINSWORTH (F. W.)—PERSONAL NARRATIVE OF THE EUPHRATES EXPEDITION. 2 vols. 8vo. 30s.

ALEXANDER (William, D.D., Bishop of Derry)—THE GREAT QUESTION, and other Sermons. Crown 8vo. 6s.

ALLIES (T. W.) M.A.—PER CRUCEM AD LUCEM. The Result of a Life. 2 vols. Demy 8vo. 25s.

A LIFE'S DECISION. Crown 8vo. 7s. 6d.

AMHERST (Rev. W. J.)—THE HISTORY OF CATHOLIC EMANCIPATION AND THE PROGRESS OF THE CATHOLIC CHURCH IN THE BRITISH ISLES (CHIEFY IN ENGLAND) FROM 1771–1820. 2 vols. Demy 8vo. 24s.

AMOS (Prof. Sheldon)—THE HISTORY AND PRINCIPLES OF THE CIVIL LAW OF ROME. Demy 8vo. 16s.

ARISTOTLE—THE NICOMACHEAN ETHICS OF ARISTOTLE. Translated by F. H. PETERS, M.A. Third Edition. Crown 8vo. 6s.

AUBERTIN (J. J.)—A FLIGHT TO MEXICO. With 7 full-page Illustrations and a Railway Map of Mexico. Crown 8vo. 7s. 6d.

SIX MONTHS IN CAPE COLONY AND NATAL. With Illustrations and Map. Crown 8vo. 6s.

A FIGHT WITH DISTANCES. With 8 Illustrations and 2 Maps. Crown 8vo. 7s. 6d.

AUCASSIN and NICOLETTE. Edited in Old French and rendered in Modern English by F. W. BOURDILLON. Fcap. 8vo. 7s. 6d.

AUCHMUTY (A. C.)—DIVES AND PAUPER, and other Sermons. Crown 8vo. 3s. 6d.

AZARIAS (Brother)—ARISTOTLE AND THE CHRISTIAN CHURCH. Small crown 8vo. 3s. 6d.

BADGER (George Percy) D.C.L.—AN ENGLISH-ARABIC LEXICON. In which the equivalents for English Words and Idiomatic Sentences are rendered into literary and colloquial Arabic. Royal 4to. 80s.

BAGEHOT (Walter)—THE ENGLISH CONSTITUTION. Fifth Edition. Crown 8vo. 7s. 6d.

LOMBARD STREET. A Description of the Money Market. Ninth Edition. Crown 8vo. 7s. 6d.

ESSAYS ON PARLIAMENTARY REFORM. Crown 8vo. 5s.

SOME ARTICLES ON THE DEPRECIATION OF SILVER, AND TOPICS CONNECTED WITH IT. Demy 8vo. 5s.

BAGOT (Alan) C.E.—ACCIDENTS IN MINES : Their Causes and Prevention. Crown 8vo. 6s.

THE PRINCIPLES OF COLLIERY VENTILATION. Second Edition, greatly enlarged, crown 8vo. 5s.

THE PRINCIPLES OF CIVIL ENGINEERING IN ESTATE MANAGEMENT. Crown 8vo. 7s. 6d.

BAIRD (Henry M.)—THE HUGUENOTS AND HENRY OF NAVARRE. 2 vols. 8vo. With Maps. 24s.

BALDWIN (Capt. J. H.)—THE LARGE AND SMALL GAME OF BENGAL AND THE NORTH-WESTERN PROVINCES OF INDIA. With 20 Illustrations. New and Cheaper Edition. Small 4to. 10s. 6d.

BALLIN (Ada S. and F. L.)—A HEBREW GRAMMAR. With Exercises selected from the Bible. Crown 8vo. 7s. 6d.

BALL (John, F.R.S.)—NOTES OF A NATURALIST IN SOUTH AMERICA. Crown 8vo. 8s. 6d.

BARCLAY (Edgar) — MOUNTAIN LIFE IN ALGERIA. Crown 4to. With numerous Illustrations by Photogravure. 16s.

BASU (K. P.) M.A.—STUDENTS' MATHEMATICAL COMPANION. Containing problems in Arithmetic, Algebra, Geometry, and Mensuration, for Students of the Indian Universities. Crown 8vo. 6s.

BAUR (Ferdinand) Dr. Ph., Professor in Maulbronn.—A PHILOLOGICAL INTRODUCTION TO GREEK AND LATIN FOR STUDENTS. Translated and adapted from the German by C. KEGAN PAUL, M.A., and the Rev. E. D. STONE, M.A. Third Edition. Crown 8vo. 6s.

BENN (Alfred W.)—THE GREEK PHILOSOPHERS. 2 vols. Demy 8vo. 28s.

BENSON (A. C.)—WILLIAM LAUD, SOMETIME ARCHBISHOP OF CANTERBURY. A Study. With Portrait. Crown 8vo. 6s.

BIBLE FOLK-LORE.—A STUDY IN COMPARATIVE MYTHOLOGY. Large crown 8vo. 10s. 6d.

BIRD (Charles) F.G.S.—HIGHER EDUCATION IN GERMANY AND ENGLAND : Being a Brief Practical Account of the Organisation and Curriculum of the German Higher Schools. With Critical Remarks and Suggestions with reference to those of England. Small crown 8vo. 2s. 6d.

BIRTH AND GROWTH OF RELIGION. A Book for Workers. Crown 8vo. cloth, 2s. ; paper covers, 1s.

BLACKBURN (Mrs. Hugh)—BIBLE BEASTS AND BIRDS. A New Edition of 'Illustrations of Scripture by an Animal Painter.' With Twenty-two Plates, Photographed from the Originals, and Printed in Platinotype. 4to. cloth extra, gilt edges, 42s.

BLOOMFIELD (The Lady)—REMINISCENCES OF COURT AND DIPLO-
MATIC LIFE. New and Cheaper Edition. With Frontispiece. Crown 8vo. 6s.

BLUNT (The Ven. Archdeacon)—THE DIVINE PATRIOT, AND OTHER
SERMONS, Preached in Scarborough and in Cannes. Crown 8vo. 4s. 6d.

BLUNT (Wilfrid S.)—THE FUTURE OF ISLAM. Crown 8vo. 6s.

IDEAS ABOUT INDIA. Crown 8vo. cloth, 6s.

BOSANQUET (Bernard)—KNOWLEDGE AND REALITY. A Criticism of
Mr. F. H. Bradley's 'Principles of Logic.' Crown 8vo. 9s.

BOUVERIE-PUSEY (S. E. B.)—PERMANENCE AND EVOLUTION. An
Inquiry into the supposed Mutability of Animal Types. Crown 8vo. 5s.

BOWEN (H. C.) M.A.—STUDIES IN ENGLISH, for the use of Modern
Schools. 7th Thousand. Small crown 8vo. 1s. 6d.

ENGLISH GRAMMAR FOR BEGINNERS. Fcp. 8vo. 1s.

SIMPLE ENGLISH POEMS. English Literature for Junior Classes. In
Four Parts. Parts I., II., and III. 6d. each; Part IV. 1s.; complete, 3s.

BRADLEY (F. H.)—THE PRINCIPLES OF LOGIC. Demy 8vo. 16s.

BRADSHAW (Henry)—MEMOIR. By G. W. PROTHERO. 8vo. 16s.

BRIDGETT (Rev. T. E.)—HISTORY OF THE HOLY EUCHARIST IN
GREAT BRITAIN. 2 vols. Demy 8vo. 18s.

BROOKE (Rev. S. A.)—LIFE AND LETTERS OF THE LATE REV. F. W.
ROBERTSON, M.A. Edited by.
   I. Uniform with Robertson's Sermons. 2 vols. With Steel Portrait, 7s. 6d.
   II. Library Edition. 8vo. With Portrait, 12s.
   III. A Popular Edition. In 1 vol. 8vo. 6s.

THE FIGHT OF FAITH. Sermons preached on various occasions.
Fifth Edition. Crown 8vo. 7s. 6d.

THE SPIRIT OF THE CHRISTIAN LIFE. Third Edition. Crown 8vo. 5s.

THEOLOGY IN THE ENGLISH POETS.—Cowper, Coleridge, Wordsworth,
and Burns. Sixth Edition. Post 8vo. 5s.

CHRIST IN MODERN LIFE. Sixteenth Edition. Crown 8vo. 5s.

SERMONS. First Series. Thirteenth Edition. Crown 8vo. 5s.

SERMONS. Second Series. Sixth Edition. Crown 8vo. 5s.

BROWN (Horatio F.)—LIFE ON THE LAGOONS. With two Illustrations
and a Map. Crown 8vo. 6s.

VENETIAN STUDIES. Crown 8vo. 7s. 6d.

BROWN (Rev. J. Baldwin) B.A.—THE HIGHER LIFE: its Reality,
Experience, and Destiny. Seventh Edition. Crown 8vo. 5s.

DOCTRINE OF ANNIHILATION IN THE LIGHT OF THE GOSPEL OF
LOVE. Five Discourses. Fourth Edition. Crown 8vo. 2s. 6d.

THE CHRISTIAN POLICY OF LIFE. A Book for Young Men of
Business. Third Edition. Crown 8vo. 3s. 6d.

BURDETT (Henry C.)—HELP IN SICKNESS : Where to Go and What
to Do. Crown 8vo. 1s. 6d.

HELPS TO HEALTH : The Habitation, The Nursery, The Schoolroom,
and The Person. With a Chapter on Pleasure and Health Resorts. Crown
8vo. 1s. 6d.

BURKE (Oliver J.)—SOUTH ISLES OF ARAN (COUNTY GALWAY). Crown 8vo. 2s. 6d.

BURKE (The late Very Rev. T. N.)—HIS LIFE. By W. J. FITZPATRICK. 2 vols. With Portrait. Demy 8vo. 30s.

BURTON (Mrs. Richard)—THE INNER LIFE OF SYRIA, PALESTINE, AND THE HOLY LAND. Post 8vo. 6s.

CANDLER (C.)—THE PREVENTION OF CONSUMPTION. A Mode of Prevention founded on a New Theory of the Nature of the Tubercle-Bacillus. Demy 8vo. 10s. 6d.

CARLYLE AND THE OPEN SECRET OF HIS LIFE. By HENRY LARKIN. Demy 8vo. 14s.

CARPENTER (W. B.) LL.D., M.D., F.R.S., &c.—THE PRINCIPLES OF MENTAL PHYSIOLOGY. With their Applications to the Training and Discipline of the Mind, and the Study of its Morbid Conditions. Illustrated. Sixth Edition. 8vo. 12s.

    NATURE AND MAN : Essays, Scientific and Philosophical. With Memoir of the Author and Portrait. Large crown 8vo. 8s. 6d.

CATHOLIC DICTIONARY—Containing some account of the Doctrine, Discipline, Rites, Ceremonies, Councils, and Religious Orders of the Catholic Church. By WILLIAM E. ADDIS and THOMAS ARNOLD, M.A. Third Edition, demy 8vo. 21s.

CHEYNE (Rev. Canon, M.A., D.D., Edin.)—JOB AND SOLOMON ; or, the Wisdom of the Old Testament. Demy 8vo. 12s. 6d.

    THE PROPHECIES OF ISAIAH. Translated with Critical Notes and Dissertations. 2 vols. Fourth Edition. Demy 8vo. 25s.

    THE BOOK OF PSALMS ; or, THE PRAISES OF ISRAEL. A New Translation, with Commentary. Demy 8vo. 16s.

CHURGRESS, THE. By The Prig. Fcp. 8vo. 3s. 6d.

CLAIRAUT—ELEMENTS OF GEOMETRY. Translated by Dr. KAINES. With 145 Figures. Crown 8vo. 4s. 6d.

CLAPPERTON (Jane Hume)—SCIENTIFIC MELIORISM AND THE EVOLUTION OF HAPPINESS. Large crown 8vo. 8s. 6d.

CLODD (Edward) F.R.A.S.—THE CHILDHOOD OF THE WORLD : a Simple Account of Man in Early Times. Eighth Edition. Crown 8vo. 3s.
    A Special Edition for Schools, 1s.

    THE CHILDHOOD OF RELIGIONS. Including a Simple Account of the Birth and Growth of Myths and Legends. Eighth Thousand. Crown 8vo. 5s.
    A Special Edition for Schools. 1s. 6d.

    JESUS OF NAZARETH. With a brief sketch of Jewish History to the Time of His Birth. Second Edition. Small crown 8vo. 6s.

COGHLAN (J. Cole) D.D.— THE MODERN PHARISEE, AND OTHER SERMONS. Edited by the Very Rev. H. H. DICKINSON, D.D., Dean of Chapel Royal, Dublin. New and Cheaper Edition. Crown 8vo. 7s. 6d.

COLERIDGE (Sara)—MEMOIR AND LETTERS OF SARA COLERIDGE. Edited by her Daughter. With Index. Cheap Edition. With one Portrait. 7s. 6d.

COLERIDGE (The Hon. Stephen)—DEMETRIUS. Crown 8vo. 5s.

COOPER (*James Fenimore*)—LIFE. By T. R. LOUNDSBURY. With Portrait. Crown 8vo. 5*s.*

CORY (*William*)—A GUIDE TO MODERN ENGLISH HISTORY. Part I.—MDCCCXV.-MDCCCXXX. Demy 8vo. 9*s.* Part II.—MDCCCXXX.-MDCCCXXXV. 15*s.*

COTTERILL (*H. B.*)—AN INTRODUCTION TO THE STUDY OF POETRY. Crown 8vo. 7*s.* 6*d.*

COTTON (*H. J. S.*)—NEW INDIA, OR INDIA IN TRANSITION. Third Edition. Crown 8vo. 4*s.* 6*d.* Popular Edition, paper covers, 1*s.*

COWIE (*Right Rev. W. G.*)—OUR LAST YEAR IN NEW ZEALAND. 1887. Crown 8vo. 7*s.* 6*d.*

COX (*Rev. Sir George W.*) *M.A., Bart.*—THE MYTHOLOGY OF THE ARYAN NATIONS. New Edition. Demy 8vo. 16*s.*

    TALES OF ANCIENT GREECE. New Edition. Small crown 8vo. 6*s.*

    A MANUAL OF MYTHOLOGY IN THE FORM OF QUESTION AND ANSWER. New Edition. Fcp. 8vo. 3*s.*

    AN INTRODUCTION TO THE SCIENCE OF COMPARATIVE MYTHOLOGY AND FOLK-LORE. Second Edition. Crown 8vo. 7*s.* 6*d.*

COX (*Rev. Sir G. W.*) *M.A., Bart., and JONES* (*Eustace Hinton*)—POPULAR ROMANCES OF THE MIDDLE AGES. Third Edition, in 1 vol. Crown 8vo. 6*s.*

COX (*Rev. Samuel*) *D.D.*—A COMMENTARY ON THE BOOK OF JOB. With a Translation. Second Edition. Demy 8vo. 15*s.*

    SALVATOR MUNDI ; or, Is Christ the Saviour of all Men? Eleventh Edition. Crown 8vo. 2*s.* 6*d.*

    THE LARGER HOPE : a Sequel to 'SALVATOR MUNDI.' Second Edition. 16mo. 1*s.*

    THE GENESIS OF EVIL, AND OTHER SERMONS, mainly expository. Third Edition. Crown 8vo. 6*s.*

    BALAAM : An Exposition and a Study. Crown 8vo. 5*s.*

    MIRACLES. An Argument and a Challenge. Crown 8vo. 2*s.* 6*d.*

CRAVEN (*Mrs.*)—A YEAR'S MEDITATIONS. Crown 8vo. 6*s.*

CRAWFURD (*Oswald*)—PORTUGAL, OLD AND NEW. With Illustrations and Maps. New and Cheaper Edition. Crown 8vo. 6*s.*

CRUISE (*F. R.*) *M.D.*—THOMAS À KEMPIS. Notes of a Visit to the Scenes in which his Life was spent, with some Account of the Examination of his Relics. Demy 8vo. Illustrated. 12*s.*

CUNNINGHAM (*W., B.D.*)—POLITICS AND ECONOMICS : An Essay on the Nature of the Principles of Political Economy, together with a Survey of Recent Legislation. Crown 8vo. 5*s.*

DARMESTETER (*Arsène*)—THE LIFE OF WORDS AS THE SYMBOLS OF IDEAS. Crown 8vo. 4*s.* 6*d.*

DAVIDSON (*Rev. Samuel*) *D.D., LL.D.*—CANON OF THE BIBLE : Its Formation, History, and Fluctuations. Third and revised Edition. Small crown 8vo. 5*s.*

    THE DOCTRINE OF LAST THINGS, contained in the New Testament, compared with the Notions of the Jews and the Statements of Church Creeds. Small crown 8vo. 3*s.* 6*d.*

DAWSON (Geo.) M.A.—Prayers, with a Discourse on Prayer. Edited by his Wife. First Series. New and Cheaper Edition. Crown 8vo. 3s. 6d.

Prayers, with a Discourse on Prayer. Edited by George St. Clair. Second Series. Crown 8vo. 6s.

Sermons on Disputed Points and Special Occasions. Edited by his Wife. Fourth Edition. Crown 8vo. 6s.

Sermons on Daily Life and Duty. Edited by his Wife. Fifth Edition. Crown 8vo. 3s. 6d.

The Authentic Gospel, and other Sermons. Edited by George St. Clair. Third Edition. Crown 8vo. 6s.

Every-day Counsels. Edited by George St. Clair, F.G.S. Crown 8vo. 6s.

Biographical Lectures. Edited by George St. Clair, F.G.S. Second Edition. Large crown 8vo. 7s. 6d.

Hakespeare, and other Lectures. Edited by George St. Clair, F.G.S. Large crown 8vo. 7s. 6d.

DE BURY (Richard)—The Philobiblon. Translated and Edited by Ernest C. Thomas.

DE JONCOURT (Madame Marie)—Wholesome Cookery. Fourth Edition. Crown 8vo. cloth, 1s. 6d. ; paper covers, 1s.

DENT (H. C.)—A Year in Brazil. With Notes on Religion, Meteorology, Natural History, &c. Maps and Illustrations. Demy 8vo. 18s.

Doctor Faust. The Old German Puppet Play, turned into English, with Introduction, etc., by T. C. H. Hedderwick. Large post 8vo. 7s. 6d.

DOWDEN (Edward) LL.D.—Shakspere: a Critical Study of his Mind and Art. Eighth Edition. Post 8vo. 12s.

Studies in Literature, 1789–1877. Fourth Edition. Post 8vo. 6s.

Transcripts and Studies. Post 8vo. 12s.

DRUMMOND (Thomas)—Life. By R. Barry O'Brien. 8vo. 14s.

Dulce Domum. Fcp. 8vo. 5s.

DU MONCEL (Count)—The Telephone, the Microphone, and the Phonograph. With 74 Illustrations. Third Edition. Small crown 8vo. 5s.

DUNN (H. Percy) F.R.C.S.—Infant Health. The Physiology and Hygiene of Early Life. Crown 8vo. 3s. 6d.

DURUY (Victor)—History of Rome and the Roman People. Edited by Professor Mahaffy, with nearly 3,000 Illustrations. 4to. 6 Vols. in 12 Parts, 30s. each volume.

Education Library. Edited by Sir Philip Magnus :—

Industrial Education. By Sir Philip Magnus.

An Introduction to the History of Educational Theories. By Oscar Browning, M.A. Second Edition. 3s. 6d.

Old Greek Education. By the Rev. Prof. Mahaffy, M.A. Second Edition. 3s. 6d.

School Management ; including a General View of the Work of Education. By Joseph Landon. Sixth Edition. 6s.

EDWARDES (Major-General Sir Herbert B.)—Memorials of his Life. By his Wife. With Portrait and Illustrations. 2 vols. 8vo. 36s.

EIGHTEENTH CENTURY ESSAYS. Selected and Edited by AUSTIN DOBSON. Fcp. 8vo. 1*s*. 6*d*.

ELSDALE (*Henry*)—STUDIES IN TENNYSON'S IDYLLS. Crown 8vo. 5*s*.

EMERSON'S (*Ralph Waldo*) LIFE. By OLIVER WENDELL HOLMES. [English Copyright Edition.] With Portrait. Crown 8vo. 6*s*.

ERANUS. A COLLECTION OF EXERCISES IN THE ALCAIC AND SAPPHIC METRES. Edited by F. W. CORNISH, Assistant Master at Eton. Second Edition. Crown 8vo. 2*s*.

FIVE O'CLOCK TEA. Containing Receipts for Cakes of every description, Savoury Sandwiches, Cooling Drinks, &c. Fcp. 8vo. 1*s*. 6*d*., or 1*s*. sewed.

FLINN (*D. Edgar*)—IRELAND : its Health Resorts and Watering-Places. With Frontispiece and Maps. Demy 8vo. 5*s*.

FORBES (*Bishop*)—A MEMOIR, by the Rev. DONALD J. MACKEY. Portrait and Map. Crown 8vo. 7*s*. 6*d*.

FORDYCE (*John*)—THE NEW SOCIAL ORDER. Crown 8vo. 3*s*. 6*d*.

FOTHERINGHAM (*James*)—STUDIES IN THE POETRY OF ROBERT BROWNING. Crown 8vo. 6*s*.

FRANKLIN (*Benjamin*)—AS A MAN OF LETTERS. By J. B. McMASTER. Crown 8vo. 5*s*.

FROM WORLD TO CLOISTER ; or, My Novitiate. By BERNARD. Crown 8vo. 5*s*.

GARDINER (*Samuel R.*) *and J. BASS MULLINGER, M.A.*— INTRODUCTION TO THE STUDY OF ENGLISH HISTORY Second Edition. Large crown 8vo. 9*s*.

GEORGE (*Henry*)—PROGRESS AND POVERTY : an Inquiry into the Causes of Industrial Depressions, and of Increase of Want with Increase of Wealth. The Remedy. Library Edition. Post 8vo. 7*s*. 6*d*. Cabinet Edition, crown 8vo. 2*s*. 6*d*.

SOCIAL PROBLEMS. Crown 8vo. 5*s*.

PROTECTION, OR FREE TRADE. An Examination of the Tariff Question, with especial regard to the Interests of Labour. Second Edition. Crown 8vo. 5*s*.

*** Also Cheap Editions of each of the above, limp cloth, 1*s*. 6*d*. ; paper covers, 1*s*.

GILBERT (*Mrs.*)—AUTOBIOGRAPHY, and other Memorials. Edited by JOSIAH GILBERT. Fifth Edition. Crown 8vo. 7*s*. 6*d*.

GILLMORE (*Col. Parker*)—DAYS AND NIGHTS BY THE DESERT. With numerous Illustrations. Demy 8vo. 10*s*. 6*d*.

GLANVILL (*Joseph*)—SCEPSIS SCIENTIFICA ; or, Confest Ignorance, th Way to Science ; in an Essay of the Vanity of Dogmatising and Confiden Opinion. Edited, with Introductory Essay, by JOHN OWEN. Elzevir 8vo. printed on hand-made paper, 6*s*.

GLASS (*Henry Alex.*)—THE STORY OF THE PSALTERS. Crown 8vo. 5*s*.

GLOSSARY OF TERMS AND PHRASES. Edited by the Rev. H. PERCY SMITH and others. Medium 8vo. 7*s*. 6*d*.

GLOVER (*F.*) *M.A.*—EXEMPLA LATINA. A First Construing Book, with Short Notes, Lexicon, and an Introduction to the Analysis of Sentences. Second Edition. Fcp. 8vo. 2*s*.

GOODENOUGH (*Commodore J. G.*)—MEMOIR OF, with Extracts from his Letters and Journals. Edited by his Widow. With Steel Engraved Portrait. Third Edition. Crown 8vo. 5*s*.

GORDON (Major-Gen. C. G.)—HIS JOURNALS AT KARTOUM. Printed from the Original MS. With Introduction and Notes by A. EGMONT HAKE. Portrait, 2 Maps, and 30 Illustrations. 2 vols. Demy 8vo. 21*s.* Also a Cheap Edition in 1 vol., 6*s.*

GORDON'S (GENERAL) LAST JOURNAL. A Facsimile of the last Journal received in England from General Gordon. Reproduced by Photo-lithography. Imperial 4to. £3. 3*s.*

EVENTS IN HIS LIFE. From the Day of his Birth to the Day of his Death. By Sir H. W. GORDON. With Maps and Illustrations. Demy 8vo. 7*s. 6d.*

GOSSE (Edmund) — SEVENTEENTH CENTURY STUDIES. A Contribution to the History of English Poetry. Demy 8vo. 10*s. 6d.*

GOULD (Rev. S. Baring) M.A.—GERMANY, PRESENT AND PAST. New and Cheaper Edition. Large crown 8vo. 7*s. 6d.*

THE VICAR OF MORWENSTOW : a Life of Robert Stephen Hawker, M.A. New and Cheaper Edition. Crown 8vo. 5*s.*

GOWAN (Major Walter E.) — A. IVANOFF'S RUSSIAN GRAMMAR. (16th Edition). Translated, enlarged, and arranged for use of Students of the Russian Language. Demy 8vo. 6*s.*

GOWER (Lord Ronald)—MY REMINISCENCES. Limp Parchment, Antique, with Etched Portrait, 10*s. 6d.*

BRIC-À-BRAC. Being some Photoprints illustrating Art objects at. Gower Lodge, Windsor. Super royal 8vo. 15*s.* ; Persian leather, 21*s.*

LAST DAYS OF MARY ANTOINETTE. An Historical Sketch. With Portrait and Facsimiles. Fcp. 4to. 10*s. 6d.*

NOTES OF A TOUR FROM BRINDISI TO YOKOHAMA, 1883–1884. Fcp. 8vo. 2*s. 6d.*

GRAHAM (William) M.A.—THE CREED OF SCIENCE, Religious, Moral, and Social. Second Edition, revised. Crown 8vo. 6*s.*

THE SOCIAL PROBLEM IN ITS ECONOMIC, MORAL, AND POLITICAL ASPECTS. Demy 8vo. 14*s.*

GRIMLEY (Rev. H. N.) M.A.—TREMADOC SERMONS, CHIEFLY ON THE SPIRITUAL BODY, THE UNSEEN WORLD, AND THE DIVINE HUMANITY. Fourth Edition. Crown 8vo. 6*s.*

THE TEMPLE OF HUMANITY, and other Sermons. Crown 8vo. 6*s.*

GURNEY (Edmund)—TERTIUM QUID : Chapters on various Disputed Questions. 2 vols. Crown 8vo. 12*s.*

HADDON (Caroline)—THE LARGER LIFE, STUDIES IN HINTON'S ETHICS. Crown 8vo. 5*s.*

HAECKEL (Prof. Ernst)—THE HISTORY OF CREATION. Translation revised by Professor E. RAY LANKESTER, M.A., F.R.S. With Coloured Plates and Genealogical Trees of the various groups of both plants and animals. 2 vols. Third Edition. Post 8vo. 32*s.*

THE HISTORY OF THE EVOLUTION OF MAN. With numerous Illustrations. 2 vols. Post 8vo. 32*s.*

A VISIT TO CEYLON. Post 8vo. 7*s. 6d.*

FREEDOM IN SCIENCE AND TEACHING. With a Prefatory Note by T. H. HUXLEY, F.R.S. Crown 8vo. 5*s.*

HALCOMBE (*J. J.*)—Gospel Difficulties due to a Displaced Section of St. Luke. Second Edition. Crown 8vo. 6*s.*

Hamilton, Memoirs of Arthur, B.A., of Trinity College, Cambridge. Crown 8vo. 6*s.*

Handbook of Home Rule, being Articles on the Irish Question by Various Writers. Edited by James Bryce, M.P. Second Edition. Crown 8vo. 1*s.* sewed, or 1*s.* 6*d.* cloth.

HART (*Rev. J. W. T.*)—Autobiography of Judas Iscariot. A Character-Study. Crown 8vo. 3*s.* 6*d.*

HAWEIS (*Rev. H. R.*) *M.A.*—Current Coin. Materialism—The Devil — Crime — Drunkenness — Pauperism — Emotion — Recreation — The Sabbath. Fifth Edition. Crown 8vo. 5*s.*

Arrows in the Air. Fifth Edition. Crown 8vo. 5*s.*

Speech in Season. Fifth Edition. Crown 8vo. 5*s.*

Thoughts for the Times. Fourteenth Edition. Crown 8vo. 5*s.*

Unsectarian Family Prayers. New Edition. Fcp. 8vo. 1*s.* 6*d.*

HAWTHORNE (*Nathaniel*)—Works. Complete in 12 vols. Large post 8vo. each vol. 7*s.* 6*d.*

Vol. I. Twice-Told Tales.
    II. Mosses from an Old Manse.
    III. The House of the Seven Gables, and The Snow Image.
    IV. The Wonder Book, Tanglewood Tales, and Grandfather's Chair.
    V. The Scarlet Letter, and The Blithedale Romance.
    VI. The Marble Faun. (Transformation.)
VII. & VIII. Our Old Home, and English Note-Books.
    IX. American Note-Books.
    X. French and Italian Note-Books.
    XI. Septimius Felton, The Dolliver Romance, Fanshawe, and, in an appendix, The Ancestral Footstep.
    XII. Tales and Essays, and other Papers, with a Biographical Sketch of Hawthorne.

HEATH (*Francis George*)—Autumnal Leaves. Third and Cheaper Edition. Large crown 8vo. 6*s.*

Sylvan Winter. With 70 Illustrations. Large crown 8vo. 14*s.*

HEGEL—The Introduction to Hegel's Philosophy of Fine Art. Translated from the German, with Notes and Prefatory Essay, by Bernard Bosanquet, M.A. Crown 8vo. 5*s.*

HEIDENHAIN (*Rudolph*) *M.D.*—Hypnotism ; or Animal Magnetism. With Preface by G. J. Romanes, F.R.S. Second Edition. Small crown 8vo. 2*s.* 6*d.*

HENNESSY (*Sir John Pope*)—Ralegh in Ireland, with his Letters on Irish Affairs and some Contemporary Documents. Large crown 8vo. printed on hand-made paper, parchment, 10*s.* 6*d.*

HENRY (*Philip*)—Diaries and Letters. Edited by Matthew Henry Lee, M.A. Large crown 8vo. 7*s.* 6*d.*

HINTON (*J.*)—The Mystery of Pain. New Edition. Fcp. 8vo. 1*s.*

Life and Letters. With an Introduction by Sir W. W. Gull, Bart., and Portrait engraved on Steel by C. H. Jeens. Fifth Edition. Crown 8vo. 8*s.* 6*d.*

HINTON (J.)—continued.

PHILOSOPHY AND RELIGION. Selections from the MSS. of the late JAMES HINTON. Edited by CAROLINE HADDON. Second Edition. Crown 8vo. 5s.

THE LAW BREAKER AND THE COMING OF THE LAW. Edited by MARGARET HINTON. Crown 8vo. 6s.

HOOPER (Mary)—LITTLE DINNERS: HOW TO SERVE THEM WITH ELEGANCE AND ECONOMY. Twentieth Edition. Crown 8vo. 2s. 6d.

COOKERY FOR INVALIDS, PERSONS OF DELICATE DIGESTION, AND CHILDREN. Fifth Edition. Crown 8vo. 2s. 6d.

EVERY-DAY MEALS. Being Economical and Wholesome Recipes for Breakfast, Luncheon, and Supper. Seventh Edition. Crown 8vo. 2s. 6d.

HOPKINS (Ellice)—WORK AMONGST WORKING MEN. Fifth Edition. Crown 8vo. 3s. 6d.

HORNADAY (W. T.)—TWO YEARS IN A JUNGLE. With Illustrations. Demy 8vo. 21s.

HOSPITALIER (E.)—THE MODERN APPLICATIONS OF ELECTRICITY. Translated and Enlarged by JULIUS MAIER, Ph.D. 2 vols. Second Edition, revised, with many additions and numerous Illustrations. Demy 8vo. 12s. 6d. each volume.

VOL. I.—Electric Generators, Electric Light.

II.—Telephone: Various Applications: Electrical Transmission of Energy.

HOWARD (Robert) M.A.—THE CHURCH OF ENGLAND AND OTHER RELIGIOUS COMMUNIONS. A Course of Lectures delivered in the Parish Church of Clapham. Crown 8vo. 7s. 6d.

HOW TO MAKE A SAINT; or, The Process of Canonisation in the Church of England. By The Prig. Fcp. 8vo. 3s. 6d.

HYNDMAN (H. M.)—THE HISTORICAL BASIS OF SOCIALISM IN ENGLAND. Large crown 8vo. 8s. 6d.

IM THURN (Everard F.)—AMONG THE INDIANS OF GUIANA. Being Sketches, chiefly Anthropologic, from the Interior of British Guiana. With 53 Illustrations and a Map. Demy 8vo. 18s.

IXORA: A Mystery. Crown 8vo. 6s.

JACCOUD (Prof. S.)—THE CURABILITY AND TREATMENT OF PULMONARY PHTHISIS. Translated and Edited by M. LUBBOCK, M.D. 8vo. 15s.

JAUNT IN A JUNK: A Ten Days' Cruise in Indian Seas. Large crown 8vo. 7s. 6d.

JENKINS (E.) and RAYMOND (J.)—THE ARCHITECT'S LEGAL HANDBOOK. Third Edition, Revised. Crown 8vo. 6s.

JENKINS (Rev. Canon R. C.)—HERALDRY: English and Foreign. With a Dictionary of Heraldic Terms and 156 Illustrations. Small crown 8vo. 3s. 6d.

STORY OF THE CARAFFA. Small crown 8vo. 3s. 6d.

JEROME (Saint)—LIFE, by Mrs. CHARLES MARTIN. Large cr. 8vo. 6s.

JOEL (L.)—A CONSUL'S MANUAL AND SHIPOWNER'S AND SHIPMASTER'S PRACTICAL GUIDE IN THEIR TRANSACTIONS ABROAD. With Definitions of Nautical, Mercantile, and Legal Terms; a Glossary of Mercantile Terms in English, French, German, Italian, and Spanish; Tables of the Money, Weights, and Measures of the Principal Commercial Nations and their Equivalents in British Standards; and Forms of Consular and Notarial Acts. Demy 8vo. 12s.

JORDAN (Furneaux) F.R.C.S.—ANATOMY AND PHYSIOLOGY IN CHARACTER. Crown 8vo. 5s.

KAUFMANN (*Rev. M.*) *M.A.*—SOCIALISM : its Nature, its Dangers, and its Remedies considered.   Crown 8vo. 7*s*. 6*d*.

UTOPIAS ; or, Schemes of Social Improvement, from Sir Thomas More to Karl Marx.   Crown 8vo. 5*s*.

CHRISTIAN SOCIALISM.   Crown 8vo.   4*s*. 6*d*.

KAY (*David*)—EDUCATION AND EDUCATORS.   Crown 8vo. 7*s*. 6*d*.

MEMORY : What it is, and how to improve it.   Crown 8vo. 6*s*.

KAY (*Joseph*)—FREE TRADE IN LAND.   Edited by his Widow.   With Preface by the Right Hon. JOHN BRIGHT, M.P.   Seventh Edition.   Crown 8vo. 5*s*.

**** Also a cheaper edition, without the Appendix, but with a Review of Recent Changes in the Land Laws of England, by the Right Hon. G. OSBORNE MORGAN, Q.C., M.P.   Cloth, 1*s*. 6*d*. ; Paper covers, 1*s*.

KELKE (*W. H. H.*)—AN EPITOME OF ENGLISH GRAMMAR FOR THE USE OF STUDENTS.   Adapted to the London Matriculation Course and Similar Examinations.   Crown 8vo. 4*s*. 6*d*.

KEMPIS (*Thomas à*)—OF THE IMITATION OF CHRIST.   Parchment Library Edition, parchment or cloth, 6*s*.; vellum, 7*s*. 6*d*.   The Red Line Edition, fcp. 8vo. cloth extra, 2*s*. 6*d*.   The Cabinet Edition, small 8vo. cloth limp, 1*s*. ; or cloth boards, red edges, 1*s*. 6*d*.   The Miniature Edition, 32mo. cloth limp, 1*s*. ; or with red lines, 1*s*. 6*d*.

**** All the above Editions may be had in various extra bindings.

KENNARD (*Rev. H. B.*)—MANUAL OF CONFIRMATION.   16mo. cloth, 1*s*.   Sewed, 3*d*.

KENDALL (*Henry*)—THE KINSHIP OF MEN : Genealogy viewed as a Science.   Crown 8vo. 5*s*.

KETTLEWELL (*Rev. S.*) *M.A.*—THOMAS À KEMPIS AND THE BROTHERS OF COMMON LIFE.   2 vols.   With Frontispieces.   Demy 8vo. 30*s*.

**** Also an Abridged Edition in 1 vol.   With Portrait.   Crown 8vo. 7*s*. 6*d*.

KIDD (*Joseph*) *M.D.*—THE LAWS OF THERAPEUTICS ; or, the Science and Art of Medicine.   Second Edition.   Crown 8vo. 6*s*.

KINGSFORD (*Anna*) *M.D.*—THE PERFECT WAY IN DIET.   A Treatise advocating a Return to the Natural and Ancient Food of Race.   Small crown 8vo. 2*s*.

KINGSLEY (*Charles*) *M.A.*—LETTERS AND MEMORIES OF HIS LIFE.   Edited by his WIFE.   With Two Steel Engraved Portraits and Vignettes.   Sixteenth Cabinet Edition, in 2 vols.   Crown 8vo. 12*s*.

**** Also a People's Edition in 1 vol.   With Portrait.   Crown 8vo. 6*s*.

ALL SAINTS' DAY, and other Sermons.   Edited by the Rev. W. HARRISON.   Third Edition.   Crown 8vo. 7*s*. 6*d*.

TRUE WORDS FOR BRAVE MEN.   A Book for Soldiers' and Sailors' Libraries.   Fourteenth Edition.   Crown 8vo. 2*s*. 6*d*.

KNOX (*Alexander A.*)—THE NEW PLAYGROUND ; or, Wanderings in Algeria.   New and Cheaper Edition.   Large crown 8vo. 6*s*.

LAMARTINE (*Alphonse de*).   By Lady MARGARET DOMVILE.   Large crown 8vo., with Portrait, 7*s*. 6*d*.

LAND CONCENTRATION AND IRRESPONSIBILITY OF POLITICAL POWER, as causing the Anomaly of a Widespread State of Want by the Side of the Vast Supplies of Nature. Crown 8vo. 5s.

LANDON (Joseph)—SCHOOL MANAGEMENT ; including a General View of the Work of Education, Organisation, and Discipline. Sixth Edition. Crown 8vo. 6s.

LAURIE (S. S.)—LECTURES ON THE RISE AND EARLY CONSTITUTION OF UNIVERSITIES. With a Survey of Mediæval Education. Crown 8vo. 6s.

LEE (Rev. F. G.) D.C.L.—THE OTHER WORLD; or, Glimpses of the Supernatural. 2 vols. A New Edition. Crown 8vo. 15s.

LEFEVRE (Right Hon. G. Shaw)—PEEL AND O'CONNELL. Demy 8vo. 10s. 6d.

INCIDENTS OF COERCION. A Journal of Visits to Ireland. Crown 8vo. 1s.

LETTERS FROM AN UNKNOWN FRIEND. By the Author of 'Charles Lowder.' With a Preface by the Rev. W. H. Cleaver. Fcp. 8vo. 1s.

LEWARD (Frank)—Edited by CHAS. BAMPTON. Crown 8vo. 7s. 6d.

LIFE OF A PRIG. By ONE. Third Edition. Fcp. 8vo. 3s. 6d.

LILLIE (Arthur) M.R.A.S.—THE POPULAR LIFE OF BUDDHA. Containing an Answer to the Hibbert Lectures of 1881. With Illustrations. Crown 8vo. 6s.

BUDDHISM IN CHRISTENDOM ; or, Jesus, the Essene. Demy 8vo. with Illustrations. 15s.

LOCHER (Carl)—EXPLANATION OF THE ORGAN STOPS, with Hints for Effective Combinations. Illustrated. Demy 8vo. 5s.

LONGFELLOW (H. Wadsworth)—LIFE. By his Brother, SAMUEL LONGFELLOW. With Portraits and Illustrations. 3 vols. Demy 8vo. 42s.

LONSDALE (Margaret)—SISTER DORA: a Biography. With Portrait. Cheap Edition. Crown 8vo. 2s. 6d.

GEORGE ELIOT : Thoughts upon her Life, her Books, and Herself. Second Edition. Small crown 8vo. 1s. 6d.

LOWDER (Charles)—A BIOGRAPHY. By the Author of 'St. Teresa.' New and Cheaper Edition. Crown 8vo. With Portrait. 3s. 6d.

LÜCKES (Eva C. E.)—LECTURES ON GENERAL NURSING, delivered to the Probationers of the London Hospital Training School for Nurses. Second Edition. Crown 8vo. 2s. 6d.

LYTTON (Edward Bulwer, Lord)—LIFE, LETTERS, AND LITERARY REMAINS. By his Son the EARL OF LYTTON. With Portraits, Illustrations, and Facsimiles. Demy 8vo. cloth. Vols. I. and II. 32s.

MACHIAVELLI (Niccolò)—HIS LIFE AND TIMES. By Prof. VILLARI. Translated by LINDA VILLARI. 4 vols. Large post 8vo. 48s.

DISCOURSES ON THE FIRST DECADE OF TITUS LIVIUS. Translated from the Italian by NINIAN HILL THOMSON, M.A. Large crown 8vo. 12s.

THE PRINCE. Translated from the Italian by N. H. T. Small crown 8vo. printed on hand-made paper, bevelled boards, 6s.

MACNEILL (J. G. Swift)—HOW THE UNION WAS CARRIED. Crown 8vo. cloth, 1s. 6d. ; paper covers, 1s.

MAGNUS (Lady)—ABOUT THE JEWS SINCE BIBLE TIMES. From the Babylonian Exile till the English Exodus. Small crown 8vo. 6s.

MAGUIRE (Thomas)—LECTURES ON PHILOSOPHY. Demy 8vo. 9*s.*

MAINTENON (Madame de). By EMILY BOWLES. With Portrait. Large crown 8vo. 7*s.* 6*d.*

MANY VOICES.—Extracts from Religious Writers, from the First to the Sixteenth Century. With Biographical Sketches. Crown 8vo. cloth extra, 6*s.*

MARKHAM (Capt. Albert Hastings) R.N.—THE GREAT FROZEN SEA : a Personal Narrative of the Voyage of the *Alert* during the Arctic Expedition of 1875-6. With 33 Illustrations and Two Maps. Sixth Edition. Crown 8vo. 6*s.*

MARTINEAU (Gertrude)—OUTLINE LESSONS ON MORALS. Small crown 8vo. 3*s.* 6*d.*

MASON (Charlotte M.)—HOME EDUCATION. A Course of Lectures to Ladies, delivered in Bradford in the winter of 1885-1886. Crown 8vo. 3*s.* 6*d.*

MATTER AND ENERGY: An Examination of the Fundamental Conceptions of Physical Force. By B. L. L. Small crown 8vo. 2*s.*

MATUCE (H. Ogram)—A WANDERER. Crown 8vo. 5*s.*

MAUDSLEY (H.) M.D.—BODY AND WILL. Being an Essay Concerning Will, in its Metaphysical, Physiological, and Pathological Aspects. 8vo. 12*s.*

    NATURAL CAUSES AND SUPERNATURAL SEEMINGS. Second Edition. Crown 8vo. 6*s.*

McGRATH (Terence)—PICTURES FROM IRELAND. New and Cheaper Edition. Crown 8vo. 2*s.*

McKINNEY (S. B. G.)—THE SCIENCE AND ART OF RELIGION. Crown 8vo. 8*s.* 6*d.*

MILLER (Edward)—THE HISTORY AND DOCTRINES OF IRVINGISM ; or, the so-called Catholic and Apostolic Church. 2 vols. Large post 8vo. 15*s.*

    THE CHURCH IN RELATION TO THE STATE. Large crown 8vo. 4*s.*

MILLS (Herbert)—POVERTY AND THE STATE ; or, Work for the Unemployed. An Enquiry into the Causes and Extent of Enforced Idleness. Cr. 8vo. 6*s.*

MINTON (Rev. Francis)—CAPITAL AND WAGES. 8vo. 15*s.*

MITCHELL (John)—LIFE. By WILLIAM DILLON. With Portrait. Demy 8vo.

MITCHELL (Lucy M.)—A HISTORY OF ANCIENT SCULPTURE. With numerous Illustrations, including six Plates in Phototype. Super royal, 42*s.*

    SELECTIONS FROM ANCIENT SCULPTURE. Being a Portfolio containing Reproductions in Phototype of 36 Masterpieces of Ancient Art, to illustrate Mrs. MITCHELL'S ' History of Ancient Sculpture.' 18*s.*

MIVART (St. George)—ON TRUTH. 8vo. 16*s.*

MOCKLER (E.)—A GRAMMAR OF THE BALOOCHEE LANGUAGE, as it is spoken in Makran (Ancient Gedrosia), in the Persia-Arabic and Roman characters. Fcp. 8vo. 5*s.*

MOHL (Julius and Mary)—LETTERS AND RECOLLECTIONS OF. By M. C. M. SIMPSON. With Portraits and Two Illustrations. Demy 8vo. 15*s.*

MOLESWORTH (W. Nassau)—HISTORY OF THE CHURCH OF ENGLAND FROM 1660. Large crown 8vo. 7*s.* 6*d.*

MORELL (J. R.)—Euclid Simplified in Method and Language. Being a Manual of Geometry. Compiled from the most important French Works, approved by the University of Paris and the Minister of Public Instruction. Fcp. 8vo. 2s. 6d.

MORISON (James Cotter)—The Service of Man. An Essay towards the Religion of the Future. Demy 8vo. 10s. 6d. ; Cheap Edition, crown 8vo. 5s.

MORSE (E. S.) Ph.D.—First Book of Zoology. With numerous Illustrations. New and Cheaper Edition. Crown 8vo. 2s. 6d.

My Lawyer : A Concise Abridgment of the Laws of England. By a Barrister-at-Law. Crown 8vo. 6s. 6d.

NELSON (J. H.) M.A.—A Prospectus of the Scientific Study of the Hindú Law. Demy 8vo. 9s.

Indian Usage and Judge-made Law in Madras. Demy 8vo. 12s.

New Social Teachings. By Politicus. Small crown 8vo. 5s.

NEWMAN (Cardinal)—Characteristics from the Writings of. Being Selections from his various Works. Arranged with the Author's personal Approval. Seventh Edition. With Portrait. Crown 8vo. 6s.

. A Portrait of Cardinal Newman, mounted for framing, can be had, 2s. 6d.

NEWMAN (Francis William)—Essays on Diet. Small crown 8vo. 2s.

Miscellanies. Vol. II. : Essays, Tracts, and Addresses, Moral and Religious. Demy 8vo. 12s.

Reminiscences of Two Exiles and Two Wars. Crown 8vo. 3s. 6d.

NICOLS (Arthur) F.G.S., F.R.G.S.—Chapters from the Physical History of the Earth : an Introduction to Geology and Palæontology. With numerous Illustrations. Crown 8vo. 5s.

NIHILL (Rev. H. D.)—The Sisters of St. Mary at the Cross : Sisters of the Poor and their Work. Crown 8vo. 2s. 6d.

NOEL (The Hon. Roden)—Essays on Poetry and Poets. Demy 8vo. 12s.

NOPS (Marianne)—Class Lessons on Euclid. Part I. containing the First Two Books of the Elements. Crown 8vo. 2s. 6d.

Nuces : Exercises on the Syntax of the Public School Latin Primer. New Edition in Three Parts. Crown 8vo. each 1s.

. The Three Parts can also be had bound together in cloth, 3s.

OATES (Frank) F.R.G.S.—Matabele Land and the Victoria Falls. A Naturalist's Wanderings in the Interior of South Africa. Edited by C. G. Oates, B.A. With numerous Illustrations and 4 Maps. Demy 8vo. 21s.

O'BRIEN (R. Barry)—Irish Wrongs and English Remedies, with other Essays. Crown 8vo. 5s.

OGLE (W.) M.D., F.R.C.P.—Aristotle on the Parts of Animals. Translated, with Introduction and Notes. Royal 8vo. 12s. 6d.

OLIVER (Robert)—Unnoticed Analogies. A Talk on the Irish Question. Crown 8vo. 3s. 6d.

O'MEARA (Kathleen)—Henri Perreyve and his Counsels to the Sick. Small crown 8vo. 5s.

One and a Half in Norway. A Chronicle of Small Beer. By Either and Both. Small crown 8vo. 3s. 6d.

O'NEIL (The late Rev. Lord).—Sermons. With Memoir and Portrait. Crown 8vo. 6s.

Essays and Addresses. Crown 8vo. 5s.

OTTLEY (*Henry Bickersteth*)—THE GREAT DILEMMA : Christ His own Witness or His own Accuser. Six Lectures. Second Edition. Crown 8vo. 3*s.* 6*d.*

OUR PRIESTS AND THEIR TITHES. By a Priest of the Province of Canterbury. Crown 8vo. 5*s.*

OUR PUBLIC SCHOOLS—ETON, HARROW, WINCHESTER, RUGBY, WEST-MINSTER, MARLBOROUGH, THE CHARTERHOUSE. Crown 8vo. 6*s.*

OWEN (*F. M.*)—JOHN KEATS : a Study. Crown 8vo. 6*s.*

PADGHAM (*Richard*)—IN THE MIDST OF LIFE WE ARE IN DEATH. Crown 8vo. 5*s.*

PALMER (*the late William*)—NOTES OF A VISIT TO RUSSIA IN 1840–41. Selected and arranged by JOHN H. CARDINAL NEWMAN. With Portrait. Crown 8vo. 8*s.* 6*d.*

EARLY CHRISTIAN SYMBOLISM. A series of Compositions from Fresco-Paintings, Glasses, and Sculptured Sarcophagi. Edited by the Rev. PROVOST NORTHCOTE, D.D., and the Rev. CANON BROWNLOW, M.A. With Coloured Plates, folio, 42*s.* ; or with plain plates, folio, 25*s.*

PARCHMENT LIBRARY. Choicely printed on hand-made paper, limp parchment antique or cloth, 6*s.* ; vellum, 7*s.* 6*d.* each volume.

CARLYLE'S SARTOR RESARTUS.

MILTON'S POETICAL WORKS. 2 vols.

CHAUCER'S CANTERBURY TALES. 2 vols. Edited by ALFRED W. POLLARD.

SELECTIONS FROM THE PROSE WRITINGS OF JONATHAN SWIFT. With a Preface and Notes by STANLEY LANE-POOLE, and Portrait.

ENGLISH SACRED LYRICS.

SIR JOSHUA REYNOLDS' DISCOURSES. Edited by EDMUND GOSSE.

SELECTIONS FROM MILTON'S PROSE WRITINGS. Edited by ERNEST MYERS.

THE BOOK OF PSALMS. Translated by the Rev. Canon CHEYNE, D.D.

THE VICAR OF WAKEFIELD. With Preface and Notes by AUSTIN DOBSON.

ENGLISH COMIC DRAMATISTS. Edited by OSWALD CRAWFURD.

ENGLISH LYRICS.

THE SONNETS OF JOHN MILTON. Edited by MARK PATTISON. With Portrait after Vertue.

FRENCH LYRICS. Selected and Annotated by GEORGE SAINTSBURY. With miniature Frontispiece, designed and etched by H. G. Glindoni.

FABLES by MR. JOHN GAY. With Memoir by AUSTIN DOBSON, and an etched Portrait from an unfinished Oil-sketch by Sir Godfrey Kneller.

SELECT LETTERS OF PERCY BYSSHE SHELLEY. Edited, with an Introduction, by RICHARD GARNETT.

THE CHRISTIAN YEAR ; Thoughts in Verse for the Sundays and Holy Days throughout the Year. With etched Portrait of the Rev. J. Keble, after the Drawing by G. Richmond, R.A.

SHAKSPERE'S WORKS. Complete in Twelve Volumes.

EIGHTEENTH CENTURY ESSAYS. Selected and Edited by AUSTIN DOBSON. With a Miniature Frontispiece by R. Caldecott.

PARCHMENT LIBRARY—continued.

Q. HORATI FLACCI OPERA. Edited by F. A. CORNISH, Assistant Master at Eton. With a Frontispiece after a design by L. ALMA TADEMA. Etched by LEOPOLD LOWENSTAM.

EDGAR ALLAN POE'S POEMS. With an Essay on his Poetry by ANDREW LANG, and a Frontispiece by Linley Sambourne.

SHAKSPERE'S SONNETS. Edited by EDWARD DOWDEN. With a Frontispiece etched by Leopold Lowenstam, after the Death Mask.

ENGLISH ODES. Selected by EDMUND GOSSE. With Frontispiece on India paper by Hamo Thornycroft, A.R.A.

OF THE IMITATION OF CHRIST. By THOMAS À KEMPIS. A revised Translation. With Frontispiece on India paper, from a Design by W. B. Richmond.

POEMS : Selected from PERCY BYSSHE SHELLEY. Dedicated to Lady Shelley. With Preface by RICHARD GARNETT and a Miniature Frontispiece.

LETTERS AND JOURNALS OF JONATHAN SWIFT. Selected and edited, with a Commentary and Notes, by STANLEY LANE POOLE.

DE QUINCEY'S CONFESSIONS OF AN ENGLISH OPIUM EATER. Reprinted from the First Edition. Edited by RICHARD GARNETT.

THE GOSPEL ACCORDING TO MATTHEW, MARK, AND LUKE.

PARSLOE (Joseph) — OUR RAILWAYS. Sketches, Historical and Descriptive. With Practical Information as to Fares and Rates, &c., and a Chapter on Railway Reform. Crown 8vo. 6*s.*

PASCAL (Blaise)—THE THOUGHTS OF. Translated from the Text of AUGUSTE MOLINIER by C. KEGAN PAUL. Large crown 8vo. with Frontispiece, printed on hand-made paper, parchment antique, or cloth, 12*s.* ; vellum, 15*s.* New Edition, crown 8vo. 6*s.*

PATON (W. A.)—DOWN THE ISLANDS ; a Voyage to the Caribbees. Illustrations. Demy 8vo. 16*s.*

PAUL (C. Kegan)—BIOGRAPHICAL SKETCHES. Printed on hand-made paper, bound in buckram. Second Edition. Crown 8vo. 7*s.* 6*d.*

PEARSON (Rev. S.)—WEEK-DAY LIVING. A Book for Young Men and Women. Second Edition. Crown 8vo. 5*s.*

PENRICE (Major J.)—ARABIC AND ENGLISH DICTIONARY OF THE KORAN. 4to. 21*s.*

PESCHEL (Dr. Oscar)—THE RACES OF MAN AND THEIR GEOGRAPHICAL DISTRIBUTION. Second Edition, large crown 8vo. 9*s.*

PETERS (F. H.)—THE NICOMACHEAN ETHICS OF ARISTOTLE. Translated by. Crown 8vo. 6*s.*

PIDGEON (D.)—AN ENGINEER'S HOLIDAY ; or, Notes of a Round Trip from Long. 0° to 0°. New and Cheaper Edition. Large crown 8vo. 7*s.* 6*d.*

OLD WORLD QUESTIONS AND NEW WORLD ANSWERS. Large crown 8vo. 7*s.* 6*d.*

PLAIN THOUGHTS FOR MEN. Eight Lectures delivered at the Foresters' Hall, Clerkenwell, during the London Mission, 1884. Crown 8vo. 1*s.* 6*d.* ; paper covers, 1*s.*

PLOWRIGHT (C. B.)—THE BRITISH UREDINEÆ AND USTILAGINEÆ. With Illustrations. Demy 8vo. 10*s.* 6*d.*

POE (*Edgar Allan*)—WORKS OF. With an Introduction and a Memoir by RICHARD HENRY STODDARD. In 6 vols. with Frontispieces and Vignettes. Large crown 8vo. 6*s.* each vol.

PRICE (*Prof. Bonamy*)—CHAPTERS ON PRACTICAL POLITICAL ECONOMY. Being the Substance of Lectures delivered before the University of Oxford. New and Cheaper Edition. Large post 8vo. 5*s.*

PRIG'S BEDE: The Venerable Bede Expurgated, Expounded, and Exposed. By the PRIG, Author of ' The Life of a Prig.' Fcp. 8vo. 3*s.* 6*d.*

PRIGMENT (THE). A Collection of ' The Prig ' Books. Crown 8vo. 6*s.*

PULPIT COMMENTARY (THE). Old Testament Series. Edited by the Rev. J. S. EXELL and the Very Rev. Dean H. D. M. SPENCE.

GENESIS. By Rev. T. WHITELAW, M.A. With Homilies by the Very Rev. J. F. MONTGOMERY, D.D., Rev. Prof. R. A. REDFORD, M.A., LL.B., Rev. F. HASTINGS, Rev. W. ROBERTS, M.A.; an Introduction to the Study of the Old Testament by the Venerable Archdeacon FARRAR, D.D., F.R.S.; and Introductions to the Pentateuch by the Right Rev. H. COTTERILL, D.D., and Rev. T. WHITELAW, M.A. Eighth Edition. One vol. 15*s.*

EXODUS. By the Rev. Canon RAWLINSON. With Homilies by Rev. J. ORR, Rev. D. YOUNG, Rev. C. A. GOODHART, Rev. J. URQUHART, and Rev. H. T. ROBJOHNS. Fourth Edition. Two vols. each 9*s.*

LEVITICUS. By the Rev. Prebendary MEYRICK, M.A. With Introductions by Rev. R. COLLINS, Rev. Professor A. CAVE, and Homilies by Rev. Prof. REDFORD, LL.B., Rev. J. A. MACDONALD, Rev. W. CLARKSON, Rev. S. R. ALDRIDGE, LL.B., and Rev. McCHEYNE EDGAR. Fourth Edition. 15*s.*

NUMBERS. By the Rev R. WINTERBOTHAM, LL.B. With Homilies by the Rev. Professor W. BINNIE, D.D., Rev. E. S. PROUT, M.A., Rev. D. YOUNG, Rev. J. WAITE; and an Introduction by the Rev. THOMAS WHITELAW, M.A. Fifth Edition. 15*s.*

DEUTERONOMY. By Rev. W. L. ALEXANDER, D.D. With Homilies by Rev. D. DAVIES, M.A., Rev. C. CLEMANCE, D.D., Rev. J. ORR, B.D., and Rev. R. M. EDGAR, M.A. Fourth Edition. 15*s.*

JOSHUA. By Rev. J. J. LIAS, M.A. With Homilies by Rev. S. R. ALDRIDGE, LL.B., Rev. R. GLOVER, Rev. E. DE PRESSENSÉ, D.D., Rev. J. WAITE, B.A. Rev. W. F. ADENEY, M.A.; and an Introduction by the Rev. A. PLUMMER, M.A. Fifth Edition. 12*s.* 6*d.*

JUDGES AND RUTH. By the Bishop of Bath and Wells and Rev. J. MORISON, D.D. With Homilies by Rev. A. F. MUIR, M.A., Rev. W. F. ADENEY, M.A., Rev. W. M. STATHAM, and Rev. Professor J. THOMSON, M.A. Fifth Edition. 10*s.* 6*d.*

1 and 2 SAMUEL. By the Very Rev. R. P. SMITH, D.D. With Homilies by Rev. DONALD FRASER, D.D., Rev. Prof. CHAPMAN, Rev. B. DALE, and Rev G. WOOD. Vol. I. Sixth Edition, 15*s.* Vol. II. 15*s.*

1 KINGS. By the Rev. JOSEPH HAMMOND, LL.B. With Homilies by the Rev. E DE PRESSENSÉ, D.D., Rev. J. WAITE, B.A., Rev. A. ROWLAND, LL.B., Rev. J. A. MACDONALD, and Rev. J. URQUHART. Fifth Edition. 15*s.*

1 CHRONICLES. By the Rev. Prof. P. C. BARKER, M.A., LL.B. With Homilies by Rev. Prof. J. R. THOMSON, M.A., Rev. R. TUCK, B.A., Rev. W. CLARKSON, B.A., Rev. F. WHITFIELD, M A., and Rev. RICHARD GLOVER. 15*s.*

PULPIT COMMENTARY (THE). Old Testament Series—continued.

EZRA, NEHEMIAH, AND ESTHER. By Rev. Canon G. RAWLINSON, M.A. With Homilies by Rev. Prof. J. R. THOMSON, M.A., Rev. Prof. R. A. REDFORD, LL.B., M.A., Rev. W. S. LEWIS, M.A., Rev. J. A. MACDONALD, Rev. A. MACKENNAL, B.A., Rev. W. CLARKSON, B.A., Rev. F. HASTINGS, Rev. W. DINWIDDIE, LL.B., Rev. Prof. ROWLANDS, B.A., Rev. G. WOOD, B.A., Rev. Prof. P. C. BARKER, LL.B., M.A., and Rev. J. S. EXELL, M.A. Sixth Edition. One vol. 12*s.* 6*d.*

ISAIAH. By the Rev. Canon G. RAWLINSON, M.A. With Homilies by Rev. Prof. E. JOHNSON, M.A., Rev. W. CLARKSON, B.A., Rev. W. M. STATHAM, and Rev. R. TUCK, B.A. Second Edition. 2 vols. each 15*s.*

JEREMIAH (Vol. I.). By the Rev. Canon CHEYNE, D.D. With Homilies by the Rev W. F. ADENEY, M.A., Rev. A. F. MUIR, M.A., Rev. S. CONWAY, B.A., Rev. J. WAITE, B.A., and Rev. D. YOUNG, B.A. Third Edition. 15*s.*

JEREMIAH (Vol. II.), AND LAMENTATIONS. By the Rev. Canon CHEYNE, D.D. With Homilies by Rev. Prof. J. R. THOMSON, M.A., Rev. W. F. ADENEY, M.A., Rev. A. F. MUIR, M.A., Rev. S. CONWAY, B.A., Rev. D. YOUNG, B.A. 15*s.*

HOSEA AND JOEL. By the Rev. Prof. J. J. GIVEN, Ph.D., D.D. With Homilies by the Rev. Prof. J. R. THOMSON, M.A., Rev. A. ROWLAND, B.A., LL.B., Rev. C. JERDAN, M.A., LL.B., Rev. J. ORR, M.A., B.D., and Rev. D. THOMAS, D.D. 15*s.*

PULPIT COMMENTARY (THE). New Testament Series.

ST. MARK. By the Very Rev. E. BICKERSTETH, D.D., Dean of Lichfield. With Homilies by the Rev. Prof. THOMSON, M.A., Rev. Prof. GIVEN, M.A., Rev. Prof. JOHNSON, M.A., Rev. A. ROWLAND, LL.B., Rev. A. MUIR, M.A., and Rev. R. GREEN. Fifth Edition. 2 vols. each 10*s.* 6*d.*

ST. JOHN. By the Rev. Prof. H. R. REYNOLDS, D.D. With Homilies by Rev. Prof. T. CROSKERY, D.D., Rev. Prof. J. R. THOMSON, Rev. D. YOUNG, Rev. B. THOMAS, and Rev. G. BROWN. 2 vols. each 15*s.*

THE ACTS OF THE APOSTLES. By the Bishop of BATH AND WELLS. With Homilies by Rev. Prof. P. C. BARKER, M.A., Rev. Prof. E. JOHNSON, M.A., Rev. Prof. R. A. REDFORD, M.A., Rev. R. TUCK, B.A., Rev. W. CLARKSON, B.A. Fourth Edition. Two vols. each 10*s.* 6*d.*

I CORINTHIANS. By the Ven. Archdeacon FARRAR, D.D. With Homilies by Rev. Ex-Chancellor LIPSCOMB, LL.D., Rev. DAVID THOMAS, D.D., Rev. DONALD FRASER, D.D., Rev. Prof. J. R. THOMSON, M.A., Rev. R. TUCK, B.A., Rev. E. HURNDALL, M.A., Rev. J. WAITE, B.A., Rev. H. BREMNER, B.D. Third Edition. 15*s.*

II CORINTHIANS AND GALATIANS. By the Ven. Archdeacon FARRAR, D.D., and Rev. Preb. E. HUXTABLE. With Homilies by Rev. Ex-Chancellor LIPSCOMB, LL.D., Rev. DAVID THOMAS, D.D., Rev. DONALD FRASER, D.D., Rev. R. TUCK, B.A., Rev. E. HURNDALL, M.A., Rev. Prof. J. R. THOMSON, M.A., Rev. R. FINLAYSON, B.A., Rev. W. F. ADENEY, M.A., Rev. R. M. EDGAR, M.A., and Rev. T. CROSKERY, D.D. 21*s.*

EPHESIANS, PHILIPPIANS, AND COLOSSIANS. By the Rev. Prof. W. G. BLAIKIE, D.D., Rev. B. C. CAFFIN, M.A., and Rev. G. G. FINDLAY, B.A. With Homilies by Rev. D. THOMAS, D.D., Rev. R. M. EDGAR, M.A., Rev. R. FINLAYSON, B.A., Rev. W. F. ADENEY, M.A., Rev. Prof. T. CROSKERY, D.D., Rev. E. S. PROUT, M.A., Rev. Canon VERNON HUTTON, and Rev. U. R. THOMAS, D.D. Second Edition. 21*s.*

PULPIT COMMENTARY (THE). New Testament Series—continued.

    THESSALONIANS, TIMOTHY, TITUS, AND PHILEMON. By the BISHOP OF BATH AND WELLS, Rev. Dr. GLOAG, and Rev. Dr. EALES. With Homilies by the Rev. B. C. CAFFIN, M.A., Rev. R. FINLAYSON, B.A., Rev. Prof. T. CROSKERY, D.D., Rev. W. F. ADENEY, M.A., Rev. W. M. STATHAM, and Rev. D. THOMAS, D.D. 15s.

    HEBREWS AND JAMES. By the Rev. J. BARMBY, D.D., and Rev. Prebendary E. C. S. GIBSON, M.A. With Homiletics by the Rev. C. JERDAN, M.A., LL.B., and Rev. Prebendary E. C. S. GIBSON. And Homilies by the Rev. W. JONES, Rev. C. NEW, Rev. D. YOUNG, B.A., Rev. J. S. BRIGHT, Rev. T. F. LOCKYER, B.A., and Rev. C. JERDAN, M.A., LL.B. Second Edition. Price 15s.

PUSEY (Dr.)—SERMONS FOR THE CHURCH'S SEASONS FROM ADVENT TO TRINITY. Selected from the published Sermons of the late EDWARD BOUVERIE PUSEY, D.D. Crown 8vo. 5s.

QUEKETT (Rev. William)—MY SAYINGS AND DOINGS, WITH REMINISCENCES OF MY LIFE. Demy 8vo. 18s.

RANKE (Leopold von)—UNIVERSAL HISTORY. The Oldest Historical Group of Nations and the Greeks. Edited by G. W. PROTHERO. Demy 8vo. 16s.

RENDELL (J. M.)—CONCISE HANDBOOK OF THE ISLAND OF MADEIRA. With Plan of Funchal and Map of the Island. Fcp. 8vo. 1s. 6d.

REYNOLDS (Rev. J. W.)—THE SUPERNATURAL IN NATURE. A Verification by Free Use of Science. Third Edition, revised and enlarged. Demy 8vo. 14s.

    THE MYSTERY OF MIRACLES. Third and Enlarged Edition. Crown 8vo. 6s.

    THE MYSTERY OF THE UNIVERSE: Our Common Faith. Demy 8vo. 14s.

    THE WORLD TO COME: Immortality a Physical Fact. Crown 8vo. 6s.

RIBOT (Prof. Th.)—HEREDITY: a Psychological Study on its Phenomena, its Laws, its Causes, and its Consequences. Second Edition. Large crown 8vo. 9s.

RIVINGTON (Luke)—AUTHORITY, OR A PLAIN REASON FOR JOINING THE CHURCH OF ROME. Crown 8vo. 3s. 6d.

ROBERTSON (The late Rev. F. W.) M.A.—LIFE AND LETTERS OF. Edited by the Rev. Stopford Brooke, M.A.

    I. Two vols., uniform with the Sermons. With Steel Portrait. Crown 8vo. 7s. 6d.

    II. Library Edition, in demy 8vo. with Portrait. 12s.

    III. A Popular Edition, in 1 vol. Crown 8vo. 6s.

    SERMONS. Four Series. Small crown 8vo. 3s. 6d. each.

    THE HUMAN RACE, and other Sermons. Preached at Cheltenham, Oxford, and Brighton. New and Cheaper Edition. Small crown 8vo. 3s. 6d.

    NOTES ON GENESIS. New and Cheaper Edition. Small crown 8vo. 3s. 6d.

    EXPOSITORY LECTURES ON ST. PAUL'S EPISTLES TO THE CORINTHIANS. A New Edition. Small crown 8vo. 5s.

    LECTURES AND ADDRESSES, with other Literary Remains. A New Edition. Small crown 8vo. 5s.

    AN ANALYSIS OF TENNYSON'S 'IN MEMORIAM.' (Dedicated by Permission to the Poet-Laureate.) Fcp. 8vo. 2s.

    THE EDUCATION OF THE HUMAN RACE. Translated from the German of Gotthold Ephraim Lessing. Fcp. 8vo. 2s. 6d.

        . A Portrait of the late Rev. F. W. Robertson, mounted for framing, can be had, 2s. 6d.

ROGERS (*William*)—REMINISCENCES. Compiled by R. H. HADDEN. With Portrait. Third Edition. Crown 8vo. 6*s.*

ROMANCE OF THE RECUSANTS. By the Author of 'Life of a Prig.' Cr. 8vo. 5*s.*

ROMANES (*G. J.*)—MENTAL EVOLUTION IN ANIMALS. With a Posthumous Essay on Instinct, by CHARLES DARWIN, F.R.S. Demy 8vo. 12*s.*

MENTAL EVOLUTION IN MAN. Vol. I. 8vo. 14*s.*

ROSMINI SERBATI (*A.*) *Founder of the Institute of Charity*—LIFE. By FATHER LOCKHART. 2 vols. Crown 8vo. 12*s.*

ROSMINI'S ORIGIN OF IDEAS. Translated from the Fifth Italian Edition of the Nuovo Saggio. *Sull' origine delle idee.* 3 vols. Demy 8vo. 10*s.* 6*d.* each.

ROSMINI'S PSYCHOLOGY. 3 vols. Demy 8vo. [Vols. I. & II. now ready, 10*s.* 6*d.* each.

ROSS (*Janet*)—ITALIAN SKETCHES. With 14 full-page Illustrations. Crown 8vo. 7*s.* 6*d.*

RULE (*Martin*) *M.A.*—THE LIFE AND TIMES OF ST. ANSELM, ARCHBISHOP OF CANTERBURY AND PRIMATE OF THE BRITAINS. 2 vols. Demy 8vo. 32*s.*

SAMUEL (*Sydney M.*)—JEWISH LIFE IN THE EAST. Small crown 8vo. 3*s.* 6*d.*

SAYCE (*Rev. Archibald Henry*)—INTRODUCTION TO THE SCIENCE OF LANGUAGE. 2 vols. Second Edition. Large post 8vo. 21*s.*

SCOONES (*W. Baptiste*)—FOUR CENTURIES OF ENGLISH LETTERS : A Selection of 350 Letters by 150 Writers, from the Period of the Paston Letters to the Present Time. Third Edition. Large crown 8vo. 6*s.*

SÉE (*Prof. Germain*)—BACILLARY PHTHISIS OF THE LUNGS. Translated and Edited for English Practitioners, by WILLIAM HENRY WEDDELL, M.R.C.S. Demy 8vo. 10*s.* 6*d.*

SELWYN (*Augustus*) *D.D.*—LIFE. By Canon G. H. CURTEIS. Crown 8vo. 6*s.*

SEYMOUR (*W. Digby*)—HOME RULE AND STATE SUPREMACY. Crown 8vo. 3*s.* 6*d.*

SHAKSPERE—WORKS. The Avon Edition, 12 vols. fcp. 8vo. cloth, 18*s.* ; in cloth box, 21*s.* ; bound in 6 vols., cloth, 15*s.*

SHAKSPERE—WORKS (An Index to). By EVANGELINE O'CONNOR. Crown 8vo. 5*s.*

SHELLEY (*Percy Bysshe*).—LIFE. By EDWARD DOWDEN, LL.D. With Portraits and Illustrations, 2 vols., demy 8vo. 36*s.*

SHILLITO (*Rev. Joseph*)—WOMANHOOD : its Duties, Temptations, and Privileges. A Book for Young Women. Third Edition. Crown 8vo. 3*s.* 6*d.*

SHOOTING, PRACTICAL HINTS ON. Being a Treatise on the Shot Gun and its Management. By ' 20-Bore.' With 55 Illustrations. Demy 8vo. 12*s.*

SISTER AUGUSTINE, Superior of the Sisters of Charity at the St. Johannis Hospital at Bonn. Cheap Edition. Large crown 8vo. 4*s.* 6*d.*

SKINNER (JAMES). A Memoir. By the Author of ' Charles Lowder.' With a Preface by Canon CARTER, and Portrait. Large crown 8vo. 7*s.* 6*d.*
  *** Also a Cheap Edition, with Portrait. Crown 8vo. 3*s.* 6*d.*

SMEATON (*Donald*).—THE LOYAL KARENS OF BURMAH. Crown 8vo. 4*s.* 6*d.*

SMITH (*Edward*) *M.D.*, *LL.B.*, *F.R.S.*—TUBERCULAR CONSUMPTION IN ITS EARLY AND REMEDIABLE STAGES. Second Edition. Crown 8vo. 6*s.*

SMITH (L. A.)—MUSIC OF THE WATERS : Sailors' Chanties, or Working Songs of the Sea of all Maritime Nations. Demy 8vo. 12s.

SMITH (Sir W. Cusack, Bart.)—OUR WAR SHIPS. A Naval Essay. Crown 8vo. 5s.

SPANISH MYSTICS. By the Editor of ' Many Voices.' Crown 8vo. 5s.

SPECIMENS OF ENGLISH PROSE STYLE FROM MALORY TO MACAULAY. Selected and Annotated, with an Introductory Essay, by GEORGE SAINTSBURY. Large crown 8vo., printed on hand-made paper, parchment antique, or cloth, 12s. ; vellum, 15s.

SPEDDING (James)—REVIEWS AND DISCUSSIONS, LITERARY, POLITICAL, AND HISTORICAL NOT RELATING TO BACON. Demy 8vo. 12s. 6d.

EVENINGS WITH A REVIEWER ; or, Bacon and Macaulay. With a Prefatory Notice by G. S. VENABLES, Q.C. 2 vols. Demy 8vo. 18s.

STRACHEY (Sir John)—LECTURES ON INDIA. 8vo. 15s.

STRAY PAPERS ON EDUCATION AND SCENES FROM SCHOOL LIFE. By B. H. Second Edition. Small crown 8vo. 3s. 6d.

STREATFEILD (Rev. G. S.) M.A.—LINCOLNSHIRE AND THE DANES. Large crown 8vo. 7s. 6d.

STRECKER-WISLICENUS—ORGANIC CHEMISTRY. Translated and Edited, with Extensive Additions, by W. R. HODGKINSON, Ph.D., and A. J. GREENAWAY, F.I.C. Demy 8vo. 12s. 6d.

SUAKIN, 1885 ; being a Sketch of the Campaign of this Year. By an Officer who was there. Second Edition. Crown 8vo. 2s. 6d.

SULLY (James) M.A.—PESSIMISM : a History and a Criticism. Second Edition. Demy 8vo. 14s.

TARRING (Charles James) M.A.—A PRACTICAL ELEMENTARY TURKISH GRAMMAR. Crown 8vo. 6s.

TAYLOR (Hugh)—THE MORALITY OF NATIONS. A Study in the Evolution of Ethics. Crown 8vo. 6s.

TAYLOR (Rev. Isaac)—THE ALPHABET. An Account of the Origin and Development of Letters. Numerous Tables and Facsimiles. 2 vols. 8vo. 36s.

LEAVES FROM AN EGYPTIAN NOTE-BOOK. Crown 8vo. 5s.

TAYLOR (Reynell) C.B., C.S.I.—A BIOGRAPHY. By E. GAMBIER PARRY. With Portrait and Map. Demy 8vo. 14s.

THOM (John Hamilton)—LAWS OF LIFE AFTER THE MIND OF CHRIST. Two Series. Crown 8vo. 7s. 6d. each.

THOMPSON (Sir H.)—DIET IN RELATION TO AGE AND ACTIVITY. Fcp. 8vo. cloth, 1s. 6d. ; Paper covers, 1s.

TIDMAN (Paul F.)—GOLD AND SILVER MONEY. Part I.—A Plain Statement. Part II.—Objections Answered. Third Edition. Crown 8vo. 1s.

MONEY AND LABOUR. 1s. 6d.

TODHUNTER (Dr. J.)—A STUDY OF SHELLEY. Crown 8vo. 7s.

TOLSTOI (Count Leo)—CHRIST'S CHRISTIANITY. Translated from the Russian. Large crown 8vo. 7s. 6d.

TRANT (William)—TRADE UNIONS ; Their Origin and Objects, Influence and Efficacy. Small crown 8vo. 1s. 6d. ; paper covers, 1s.

TRENCH (The late R. C., Archbishop)—LETTERS AND MEMORIALS. Edited by the Author of 'Charles Lowder, a Biography,' &c. With two Portraits. 2 vols. demy 8vo. 21s.

SERMONS NEW AND OLD. Crown 8vo. 6s.

WESTMINSTER AND DUBLIN SERMONS. Crown 8vo. 6s.

NOTES ON THE PARABLES OF OUR LORD. Fourteenth Edition. 8vo. 12s.; Popular Edition, crown 8vo. 7s. 6d.

NOTES ON THE MIRACLES OF OUR LORD. Twelfth Edition. 8vo. 12s.; Popular Edition, crown 8vo. 7s. 6d.

STUDIES IN THE GOSPELS. Fifth Edition, Revised. 8vo. 10s. 6d.

BRIEF THOUGHTS AND MEDITATIONS ON SOME PASSAGES IN HOLY Scripture. Third Edition. Crown 8vo. 3s. 6d.

SYNONYMS OF THE NEW TESTAMENT. Tenth Edition, Enlarged. 8vo. 12s.

ON THE AUTHORISED VERSION OF THE NEW TESTAMENT. Second Edition. 8vo. 7s.

COMMENTARY ON THE EPISTLE TO THE SEVEN CHURCHES IN ASIA. Fourth Edition, Revised. 8vo. 8s. 6d.

THE SERMON ON THE MOUNT. An Exposition drawn from the Writings of St. Augustine, with an Essay on his Merits as an Interpreter of Holy Scripture. Fourth Edition, Enlarged. 8vo. 10s. 6d.

SHIPWRECKS OF FAITH. Three Sermons preached before the University of Cambridge in May 1867. Fcp. 8vo. 2s. 6d.

LECTURES ON MEDIÆVAL CHURCH HISTORY. Being the Substance of Lectures delivered at Queen's College, London. Second Edition. 8vo. 12s.

ENGLISH, PAST AND PRESENT. Thirteenth Edition, Revised and Improved. Fcp. 8vo. 5s.

ON THE STUDY OF WORDS. Nineteenth Edition, Revised. Fcp. 8vo. 5s.

SELECT GLOSSARY OF ENGLISH WORDS USED FORMERLY IN SENSES DIFFERENT FROM THE PRESENT. Sixth Edition, Revised and Enlarged. Fcp. 8vo. 5s.

PROVERBS AND THEIR LESSONS. Seventh Edition, Enlarged. Fcp. 8vo. 4s.

POEMS. Collected and Arranged Anew. Ninth Edition. Fcp. 8vo. 7s. 6d.

POEMS. Library Edition. 2 vols. Small crown 8vo. 10s.

SACRED LATIN POETRY. Chiefly Lyrical, Selected and Arranged for Use. Third Edition, Corrected and Improved. Fcp. 8vo. 7s.

A HOUSEHOLD BOOK OF ENGLISH POETRY. Selected and Arranged, with Notes. Fourth Edition, Revised. Extra fcp. 8vo. 5s. 6d.

AN ESSAY ON THE LIFE AND GENIUS OF CALDERON. With Translations from his 'Life's a Dream' and 'Great Theatre of the World.' Second Edition, Revised and Improved. Extra fcp. 8vo. 5s. 6d.

GUSTAVUS ADOLPHUS IN GERMANY, AND OTHER LECTURES ON THE THIRTY YEARS' WAR. Third Edition, Enlarged. Fcp. 8vo. 4s.

PLUTARCH: HIS LIFE, HIS LIVES, AND HIS MORALS. Second Edition, Enlarged. Fcp. 8vo. 3s. 6d.

REMAINS OF THE LATE MRS. RICHARD TRENCH. Being Selections from her Journals, Letters, and other Papers. New and Cheaper Issue. With Portrait. 8vo. 6s.

TUTHILL (C. A. H.)—ORIGIN AND DEVELOPMENT OF CHRISTIAN DOGMA. Crown 8vo. 3s. 6d.

TWINING (Louisa)—WORKHOUSE VISITING AND MANAGEMENT DURING TWENTY-FIVE YEARS. Small crown 8vo. 2s.

TWO CENTURIES OF IRISH HISTORY. Edited by JAMES BRYCE, M.P. 8vo. 16s.

UMLAUFT (F.)—THE ALPS. Illustrated. 8vo.

VAL D'EREMAO (J. P.) D.D.—THE SERPENT OF EDEN. Crown 8vo. 4s. 6d.

VAUGHAN (H. Halford)—NEW READINGS AND RENDERINGS OF SHAKESPEARE'S TRAGEDIES. 3 vols. Demy 8vo. 12s. 6d. each.

VICARY (J. Fulford)—SAGA TIME. With Illustrations. Cr. 8vo. 7s. 6d.

VOLCKXSOM (E. W. v.)—CATECHISM OF ELEMENTARY MODERN CHEMISTRY. Small crown 8vo. 3s.

WALPOLE (Chas. George)—A SHORT HISTORY OF IRELAND FROM THE EARLIEST TIMES TO THE UNION WITH GREAT BRITAIN. With 5 Maps and Appendices. Third Edition. Crown 8vo. 6s.

WARD (William George) Ph.D. — ESSAYS ON THE PHILOSOPHY OF THEISM. Edited, with an Introduction, by WILFRID WARD. 2 vols. demy 8vo. 21s.

WARD (Wilfrid)—THE WISH TO BELIEVE: A Discussion concerning the Temper of Mind in which a reasonable Man should undertake Religious Inquiry. Small crown 8vo. 5s.

WARNER (Francis) M.D.—LECTURES ON THE ANATOMY OF MOVEMENT. Crown 8vo. 4s. 6d.

WARTER (J. W.)—AN OLD SHROPSHIRE OAK. 2 vols. demy 8vo. 28s.

WEDMORE (Frederick)—THE MASTERS OF GENRE PAINTING. With Sixteen Illustrations. Post 8vo. 7s. 6d.

WHIBLEY (Charles)—CAMBRIDGE ANECDOTES. Crown 8vo. 7s. 6d.

WHITMAN (Sidney)—CONVENTIONAL CANT: Its Results and Remedy. Crown 8vo. 6s.

WHITNEY (Prof. William Dwight)—ESSENTIALS OF ENGLISH GRAMMAR, for the Use of Schools. Second Edition, crown 8vo. 3s. 6d.

WHITWORTH (George Clifford)—AN ANGLO-INDIAN DICTIONARY: a Glossary of Indian Terms used in English. Demy 8vo. cloth, 12s.

WILBERFORCE (Samuel) D.D.—LIFE. By R. G. WILBERFORCE. Crown 8vo. 6s.

WILSON (Mrs. R. F.)—THE CHRISTIAN BROTHERS: THEIR ORIGIN AND WORK. Crown 8vo. 6s.

WOLTMANN (Dr. Alfred), and WOERMANN (Dr. Karl)—HISTORY OF PAINTING. Vol. I. Ancient, Early, Christian, and Mediæval Painting. With numerous Illustrations. Super-royal 8vo. 28s.; bevelled boards, gilt leaves, 30s. Vol. II. The Painting of the Renascence. Cloth, 42s.; cloth extra, bevelled boards, 45s.

WORDS OF JESUS CHRIST TAKEN FROM THE GOSPELS. Small crown 8vo. 2s. 6d.

YOUMANS (Eliza A.)—FIRST BOOK OF BOTANY. Designed to cultivate the Observing Powers of Children. With 300 Engravings. New and Cheaper Edition. Crown 8vo. 2s. 6d.

YOUMANS (Edward L.) M.D.—A CLASS BOOK OF CHEMISTRY, on the Basis of the New System. With 200 Illustrations. Crown 8vo. 5s.

YOUNG (Arthur).—AXIAL POLARITY OF MAN'S WORD-EMBODIED IDEAS, AND ITS TEACHING. Demy 4to. 15s.

THE INTERNATIONAL SCIENTIFIC SERIES.

I. FORMS OF WATER : a Familiar Exposition of the Origin and Phenomena of Glaciers. By J. Tyndall, LL.D., F.R.S. With 25 Illustrations. Ninth Edition. Crown 8vo. 5s.

II. PHYSICS AND POLITICS ; or, Thoughts on the Application of the Principles of 'Natural Selection' and 'Inheritance' to Political Society. By Walter Bagehot. Eighth Edition. Crown 8vo. 5s.

III. FOODS. By Edward Smith, M.D., LL.B., F.R.S. With numerous Illustrations. Ninth Edition. Crown 8vo. 5s.

IV. MIND AND BODY : the Theories and their Relation. By Alexander Bain, LL.D. With Four Illustrations. Eighth Edition. Crown 8vo. 5s.

V. THE STUDY OF SOCIOLOGY. By Herbert Spencer. Thirteenth Edition. Crown 8vo. 5s.

VI. ON THE CONSERVATION OF ENERGY. By Balfour Stewart, M.A., LL.D., F.R.S. With 14 Illustrations. Seventh Edition. Crown 8vo. 5s.

VII. ANIMAL LOCOMOTION ; or, Walking, Swimming, and Flying. By J. B. Pettigrew, M.D., F.R.S., &c. With 130 Illustrations. Third Edition. Crown 8vo. 5s.

VIII. RESPONSIBILITY IN MENTAL DISEASE. By Henry Maudsley, M.D. Fourth Edition. Crown 8vo. 5s.

IX. THE NEW CHEMISTRY. By Professor J. P. Cooke. With 31 Illustrations. Ninth Edition, remodelled and enlarged. Crown 8vo. 5s.

X. THE SCIENCE OF LAW. By Professor Sheldon Amos. Sixth Edition. Crown 8vo. 5s.

XI. ANIMAL MECHANISM: a Treatise on Terrestrial and Aërial Locomotion. By Professor E. J. Marey. With 117 Illustrations. Third Edition. Crown 8vo. 5s.

XII. THE DOCTRINE OF DESCENT AND DARWINISM. By Professor Oscar Schmidt. With 26 Illustrations. Seventh Edition. Crown 8vo. 5s.

XIII. THE HISTORY OF THE CONFLICT BETWEEN RELIGION AND SCIENCE. By J. W. Draper, M.D., LL.D. Twentieth Edition. Crown 8vo. 5s.

XIV. FUNGI: their Nature, Influences, Uses, &c. By M. C. Cooke, M.D., LL.D. Edited by the Rev. M. J. Berkeley, M.A., F.L.S. With numerous Illustrations. Fourth Edition. Crown 8vo. 5s.

XV. THE CHEMICAL EFFECTS OF LIGHT AND PHOTOGRAPHY. By Dr. Hermann Vogel. Translation thoroughly revised. With 100 Illustrations. Fifth Edition. Crown 8vo. 5s.

XVI. THE LIFE AND GROWTH OF LANGUAGE. By Professor William Dwight Whitney. Fifth Edition. Crown 8vo. 5s.

XVII. MONEY AND THE MECHANISM OF EXCHANGE. By W. Stanley Jevons, M.A., F.R.S. Eighth Edition. Crown 8vo. 5s.

XVIII. THE NATURE OF LIGHT. With a General Account of Physical Optics. By Dr. Eugene Lommel. With 188 Illustrations and a Table of Spectra in Chromo-lithography. Fourth Edit. Crown 8vo. 5s.

XIX. ANIMAL PARASITES AND MESSMATES. By P. J. Van Beneden. With 83 Illustrations. Third Edition. Crown 8vo. 5s.

XX. FERMENTATION. By Professor Schützenberger. With 28 Illustrations. Fourth Edition. Crown 8vo. 5s.

XXI. THE FIVE SENSES OF MAN. By Professor Bernstein. With 91 Illustrations. Fifth Edition. Crown 8vo. 5s.

XXII. THE THEORY OF SOUND IN ITS RELATION TO MUSIC. By Professor Pietro Blaserna. With numerous Illustrations. Third Edition. Crown 8vo. 5s.

XXIII. STUDIES IN SPECTRUM ANALYSIS. By J. Norman Lockyer, F.R.S. Fourth Edition. With six Photographic Illustrations of Spectra, and numerous Engravings on Wood. Crown 8vo. 6s. 6d.

XXIV. A HISTORY OF THE GROWTH OF THE STEAM ENGINE. By Professor R. H. Thurston. With numerous Illustrations. Fourth Edition. Crown 8vo. 5*s.*

XXV. EDUCATION AS A SCIENCE. By Alexander Bain, LL.D. Sixth Edition. Crown 8vo. 5*s.*

XXVI. THE HUMAN SPECIES. By Prof. A. De Quatrefages. Fourth Edition. Crown 8vo. 5*s.*

XXVII. MODERN CHROMATICS. With Applications to Art and Industry. By Ogden N. Rood. With 130 original Illustrations. Second Edition. Crown 8vo. 5*s.*

XXVIII. THE CRAYFISH: an Introduction to the Study of Zoology. By Professor T. H. Huxley. With 82 Illustrations. Fourth Edition. Crown 8vo. 5*s.*

XXIX. THE BRAIN AS AN ORGAN OF MIND. By H. Charlton Bastian, M.D. With numerous Illustrations. Third Edition. Crown 8vo. 5*s.*

XXX. THE ATOMIC THEORY. By Prof. Wurtz. Translated by G. Cleminshaw, F.C.S. Fifth Edition. Crown 8vo. 5*s.*

XXXI. THE NATURAL CONDITIONS OF EXISTENCE AS THEY AFFECT ANIMAL LIFE. By Karl Semper. With 2 Maps and 106 Woodcuts. Third Edition. Crown 8vo. 5*s.*

XXXII. GENERAL PHYSIOLOGY OF MUSCLES AND NERVES. By Prof. J. Rosenthal. Third Edition. With Illustrations. Crown 8vo. 5*s.*

XXXIII. SIGHT: an Exposition of the Principles of Monocular and Binocular Vision. By Joseph Le Conte, LL.D. Second Edition. With 132 Illustrations. Crown 8vo. 5*s.*

XXXIV. ILLUSIONS: a Psychological Study. By James Sully. Third Edition. Crown 8vo. 5*s.*

XXXV. VOLCANOES: WHAT THEY ARE AND WHAT THEY TEACH. By Professor J. W. Judd, F.R.S. With 92 Illustrations on Wood. Fourth Edition. Crown 8vo. 5*s.*

XXXVI. SUICIDE: an Essay on Comparative Moral Statistics. By Prof. H. Morselli. Second Edition. With Diagrams. Crown 8vo. 5*s.*

XXXVII. THE BRAIN AND ITS FUNCTIONS. By J. Luys. Second Edition. With Illustrations. Crown 8vo. 5*s.*

XXXVIII. MYTH AND SCIENCE: an Essay. By Tito Vignoli. Third Edition. Crown 8vo. 5*s.*

XXXIX. THE SUN. By Professor Young. With Illustrations. Third Edition. Crown 8vo. 5*s.*

XL. ANTS, BEES, AND WASPS: a Record of Observations on the Habits of the Social Hymenoptera. By Sir John Lubbock, Bart., M.P. With 5 Chromolithographic Illustrations. Ninth Edition. Crown 8vo 5*s.*

XLI. ANIMAL INTELLIGENCE. By G. J. Romanes, LL.D., F.R.S. Fourth Edition. Crown 8vo. 5*s.*

XLII. THE CONCEPTS AND THEORIES OF MODERN PHYSICS. By J. B. Stallo. Third Edition. Crown 8vo. 5*s.*

XLIII. DISEASES OF MEMORY: an Essay in the Positive Pyschology. By Prof. Th. Ribot. Third Edition. Crown 8vo. 5*s.*

XLIV. MAN BEFORE METALS. By N. Joly. Fourth Edition. Crown 8vo. 5*s.*

XLV. THE SCIENCE OF POLITICS. By Prof. Sheldon Amos. Third Edit. Crown. 8vo. 5*s.*

XLVI. ELEMENTARY METEOROLOGY. By Robert H. Scott. Fourth Edition. With numerous Illustrations. Crown 8vo. 5*s.*

XLVII. THE ORGANS OF SPEECH AND THEIR APPLICATION IN THE FORMATION OF ARTICULATE SOUNDS By Georg Hermann von Meyer. With 47 Woodcuts. Crown 8vo. 5*s.*

XLVIII. FALLACIES: a View of Logic from the Practical Side. By Alfred Sidgwick. Second Edition. Crown 8vo. 5*s.*

XLIX. ORIGIN OF CULTIVATED PLANTS. By Alphonse de Candolle. Second Edition. Crown 8vo. 5*s.*

L. JELLY FISH, STAR FISH, AND SEA URCHINS. Being a Research on Primitive Nervous Systems. By G. J. Romanes. Crown 8vo. 5*s.*

LI. THE COMMON SENSE OF THE EXACT SCIENCES. By the late William Kingdon Clifford. Second Edition. With 100 Figures. 5*s.*

LII. PHYSICAL EXPRESSION: ITS MODES AND PRINCIPLES. By Francis Warner, M.D., F.R.C.P. With 50 Illustrations. 5*s.*

LIII. ANTHROPOID APES. By Robert Hartmann. With 63 Illustrations. 5*s.*

LIV. THE MAMMALIA IN THEIR RELATION TO PRIMEVAL TIMES. By Oscar Schmidt. With 51 Woodcuts. 5*s.*

LV. COMPARATIVE LITERATURE. By H. Macaulay Posnett, LL.D. 5*s.*

LVI. EARTHQUAKES AND OTHER EARTH MOVEMENTS. By Prof. JOHN MILNE. With 38 Figures. Second Edition. 5*s.*

LVII. MICROBES, FERMENTS, AND MOULDS. By E. L. TROUESSART. With 107 Illustrations. 5*s.*

LVIII. GEOGRAPHICAL AND GEOLOGICAL DISTRIBUTION OF ANIMALS. By Professor A. Heilprin. With Frontispiece. 5*s.*

LIX. WEATHER. A Popular Exposition of the Nature of Weather Changes from Day to Day. By the Hon. Ralph Abercromby. With 96 Illustrations. Second Edition. 5*s.*

LX. ANIMAL MAGNETISM. By Alfred Binet and Charles Féré. 5*s.*

LXI. MANUAL OF BRITISH DISCOMYCETES, with descriptions of all the Species of Fungi hitherto found in Britain included in the Family, and Illustrations of the Genera. By William Phillips, F.L.S. 5*s.*

LXII. INTERNATIONAL LAW. With Materials for a Code of International Law. By Professor Leone Levi. 5*s.*

LXIII. THE GEOLOGICAL HISTORY OF PLANTS. By Sir J. William Dawson. With 80 Illustrations. 5*s.*

LXIV. THE ORIGIN OF FLORAL STRUCTURES THROUGH INSECT AND OTHER AGENCIES. By Professor G. Henslow.

LXV. ON THE SENSES, INSTINCTS, AND INTELLIGENCE OF ANIMALS. With special Reference to Insects. By Sir John Lubbock, Bart., M.P. 100 Illustrations. 5*s.*

MILITARY WORKS.

BARRINGTON (Capt. J. T.)—ENGLAND ON THE DEFENSIVE; or, the Problem of Invasion Critically Examined. Large crown 8vo. with Map, 7*s.* 6*d.*

BRACKENBURY (Col. C. B.) R.A.—MILITARY HANDBOOKS FOR REGIMENTAL OFFICERS:

I. MILITARY SKETCHING AND RECONNAISSANCE. By Colonel F. J. Hutchison and Major H. G. MacGregor. Fifth Edition. With 15 Plates. Small crown 8vo. 4*s.*

II. THE ELEMENTS OF MODERN TACTICS PRACTICALLY APPLIED TO ENGLISH FORMATIONS. By Lieut.-Col. Wilkinson Shaw. Sixth Edit. With 25 Plates and Maps. Small crown 8vo. 9*s.*

III. FIELD ARTILLERY: its Equipment, Organisation, and Tactics. By Major Sisson C. Pratt, R.A. With 12 Plates. Third Edition. Small crown 8vo. 6*s.*

IV. THE ELEMENTS OF MILITARY ADMINISTRATION. First Part: Permanent System of Administration. By Major J. W. Buxton. Small crown 8vo. 7*s.* 6*d.*

BRACKENBURY (Col. C. B.) R.A.—continued.

V. MILITARY LAW: its Procedure and Practice. By Major Sisson C. Pratt, R.A. Third Edition. Small crown 8vo. 4*s.* 6d.

VI. CAVALRY IN MODERN WAR. By Major-General F. Chenevix Trench. Small crown 8vo. 6*s.*

VII. FIELD WORKS. Their Technical Construction and Tactical Application. By the Editor, Col. C. B. Brackenbury, R.A. Small crown 8vo.

BROOKE (Major C. K.)—A SYSTEM OF FIELD TRAINING. Small crown 8vo. 2*s.*

CLERY (Col. C. Francis) C.B.—MINOR TACTICS. With 26 Maps and Plans. Eighth Edition. Crown 8vo. 9*s.*

COLVILE (Lieut.-Col. C. F.)—MILITARY TRIBUNALS. Sewed, 2*s.* 6*d.*

CRAUFURD (Capt. H. J.)—SUGGESTIONS FOR THE MILITARY TRAINING OF A COMPANY OF INFANTRY. Crown 8vo. 1*s.* 6*d.*

HAMILTON (*Capt. Ian*) *A.D.C.*—THE FIGHTING OF THE FUTURE. 1*s.*

HARRISON (*Lieut.-Col. R.*) — THE OFFICER'S MEMORANDUM BOOK FOR PEACE AND WAR. Fourth Edition. Oblong 32mo. roan, with pencil, 3*s.* 6*d.*

NOTES ON CAVALRY TACTICS, ORGANISATION, &c. By a Cavalry Officer. With Diagrams. Demy 8vo. 12*s.*

PARR (*Col. H. Hallam*) *C.M.G.*—THE DRESS, HORSES, AND EQUIPMENT OF INFANTRY AND STAFF OFFICERS. Crown 8vo. 1*s.*

FURTHER TRAINING AND EQUIPMENT OF MOUNTED INFANTRY. Crown 8vo. 1*s.*

SCHAW (*Col. H.*)—THE DEFENCE AND ATTACK OF POSITIONS AND LOCALITIES. Third Edition, revised and corrected. Crown 8vo. 3*s.* 6*d.*

STONE (*Capt. F. Gleadowe*) *R.A.*—TACTICAL STUDIES FROM THE FRANCO-GERMAN WAR OF 1870-71. With 22 Lithographic Sketches and Maps. Demy 8vo. 10*s.* 6*d.*

THE CAMPAIGN OF FREDERICKSBURG, November–December, 1862 : a Study for Officers of Volunteers. By a Line Officer. Second Edition. Crown 8vo. With Five Maps and Plans. 5*s.*

WILKINSON (*H. Spenser*) *Capt. 20th Lancashire R.V.*—CITIZEN SOLDIERS. Essays towards the Improvement of the Volunteer Force. Cr. 8vo. 2*s.* 6*d.*

POETRY.

ADAM OF ST. VICTOR—THE LITURGICAL POETRY OF ADAM OF ST. VICTOR. From the text of Gautier. With Translations into English in the Original Metres, and Short Explanatory Notes. By Digby S. Wrangham, M.A. 3 vols. Crown 8vo. printed on hand-made paper, boards, 21*s.*

ALEXANDER (*William*) *D.D.*, *Bishop of Derry*—ST. AUGUSTINE'S HOLIDAY, and other Poems. Crown 8vo. 6*s.*

AUCHMUTY (*A. C.*)—POEMS OF ENGLISH HEROISM : From Brunanburgh to Lucknow ; from Athelstan to Albert. Small crown 8vo. 1*s.* 6*d.*

BARNES (*William*)—POEMS OF RURAL LIFE, IN THE DORSET DIALECT. New Edition, complete in one vol. Crown 8vo. 6*s.*

BAYNES (*Rev. Canon H. R.*)—HOME SONGS FOR QUIET HOURS. Fourth and cheaper Edition. Fcp. 8vo. 2*s.* 6*d.*

BEVINGTON (*L. S.*)—KEY NOTES. Small crown 8vo. 5*s.*

BLUNT (*Wilfrid Scawen*)—THE WIND AND THE WHIRLWIND. Demy 8vo. 1*s.* 6*d.*

THE LOVE SONNETS OF PROTEUS. Fifth Edition. 18mo. cloth extra, gilt top, 5*s.*

BOWEN (*H. C.*) *M.A.*—SIMPLE ENGLISH POEMS. English Literature for Junior Classes. In Four Parts. Parts I. II. and III. 6*d.* each, and Part IV. 1*s.*, complete 3*s.*

BRYANT (*W. C.*) — POEMS. Cheap Edition, with Frontispiece. Small crown 8vo. 3*s.* 6*d.*

CALDERON'S DRAMAS : the Wonder-working Magician—Life is a Dream—the Purgatory of St. Patrick. Translated by Denis Florence MacCarthy. Post 8vo. 10*s.*

CAMPBELL (*Lewis*)—SOPHOCLES. The Seven Plays in English Verse. Crown 8vo. 7*s.* 6*d.*

CERVANTES. — JOURNEY TO PARNASSUS. Spanish Text, with Translation into English Tercets, Preface, and Illustrative Notes, by JAMES Y. GIBSON. Crown 8vo. 12*s.*

NUMANTIA ; a Tragedy. Translated from the Spanish, with Introduction and Notes, by JAMES Y. GIBSON. Crown 8vo., printed on hand-made paper, 5*s.*

CID BALLADS, and other Poems. Translated from Spanish and German by J. Y. Gibson. 2 vols. Crown 8vo. 12*s.*

CHRISTIE (*A. J.*)—THE END OF MAN. Fourth Edition. Fcp. 8vo. 2*s.* 6*d.*

COXHEAD (*Ethel*)—BIRDS AND BABIES. Imp. 16mo. With 33 Illustrations. 1*s.*

DANTE—THE DIVINA COMMEDIA OF DANTE ALIGHIERI. Translated, line for line, in the 'Terza Rima' of the original, with Notes, by FREDERICK K. H. HASELFOOT, M.A. Demy 8vo. 16*s.*

DE BERANGER.—A Selection from his Songs. In English Verse. By William Toynbee. Small crown 8vo. 2s. 6d.

DENNIS (*J.*) — English Sonnets. Collected and Arranged by. Small crown 8vo. 2s. 6d.

DE VERE (*Aubrey*)—Poetical Works:
I. The Search after Proserpine, &c. 6s.
II. The Legends of St. Patrick, &c. 6s.
III. Alexander the Great, &c. 6s.

The Foray of Queen Meave, and other Legends of Ireland's Heroic Age. Small crown 8vo. 5s.

Legends of the Saxon Saints. Small crown 8vo. 6s.

Legends and Records of the Church and the Empire. Small crown 8vo. 6s.

DOBSON (*Austin*)—Old World Idylls, and other Verses. Eighth Edition. Elzevir 8vo. cloth extra, gilt tops, 6s.

At the Sign of the Lyre. Fifth Edition. Elzevir 8vo., gilt top, 6s.

DOWDEN (*Edward*) *LL.D.*—Shakspere's Sonnets. With Introduction and Notes. Large post 8vo. 7s. 6d.

DUTT (*Toru*)—A Sheaf Gleaned in French Fields. New Edition. Demy 8vo. 10s. 6d.

Ancient Ballads and Legends of Hindustan. With an Introductory Memoir by Edmund Gosse. Second Edition. 18mo. Cloth extra, gilt top, 5s.

ELLIOTT (*Ebenezer*), *The Corn Law Rhymer*—Poems. Edited by his Son, the Rev. Edwin Elliott, of St. John's, Antigua. 2 vols. crown 8vo. 18s.

English Verse. Edited by W. J. Linton and R. H. Stoddard. In 5 vols. Crown 8vo. each 5s.
1. Chaucer to Burns.
2. Translations.
3. Lyrics of the Nineteenth Century.
4. Dramatic Scenes and Characters.
5. Ballads and Romances.

EVANS (*Anne*)—Poems and Music. With Memorial Preface by Ann Thackeray Ritchie. Large crown 8vo. 7s.

GOSSE (*Edmund W.*)—New Poems. Crown 8vo. 7s. 6d.

Firdausi in Exile, and other Poems. Elzevir 8vo. gilt top, 6s.

GURNEY (*Rev. Alfred*)—The Vision of the Eucharist, and other Poems. Crown 8vo. 5s.

A Christmas Faggot. Small crown 8vo. 5s.

HARRISON (*Clifford*)—In Hours of Leisure. Second Edition. Crown 8vo. 5s.

KEATS (*John*) — Poetical Works. Edited by W. T. Arnold. Large crown 8vo. choicely printed on hand-made paper, with Portrait in *eau forte*. Parchment, or cloth, 12s.; vellum, 15s.

Also, a smaller Edition. Crown 8vo. 3s. 6d.

KING (*Mrs. Hamilton*)—The Disciples. Eighth Edition, with Portrait and Notes. Crown 8vo. 5s. Elzevir Edition, 6s.

A Book of Dreams. Third Edition. Crown 8vo. 3s. 6d.

The Sermon in the Hospital. Reprinted from 'The Disciples.' Fcp. 8vo. 1s. Cheap Edition, 3d., or 20s. per 100.

KNOX (*The Hon. Mrs. O. N.*)—Four Pictures from a Life, and other Poems. Small crown 8vo. 3s. 6d.

LANG (*A.*)—XXXII Ballades in Blue China. Elzevir 8vo. parchment, or cloth, 5s.

Rhymes à la Mode. With Frontispiece by E. A. Abbey. Elzevir 8vo. cloth extra, gilt top, 5s.

LAWSON (*Right Hon. Mr. Justice*)—Hymni Usitati Latine Redditi, with other Verses. Small 8vo. parchment, 5s.

Living English Poets. MDCCCLXXXII. With Frontispiece by Walter Crane. Second Edition. Large crown 8vo. printed on hand-made paper. Parchment, or cloth, 12s.; vellum, 15s.

LOCKER (*F.*)—London Lyrics. New Edition, with Portrait. 18mo. cloth extra, gilt tops, 5s.

Love in Idleness. A Volume of Poems. With an etching by W. B. Scott. Small crown 8vo. 5s.

LUMSDEN (*Lieut.-Col. H. W.*)—Beo-wulf: an Old English Poem. Translated into Modern Rhymes. Second and revised Edition. Small crown 8vo. 5s.

MAGNUSSON (*Eirikr*) *M.A., and PALMER* (*E. H.*) *M.A.*—Johan Ludvig Runeberg's Lyrical Songs, Idylls, and Epigrams. Fcp. 8vo. 5s.

MEREDITH (*Owen*) [*The Earl of Lytton*]—Lucile. New Edition. With 32 Illustrations. 16mo. 3s. 6d. ; cloth extra, gilt edges, 4s. 6d.

MORRIS (*Lewis*) — Poetical Works. New and Cheaper Editions, with Portrait, complete in 4 vols. 5s. each.
Vol. I. contains Songs of Two Worlds. Twelfth Edition.
Vol. II. contains The Epic of Hades. Twenty-second Edition.
Vol. III. contains Gwen and the Ode of Life. Seventh Edition.
Vol. IV. contains Songs Unsung and Gycia. Fifth Edition.
Songs of Britain. Third Edition. Fcp. 8vo. 5s.
The Epic of Hades. With 16 Auto-type Illustrations after the drawings by the late George R. Chapman. 4to. cloth extra, gilt leaves, 21s.
The Epic of Hades. Presentation Edit. 4to. cloth extra, gilt leaves, 10s. 6d.
The Lewis Morris Birthday Book. Edited by S. S. Copeman. With Frontispiece after a design by the late George R. Chapman. 32mo. cloth extra, gilt edges, 2s.; cloth limp, 1s. 6d.

MORSHEAD (*E. D. A.*)—The House of Atreus. Being the Agamemnon, Libation-Bearers, and Furies of Æschylus. Translated into English Verse. Crown 8vo. 7s.
The Suppliant Maidens of Æschylus. Crown 8vo. 3s. 6d.

MULHOLLAND (*Rosa*). — Vagrant Verses. Small crown 8vo. 5s.

NADEN (*Constance C. W.*)—A Modern Apostle, and other Poems. Small crown 8vo. 5s.

NOEL (*The Hon. Roden*)—A Little Child's Monument. Third Edition. Small crown 8vo. 3s. 6d.
The Red Flag, and other Poems. New Edition. Small crown 8vo. 6s.
The House of Ravensburg. New Edition. Small crown 8vo. 6s.

NOEL (*The Hon. Roden*)—continued.
Songs of the Heights and Deeps. Crown 8vo. 6s.
A Modern Faust. Small crown 8vo.

O'BRIEN (*Charlotte Grace*) — Lyrics. Small crown 8vo. 3s. 6d.

O'HAGAN (*John*) — The Song of Roland. Translated into English Verse. New and Cheaper Edition. Crown 8vo. 5s.

PFEIFFER (*Emily*)—The Rhyme of the Lady of the Rock and How it Grew. Small crown 8vo. 3s. 6d.
Gerard's Monument, and other Poems. Second Edition. Crown 8vo. 6s.
Under the Aspens: Lyrical and Dramatic. With Portrait. Crown 8vo. 6s.

PIATT (*J. J.*)—Idyls and Lyrics of the Ohio Valley. Crown 8vo. 5s.

PIATT (*Sarah M. B.*)—A Voyage to the Fortunate Isles, and other Poems. 1 vol. Small crown 8vo. gilt top, 5s.
In Primrose Time. A New Irish Garland. Small crown 8vo. 2s. 6d.

Rare Poems of the 16th and 17th Centuries. Edited by W. J. Linton. Crown 8vo. 5s.

RHOADES (*James*)—The Georgics of Virgil. Translated into English Verse. Small crown 8vo. 5s.

ROBINSON (*A. Mary F.*)—A Handful of Honeysuckle. Fcp. 8vo. 3s. 6d.
The Crowned Hippolytus. Translated from Euripides. With New Poems. Small crown 8vo. cloth, 5s.
Shakspere's Works. The Avon Edition, 12 vols. fcp. 8vo. cloth, 18s. ; and in box, 21s. ; bound in 6 vols. cloth, 15s.
Sophocles: The Seven Plays in English Verse. Translated by Lewis Campbell. Crown 8vo. 7s. 6d.

SYMONDS (*John Addington*) — Vaga-bunduli Libellus. Crown 8vo. 6s.

TAYLOR (*Sir H.*)—Works Complete in Five Volumes. Crown 8vo. 30s.
Philip van Artevelde. Fcp. 8vo. 3s. 6d.
The Virgin Widow, &c. Fcp. 8vo. 3s. 6d.
The Statesman. Fcp. 8vo. 3s. 6d.

TODHUNTER (Dr. J.) — LAURELLA, and other Poems. Crown 8vo. 6s. 6d.

FOREST SONGS. Small crown 8vo. 3s. 6d.

THE TRUE TRAGEDY OF RIENZI: a Drama. Crown 8vo. 3s. 6d.

ALCESTIS: a Dramatic Poem. Extra fcp. 8vo. 5s.

HELENA IN TROAS. Small crown 8vo. 2s. 6d.

TYNAN (Katherine) — LOUISE DE LA VALLIERE, and other Poems. Small crown 8vo. 3s. 6d.

SHAMROCKS. Small crown 8vo. 5s.

VICTORIAN HYMNS: English Sacred Songs of Fifty Years. Dedicated to the Queen. Large post 8vo. 10s. 6d.

WATTS (Alaric Alfred and Emma Mary Howitt) — AURORA: a Medley of Verse. Fcp. 8vo. 5s.

WORDSWORTH — SELECTIONS. By Members of the Wordsworth Society. Large crown 8vo. parchment, 12s.; vellum, 15s. Also, cr. 8vo. cl. 4s. 6d.

WORDSWORTH BIRTHDAY BOOK, THE. Edited by ADELAIDE and VIOLET WORDSWORTH. 32mo. limp cloth, 1s. 6d.; cloth extra, 2s.

WORKS OF FICTION.

'ALL BUT:' a Chronicle of Laxenford Life. By PEN OLIVER, F.R.C.S. With 20 Illustrations. Second Edit. Crown 8vo. 6s.

BANKS (Mrs. G. L.) — GOD'S PROVIDENCE HOUSE. New Edition. Crown 8vo. 6s.

CHICHELE (Mary) — DOING AND UNDOING: a Story. Crown 8vo. 4s. 6d.

CRAWFURD (Oswald) — SYLVIA ARDEN. Crown 8vo. 6s.

GARDINER (Linda) — HIS HERITAGE. Crown 8vo. 6s.

GRAY (Maxwell) — THE SILENCE OF DEAN MAITLAND. Fourth Edition. Crown 8vo. 6s.

GREY (Rowland) — BY VIRTUE OF HIS OFFICE. Crown 8vo. 6s.

IN SUNNY SWITZERLAND. Small crown 8vo. 5s.

LINDENBLUMEN, and other Stories. Small crown 8vo. 5s.

HUNTER (Hay) — CRIME OF CHRISTMAS DAY. A Tale of the Latin Quarter. By the Author of 'My Ducats and My Daughter.' 1s.

HUNTER (Hay) and *WHYTE (Walter)* MY DUCATS AND MY DAUGHTER. New and Cheaper Edition. With Frontispiece. Crown 8vo. 6s.

INGELOW (Jean) — OFF THE SKELLIGS. A Novel. With Frontispiece. Second Edition. Crown 8vo. 6s.

IXORA. A Mystery. Crown 8vo. 6s.

JENKINS (Edward) — A SECRET OF TWO LIVES. . Crown 8vo. 2s. 6d.

KIELLAND (Alexander L.) — GARMAN AND WORSE. A Norwegian Novel. Authorised Translation by W. W. Kettlewell. Crown 8vo. 6s.

LANG (Andrew) — IN THE WRONG PARADISE, and other Stories. Crown 8vo. 6s.

MACDONALD (G.) — DONAL GRANT. Crown 8vo. 6s.

CASTLE WARLOCK. Crown 8vo. 6s.

MALCOLM. With Portrait of the Author engraved on Steel. Crown 8vo. 6s.

THE MARQUIS OF LOSSIE. Crown 8vo. 6s.

ST. GEORGE AND ST. MICHAEL. Crown 8vo. 6s.

PAUL FABER, SURGEON. Crown 8vo. 6s.

THOMAS WINGFOLD, CURATE. Crown 8vo. 6s.

WHAT'S MINE'S MINE. Second Edition. Crown 8vo. 6s.

ANNALS OF A QUIET NEIGHBOURHOOD. Crown 8vo. 6s.

THE SEABOARD PARISH: a Sequel to 'Annals of a Quiet Neighbourhood.' Crown 8vo. 6s.

WILFRED CUMBERMEDE. An Autobiographical Story. Crown 8vo. 6s.

THE ELECT LADY. Crown 8vo. 6s.

MALET (Lucas) — COLONEL ENDERBY'S WIFE. Crown 8vo. 6s.

A COUNSEL OF PERFECTION. Crown 8vo. 6s.

MULHOLLAND (Rosa) — MARCELLA GRACE. An Irish Novel. Crown 8vo. 6s.

A FAIR EMIGRANT. Crown 8vo. 6s.

OGLE (A. C.) ('Ashford Owen.') A LOST LOVE. Small crown 8vo. 2s. 6d.

PALGRAVE (*W. Gifford*)—HERMANN AGHA: an Eastern Narrative. Third Edition. Crown 8vo. 6s.

SEVERNE (*Mrs.*)—THE PILLAR HOUSE. With Frontispiece. Crown 8vo. 6s.

SHAW (*Flora L.*)—CASTLE BLAIR; a Story of Youthful Days. New and Cheaper Edition. Crown 8vo. 3s. 6d.

STRETTON (*Hesba*) — THROUGH A NEEDLE'S EYE. A Story. New and Cheaper Edition, with Frontispiece. Crown 8vo. 6s.

TAYLOR (*Col. Meadows*) *C.S.I., M.R.I.A.* SEETA. A Novel. New and Cheaper Edition. With Frontispiece. Crown 8vo. 6s.

TAYLOR (*Col. Meadows*) *C.S.I., M.R.I.A.* —continued.
TIPPOO SULTAUN: a Tale of the Mysore War. New Edition, with Frontispiece. Crown 8vo. 6s.
RALPH DARNELL. New and Cheaper Edition. With Frontispiece. Crown 8vo. 6s.
A NOBLE QUEEN. New and Cheaper Edition. With Frontispiece. Crown 8vo. 6s.
THE CONFESSIONS OF A THUG. Crown 8vo. 6s.
TARA: a Mahratta Tale. Crown 8vo. 6s.

WITHIN SOUND OF THE SEA. New and Cheaper Edition, with Frontispiece. Crown 8vo. 6s.

BOOKS FOR THE YOUNG.

BRAVE MEN'S FOOTSTEPS. A Book of Example and Anecdote for Young People. By the Editor of 'Men who have Risen.' With Four Illustrations by C. Doyle. Eighth Edition. Crown 8vo. 2s. 6d.

COXHEAD (*Ethel*)—BIRDS AND BABIES. With 33 Illustrations. Imp. 16mo. cloth gilt, 1s.

DAVIES (*G. Christopher*) — RAMBLES AND ADVENTURES OF OUR SCHOOL FIELD CLUB. With Four Illustrations. New and Cheaper Edition. Crown 8vo. 3s. 6d.

EDMONDS (*Herbert*) — WELL-SPENT LIVES: a Series of Modern Biographies. New and Cheaper Edition. Crown 8vo. 3s. 6d.

EVANS (*Mark*)—THE STORY OF OUR FATHER'S LOVE, told to Children. Sixth and Cheaper Edition of Theology for Children. With Four Illustrations. Fcp. 8vo. 1s. 6d.

MAC KENNA (*S. J.*)—PLUCKY FELLOWS. A Book for Boys. With Six Illustrations. Fifth Edition. Crown 8vo. 3s. 6d.

MALET (*Lucas*)—LITTLE PETER. A Christmas Morality for Children of any Age. With numerous Illustrations. 5s.

REANEY (*Mrs. G. S.*)—WAKING AND WORKING; or, From Girlhood to Womanhood. New and Cheaper Edition. With a Frontispiece. Cr. 8vo. 3s. 6d.
BLESSING AND BLESSED: a Sketch of Girl Life. New and Cheaper Edition. Crown 8vo. 3s. 6d.
ROSE GURNEY'S DISCOVERY. A Book for Girls. Dedicated to their Mothers. Crown 8vo. 3s. 6d.
ENGLISH GIRLS: Their Place and Power. With Preface by the Rev. R. W. Dale. Fourth Edition. Fcp. 8vo. 2s. 6d.
JUST ANYONE, and other Stories. Three Illustrations. Royal 16mo. 1s. 6d.
SUNBEAM WILLIE, and other Stories. Three Illustrations. Royal 16mo. 1s. 6d.
SUNSHINE JENNY, and other Stories. Three Illustrations. Royal 16mo. 1s. 6d.

STORR (*Francis*) *and TURNER* (*Hawes*). CANTERBURY CHIMES; or, Chaucer Tales Re-told to Children. With Six Illustrations from the Ellesmere MS. Third Edition. Fcp. 8vo. 3s. 6d.

STRETTON (*Hesba*)—DAVID LLOYD'S LAST WILL. With Four Illustrations. New Edition. Royal 16mo. 2s. 6d.

WHITAKER (*Florence*)—CHRISTY'S INHERITANCE: A London Story. Illustrated. Royal 16mo. 1s. 6d.